Somebody
HAS TO PAY

Dear Reader:

Pat Tucker is known to create stories based on today's headlines and incorporating her experience as a former TV news reporter. She's now capturing the whole baby mama and daddy drama with titles such as *Daddy by Default* and *Daddy's Maybe*. Her latest, *Somebody Has To Pay*, continues this thread of tales about paternity. Now it comes with a twist where Dani intentionally falsely identifies the father of her baby as Keeling. And when it's exposed for all to see on a highly popular TV show, *DNA Revealed*, she suffers the consequences while Keeling and his meddlesome mom seek revenge.

In addition to the woes of Dani and Keeling, readers can follow a married couple, Mark and Zaneda who constantly deal with Arlene, his daughter's mother who makes life miserable for the duo. Throw in continuous plot twists and you have plenty of schemes and drama. In fact, Pat has created the handle #ChildSupportDrama for social media.

As always, thanks for supporting myself and the Strebor Books family. We strive to bring you the most cutting-edge, out-of-the-box material on the market. You can find me on Facebook @AuthorZane or you can email me at zane@eroticanoir.com.

Blessings,

Zane

Publisher
Strebor Books
www.simonandschuster.com

ZANE PRESENTS

Somebody
HAS TO PAY

A Novel

PAT TUCKER

SBI

STREBOR BOOKS

NEW YORK LONDON TORONTO SYDNEY

Strebor Books
P.O. Box 6505
Largo, MD 20792
http://www.streborbooks.com

ISBN 978-1-59309-592-5
ISBN 978-1-4767-7577-7 (ebook)
LCCN 2015934965

First Strebor Books trade paperback edition November 2015

Cover design: www.mariondesigns.com
Cover photograph: © Keith Saunders/Keith Saunders Photos
DNA helix © djem/Shutterstock.com

10 9 8 7 6 5 4 3 2 1

Manufactured in the United States of America

For information regarding special discounts for bulk purchases, please contact Simon & Schuster Special Sales at 1-866-506-1949

The Simon & Schuster Speakers Bureau can bring authors to your live event. For more information or to book an event, contact the Simon & Schuster Speakers Bureau at 1-866-248-3049 or visit our website at www.simonspeakers.com.

Dedicated to the reader. Thank you for your support!

CHAPTER ONE

Dani

A wkward couldn't begin to express how I felt. I was nervous to the umpteenth degree, probably worse than a street walker who accidently stumbled into communion. The loud claps and cheers finally quieted down, but I was still a hot mess.

Sweat poured from my lace-front wig in buckets, which meant my makeup was a disaster. My head hurt. I was anxious and frustrated. I could barely catch my breath. The lights, the cameras, all of it, the people who stared at me. It was just too damn much! I didn't know what I thought it was gonna be like, but I never expected all of that. My eyes darted around at the people who sat in the audience and all of a sudden I started to feel strange.

It was like all of 'em, they were hungry for some drama and that was why I had been invited, to feed their starvation. Only, I didn't wanna go through with it anymore. I was about to make an ass of myself and my baby daddy, Keeling, too.

What in the world made me think that *ish* was a good idea in the first place? How come nobody told me it was not the business? Lulu and Niecy, my road-dawgs, probably just wanted the free trip.

Truth be told, I couldn't blame them. The show did set it out for us. Round trip tickets to Burbank, limo ride to and from the airport, and two nights in a bomb-ass hotel. On top of that, the show's producers laced me with five hundred dollars in cash, and if that wasn't enough, they hired a car to take us around to all the hottest tourist spots.

Yeah, at the time, when they gave us the royal treatment, it seemed like this would be easy-breezy; come in, talk about my baby-daddy drama, the child support mess, and let them beat up on him a little. Besides, he kinda deserved it anyway. If not him directly, he definitely deserved it because of that vicious ratchet mama of his. Keeling's mama, Kelsa, hated me something fierce. And she had put me through hell.

At first, I told myself it was no biggie. People would forget all about us and our story before the credits rolled.

But once I made it out to the stage, those damned lights were the real game changer. There was something about being under those hot lights that made me rethink a thing or two. What really did it, was when I had to sit and listen as the host Reece Renaldo, read from those colorful little index cards.

She had him arrested for nonpayment of child support.

Ummm…that wasn't me. That was the attorney general's office.

When the judge asked what he had done since the child was born, she was quick to say, "not a damn thing."

Well…I was just keeping it real.

The audience roared with wild cheers and laughter. Some people looked like they'd fall from their chairs because they laughed so hard. I started to get excited, but not in a good way.

She blamed him for the welfare she had to accept.

I never said that. It was the producer who said that.

And when she found out that he had fathered another child, she did the right thing; she reached out to DNA Revealed.

My eyebrows went up.

Keeling ain't got no other kids. I never said nothing about another child. I rolled my eyes. Besides, I didn't call them, they called me. And I ain't never told nobody that I went on welfare. But I didn't say anything. I sat back and listened as she read from those index cards.

It seemed as if the more she rattled off information about my life, the more riled up and hyped the audience became.

People yelled stuff out. Some whistled, jumped up from their seats and pumped their fists in the air. It was all so wild.

And all of it made me feel nauseous.

"Stay with us, because right after the break, we let you in on Dani Patnett's big secret. You don't want to miss this," Reece Renaldo promised.

She had me hyped, at first. But it didn't take long for things to add up in my head. The talk show *DNA Revealed* was like a combination of *Jerry Springer* and *Maury*. I was the Dani Patnett who had a secret, and the host promised it would be revealed after the break.

Lawwwd, help us all!

I jumped when Reece Renaldo, probably not her real name, touched my leg. "Oh, honey, it's okay. We're in commercial. You okay? Looks like you could use some water or something." That made me feel even more nervous and out of place.

"Oh, naw. I'm good," I lied. My eyes darted around at the audience again. Some people leaned in and whispered to one another. I noticed other people as they talked and threw major shade my way. Their evil eyes spoke volumes.

My cheeks started to hurt. I wasn't sure why it took so long, but all of a sudden, something told me, the show was probably not gonna end well for me.

When the commercial was over and the show was back on again, I looked around the studio and all the eyes were fixed squarely on me. That made me seriously think about what would happen if I got up and walked out, but I couldn't. Could I?

"So, are you ready to bring Keeling out here?" Reece asked the audience.

The crowd went bonkers.

It felt like a massive tumbleweed had somehow made its way down my throat. Because I had talked Keeling into coming on the show, we'd get an extra five hundred dollars each when the episode finally came on TV.

Again, at the time, all I thought about was the cash and the free trip. I knew Keeling would probably be down because he had just gotten out of jail, and he needed the money.

But, as I sat there and listened to Reece remind the audience that although Keeling was here, he had been kept in a soundproof booth wearing a blindfold, and had no idea why he had been invited to the show, I really wanted to run for cover.

When Reece asked the audience whether they were ready for Keeling, they clapped, screamed, and some people even whistled.

Thoughts of the lie I had told him to get him on the show ran through my mind, but I pushed them away. It was way too late for regrets.

Moments later, two big guys walked Keeling out and on to the stage.

I watched nervously as the guys led him to an empty seat on the other side of Reece. I felt a bit relieved that there was at least a little distance between us. But my stomach rumbled like lunch might leave at any moment.

I exhaled and rubbed my palms on top of my thighs.

"Keeling is here, everyone, and when we drop this bomb, we know for sure you'll never again look at *DNA Revealed* the same. We talk to Keeling himself right after this break. Stay with us."

Reece smiled, then suddenly stopped. That's how I knew we were in another commercial break. She turned that personality of hers on and off like a faucet, and poured it on for the cameras.

"Uh. So what's up?" Keeling asked. His voice sounded a bit shaky too.

A few people from the audience laughed.

"You need anything?" Reece asked in Keeling's direction.

"Uh. Naw. I'm good. Wish I knew what was what," he said. "Why I gotta sit here in this blindfold?"

"Don't worry. It's coming off real soon," Reece said. "We're coming back from a commercial break in a few, so you won't have to wait much longer." When I looked over at Keeling, something hit me. I knew I had done a lot to him, but in that moment, I felt like this was probably gonna go on record as the lowest of the low.

As I sat on the stage in front of all those strangers, there was no way for me to know how much my life would be turned upside down simply because I agreed to go on the talk show, *DNA Revealed*.

CHAPTER TWO

Arlene

"Nooooooo, Mommy, no. I wanna stay!" Markeesa cried, as she clutched my shirt tightly.

My heart melted into pieces. I had to try to stay calm because I knew all eyes were on my every move. I tried to pull her small hands away, but despite their size, her grip was strong and tight.

"It's okay, baby. It's gonna be okay," I whispered. "I need you to calm down."

"No. I don't wanna go. I wanna stay home with you and Grams. Please, Mommy, pleeeaaassse," she begged.

I pulled her small arms together and moved her in front of me so I could look directly into her tear-filled eyes.

"Listen to Mommy. Markeesa, stop crying and listen to me, okay?" I said. "The judge says you have to go with him. Now, I need you to get it together," I said.

Her lips trembled uncontrollably. She sniffled a couple of times and tried to compose herself as much as a six-year-old could. "You have to go and spend some time with your daddy," I said.

"But, Mommy, you said…"

"Enough of that!" I cut her off. I didn't need her to repeat any of our private conversations about her daddy in front of mixed company. "I need you to listen to what I'm saying now."

Confusion settled into my child's features as she frowned and looked at me.

"Now, I want you to be a big girl like we talked about. You go over there and you listen to what your daddy says."

My daughter sniffled a few more times. "But, Mom, what if…"

"Markeesa. Now you listen to me and remember what Grams and I told you. You have to try, honey," I said. She looked so lost, as I stared into her eyes.

The loud knock startled me, and pulled me away from the horrible memory of what we had gone through a few months ago.

The noise rattled my front door. The thought of what was to come sent a shiver through me, but I still got up from the chair and walked out of the kitchen. My daughter was sleeping in her room and I had no intentions of waking her.

The booming noise sounded again, like someone was anxious to warn us about an out-of-control fire. At the door, I snatched it open and barked at the man who stood there.

"Why you banging on my door like you've lost your ever-loving mind?" I asked. My body stiffened, and the heat that crawled up my back threatened to sear my hairline. Hatred boiled through my veins like hot oil in a pressure cooker that was eager to explode. I pulled the door close to my body, squared my shoulders, and planted my feet where I stood. My frown was plastered securely in place.

"We're here for Markeesa," Mark, my ex, said. "I hope she's ready, 'cause we're in a hurry."

Mark Clyburn's six-foot, five-inch, muscled frame towered over mine, as it darkened my doorway. His chiseled jawline was perfect and made him photogenic even when there was no camera around. His massive, wide shoulders could carry the world on one side and the moon on the other.

Mark's dreamy, deep-set eyes were nothing less than hypnotic. He was everything—his smile, his mannerisms, not to mention his money—absolutely everything about him was what most women wanted in a man.

He was supposed to be my ticket to a better life. Mark was an NFL superstar who was completely down-to-earth. He behaved like any ordinary man. I had it all planned. Markeesa would have both her mommy and daddy, and several nannies under one roof. I'd make sure our home life was as close to fairytale-like, as possible. Our closets would be filled with the latest designer clothes, shoes, and accessories. And our family would be the one by which others would be measured. We were supposed to be sharing his lavish, sprawling home. And our life together would've been close to perfection.

But a life with Mark wasn't just about the material things. Being with Mark meant so much more than all of the tangible things his money could buy.

If things had gone the way I'd planned, I would've been the first in my family's history to have enough money to do whatever I felt like doing. But Mark had screwed it all up. And ever since he had, nothing in my life seemed to go the way I wanted.

"We?" I snarled.

Before he answered my question, a voice that haunted my dreams night and day, screamed out. I looked up to see Ms. *Thang* as she slid out of her metallic-gold Bentley, and pranced up in what had to be the cutest Gucci shorts romper I had ever seen. She stood at my door in all her designer glory as if she were a contestant on *America's Next Top Model*. The sight of her made me want to throw up in my own mouth.

"Good help has always been hard to find. Mark, what's taking so long? Is the kid ready?" she asked. "We need to leave now if we're..." The moment her eyes connected with mine Zaneda stopped, and her tone changed instantly.

Her neck began to swivel. She said, "Arlene, we ain't got time for your foolishness today. You were supposed to have the child ready at three thirty. It's four. Please go get her, now."

"What the hell is she doing here?" I ignored her and spoke directly to Mark. Her no-nonsense tone didn't do a damn thing except piss me off even more.

"Look," Mark said.

"Look, my ass! I told you she ain't invited near my place. This is the kind of mess I was talking about in court. This is between me, you, and Markeesa. Why she gotta be here?"

"Where's Markeesa?" Mark asked.

"She's not feeling too good, so I don't think she's gonna be able to make it today," I said.

Mark's eyes turned into slits.

"See, what'd I tell you?" Zaneda said. "I knew she was up to something. I am so sick of her and this mess."

I wanted to tell her what she could do with her sick behind, but I held my tongue.

"Well, Zaneda, why don't you leave? Nobody told you to keep coming around anyway," I said.

"Arlene, you gotta stop this. We have a court order. You can't just change your mind when you feel like it. Please, go get Markeesa so we can take her like we're supposed to," Mark said.

The stand-off between the three of us was nothing new. I had already told Mark that bringing his wife to my house to pick up our daughter was completely disrespectful and I wasn't putting up with it.

"So, this is how we're doing this?" Mark asked.

I pursed my lips, crossed my arms at my chest, and leaned against the doorframe.

"You know what, babe? Don't trip. Just call the police. Let them deal with this trick," Zaneda chimed in.

"I don't know who you think you calling a 'trick,'" I snarled in her direction.

Zaneda's eyebrows and upper lip twisted upward. "Last time I checked, a trick is someone who screws the man who's paying her to clean his house and watch after his children," she said.

"That makes no sense! You are so stupid! Get off my porch before I call the police on you for trespassing!" I screamed.

"Trick, I dare you," she said, and motioned in my direction.

Mark stepped between us.

"That's why I fired your hoish ass," Zaneda muttered.

CHAPTER THREE

Keeling

Sitting on a stage blindfolded in front of a live studio audience could mess with anybody's head. And that's exactly what it did to mine. I thought about all kinds of stuff. But most importantly, I wondered what I had been thinking on this one. I had no idea why I let Dani talk me into going on the show, but it was what it was. Well, I know why; it was because I needed the money. It was that simple.

The little bit of change wasn't gonna make a brotha rich, but it would help. It was real hard trying to get back on my feet, since I got out, and if I didn't have my moms, I would've been on my buddy Roger's couch or out on the streets somewhere.

When the corny music came back on, I thought about being on national TV and telling a bunch of strangers all my business. The pace picked up and I started to get hyped. Maybe it wouldn't be so bad after all.

Before Dani told me about it, I had never even heard of the show. A few seconds later, the host started talking again.

"Welcome back to *DNA Revealed*, everyone. Thanks for staying with us," she said. "If you're just joining us, let me bring you up to speed. Our guest this hour, Dani Patnett, is here. She told us all about her baby-daddy drama. She has a three-year-old with Keeling

Lake. And Dani's not shy about saying how their relationship has been nothing but drama, drama, and more drama."

People in the audience laughed.

As the host talked, I realized Dani didn't give a damn about putting it all out there.

The host kept talking, "She told us how after Keeling fell behind with his child support, she reported him, and had him arrested."

The audience booed.

"She also told us how Dani and Keeling's mother hate each other, so much so that the two of them have nearly come to blows several times," the host said.

As if on cue, the audience sighed collectively.

My palms became moist and clammy, and I began to sweat.

"Well, once we heard Dani's story and all that she had gone through, we invited her, and her baby's daddy, Keeling, on the show."

Suddenly, I felt the tie loosen around my head. The blindfold had come off.

"Keeling Lake, welcome to *DNA Revealed*," the host said.

The audience clapped and cheered like I was a superstar athlete or somebody big like that. I gotta admit, the attention made me feel like I was the *man*.

Dani looked like she was nervous, but she looked good. With me staying by my moms, we didn't really see each other too much, even since I've been out. My mother hated Dani, so it wasn't an option to have her over or anything like that. And that bad blood between them was there long before I went to jail.

"So, Keeling. Tell us about your experience in jail," the lady said to me.

My eyebrows went up.

"Ah, what you wanna know?" I asked.

"Well, tell us what happened. You went to jail. What'd you do?"

"Man, I didn't do nothing. I did my time," I said, and shifted in my chair.

"Oh. Okay, yes, we get that. But, Keeling, what did you think when the judge ordered you arrested? And for not paying child support?" she asked. The lady acted all dramatic and over the top. She made her eyes wide, then when she asked the question, she leaned in close to me.

I shrugged. "Man, it wasn't really like that. I mean it didn't happen in court. I went out with one of my boys. It was kinda late, so I crashed at his place. At like five or something in the morning, there was a knock at his door. The cops busted in talking about some kinda' roundup. Next thing I knew, they were checking everybody's driver's licenses and one of 'em said something about an outstanding warrant for me."

"Whoa!" the host said. She glanced at the audience, then back at me.

The audience gasped again. Then all of a sudden, they started to talk to each other, until the host turned to them and said, "Sssssh."

"So, you come in after a night out with the fellas, and wind up behind bars?" Her voice went up and then down at just the right time.

"Yeah, pretty much." I looked at her, and shrugged. I didn't feel like she needed to know I was picked up at work. So, I ran with the story about being with the fellas.

"Keeling, we also heard you lost more than just your freedom for nine months," the host said.

This time, when she talked, she lowered her voice at the end and looked at me with sad eyes.

"Yeah, that's right. My grandma died away while I was locked up," I said. It still made me a little choked up because I was close to my grandmother, but they wouldn't let me out to go to her funeral. I didn't think the audience needed to know that.

"So, all of this, the embarrassment of jail, the loss of your freedom, the heartbreak of not saying a final goodbye to your grandmother…" she said.

I wondered where all of this was going. And just when I thought I was about to find out, she asked another question.

"Okay, so, since you've done your time, does that mean your slate is clean? I mean, you're all caught up on your child support payments, right?"

"Well, here's the thing. When I went to jail, I lost my job and kinda fell behind again," I said.

That sent her over the edge. When she talked, she waved her hands all over the place. Her eyes got all big and her mouth fell open. She was a bonafide drama queen.

I wasn't sure if she was acting like that because she was really shocked, or if she was playing it up for the cameras.

"Hold up a minute here!" she yelled. "Did you say you lost your job when you went to jail?"

The audience gasped again.

"Ah. Yes, ma'am. I did," I said.

"Well, Keeling, we've got some additional news for you. You've already been through so much, but we thought you should know exactly what the DNA test has revealed."

When she said the last part, music blared through some speakers.

I sat upright and noticed people in the audience looked like they were on the edge of their seats.

"Uh, okay," I said.

"Keeling. Our latest DNA test has revealed that you are *not* that child's father," the host said.

CHAPTER FOUR

Mark

In the heat of the day, a pick-up game at Peggy Park in Houston's Third Ward was usually exactly what I needed to get my mind straight. Today was no different. There was something about going back to my old stomping grounds. It was like I had gone back to the village, kind of like a native son returns home. Players on the court included street hustlers and business professionals alike, all with one thing in common: a love for the game.

My body was drenched in sweat and my muscles screamed from the fierce workout. But I was still hungry for more.

"That's game, dude," a scrawny, boyish man yelled as he palmed the basketball like a pro. He could've been right. I didn't know because I had been in my zone for the past thirty minutes.

My breathing was hard and labored. I was outta shape for the kind of game they played.

"Damn, Mark, I see playing ball in the NFL don' made you soft," Nebo, one of the regulars and my friend, chided me. He put his fist out for some dap.

"Naw, it ain't nothing like that," I said, as I pounded his fist.

"What's up? Y'all done? We just getting started!" another dude yelled. He dribbled his ball between his legs and did a few fancy moves. "I know y'all not tired," he said, as he looked up in our direction.

Nebo and I looked at each other. I was tired as hell, but my breathing had returned to normal and the sweat that covered my body was gone from my head and shoulders. I tossed my towel over to my duffle bag and got ready to get back in the game.

"What's up, big man?" Nebo asked.

I shrugged.

"Another ass whopping ain't never hurt nobody. Let's make it do what it do," I said.

"Bet that!" Nebo said excitedly. He rushed around the court and gathered up the members of our team who still lingered around.

We were down by eight points when I heard my cell phone ring. Usually I would've ignored the call, but my throat felt drier than the Mohave Desert, so it was a good time for a water break.

"Hold up a sec," I said, and jogged toward the bag. I dug in the side pocket for my phone.

"What the hell?" I heard one of the players groan.

When my eyes connected with the number on the screen, my heart raced with fear. I missed the call, but unlocked my phone and dialed home. My wife, Zaneda, knew not to call while I balled with the fellas.

"C'mon, bruh. You holdin' up the game!" another player yelled.

"Give me five," I said. The phone rang in my ear and I wondered what took Zaneda so long to answer. I ended the call and dialed home again.

She answered on the second ring this time.

"Hello?" My wife's voice was shaky like she was nervous, distracted, or both.

One of us had to stay calm. "Aye, what's up? I saw a missed call from you and you didn't answer when I called back," I said.

The guys still tried to ride me about the way I held up the game, but trouble at home had my attention and was a priority.

"Mark, um, I think you need to hurry up and get home. It's the po-police. They're here," Zaneda stammered.

My face twisted in confusion. I heard what she said, but couldn't wrap my mind around what she meant. Why would the police be at our house?

"What are the police doing there?" I asked. Before I heard her answer, I turned my head to the guys and said over my shoulder, "That's game for me, guys. Gotta run."

"Aww. C'mon, dude!" someone said.

"He didn't want that ass whuppin'," another player chimed in as he tried to egg me on.

Nebo jogged over and looked at me with concern all over his face. "Hey, dawg, what's up? Is everything okay?"

"Naw. I need to run to the house. I'll catch up with you later," I said as I grabbed the towel and my bag.

"Okay. You good to drive, man?" Nebo glanced around as if a driver might magically appear.

"Yeah, thanks. I'll call and let you know what's up," I said.

I threw the strap of my bag over my head and across my body, then rushed to my truck. I got my wife on the phone again. "Zaneda, what's going on?"

"Just hurry," she begged.

"I am. But you need to tell me what's going on over there."

"I didn't know what to do. I tried to call you. They knocked on the door, but I didn't open it. I was scared. The first person I saw was the police officer, then she stood next to him with a clipboard in her hands," Zaneda said. "I didn't know what to do so I told them I needed to call my husband."

Zaneda and I had been married for nine years. We had two boys together, but I had a six-year-old daughter who didn't live with us.

Her words came out so fast, I tried to take it all in. What she said didn't make sense. Why wouldn't she open the door for the police? I knew better than to question her decision; it would've only made matters worse.

"Okay; calm down. Where are they now, and what's going on?" I asked.

"Mark, I don't know. I just knew that I didn't have to let them in, so I ran to get my cell phone and that's when I called you."

"What did the police say?"

My voice was calm as I talked to my wife. I wanted her to follow my lead, but I could hear the fear in her voice. "Well. It was the lady who did all the talking. She said she was with Child Protective Services and she needed to come inside so she could see Mark Junior," Zaneda said.

Her voice cracked as she talked. I hated that I hadn't been there.

"Mark Junior?" I repeated, confused.

"Where are you, and how far away are you?" I could tell she was struggling to hold it together.

"I'm on I-10 now. I'm on my way, babe. I'll be there as quickly as I can," I said.

"Oh God, Mark! You're all the way in the Third Ward?" She sighed hard.

"Calm down. I'm already at the Beltway. I'll be there soon."

"Mark, this has Arlene written all over it. Who in the hell else would've called CPS on us?" Zaneda asked. "Do you think they're gonna try and take the kids because I didn't let them in?"

"Babe, I wanna stay on the phone with you, but I really need to call our attorney. If you didn't let them in, I know for a fact they'll be back and we need to be ready when they return," I said.

CHAPTER FIVE

Dani

"Hey!"

This chick I didn't know yelled in my direction.

She scared the mess outta me. I let go of a breath I didn't know I held in my chest, and glared in her direction. The store was mad-busy and I didn't want to get stuck in that after-work crowd that rushed the grocery store, so she needed to make it quick.

"You talking to me?" I asked.

"Yeah. Wasn't you on that show, *DNA Revealed?*" she asked.

I looked around the crowded store and saw two other females who stood off to the side and snickered as they watched her talk to me. I was so tired of feeling like a Z-list celebrity. It felt like everywhere I went, someone had seen that damn episode. Who knew so many people watched the stupid show?!

"Yeah, that was me," I said, and rolled my eyes. I didn't give her a chance to say anything else. I quickly grabbed my bags and headed toward the automatic doors. She turned and walked back to where her friends stood, and giggled with them.

"Umph, I knew it was that THOT. Told y'all it was that ratchet ho," I heard her say.

"Did you say it was *that ho over there*, like all loud, where she could hear you?"

"She knows what THOT means," the girl answered.

"I can't believe you asked her," the other female said.

They all laughed.

I kept it moving. It had been two weeks since my episode first aired, and my life had been like a living hell ever since. The money was long gone, but it felt like my problems had just started.

Not a single day had passed without someone, or something that reminded me of the complete ass I had made of myself when I appeared on the national talk show.

Once I made it to the car, I noticed the chick and her friends as they stared at me. The tricks laughed and pointed in my direction. I wanted to wave to them with my middle finger, but told myself they weren't worth the energy.

Every day was an exercise in patience because I had to struggle to put my appearance on *DNA Revealed* behind me. It had so not been worth it, and I wish someone would've talked me out of it.

I pulled up to the mailbox, and forced myself to ignore thoughts of the girls from the store. I opened the mailbox and found a strange-looking envelope mixed in with junk mail and the other envelopes. It had my name on it, but my name was spelled wrong, and it looked like a *retard* had written it.

Curiosity caused me to rip the strange letter open first, but when I did, what I saw made me sick.

Dear Danny,

Consider this letter a death threat! Bitches like you deserve to die a slow and pain-filled death. You make all women look bad. I wish the president would sign an executive order and have all hood rats like you sterilized. You should not be allowed to procreate ever again. I don't know how you look at yourself in the mirror, you stank tramp!

Signed,

A woman who hates Danny Patnett!

I read the letter, looked around, and rolled my eyes. "People need to get a life!" I ripped the letter to pieces, stuffed it back into the envelope, and flipped through the stack of bills.

All of that made me think about the moment I hated most about our appearance on the show. It seemed like any little thing took me back to that moment and it was like I was right back there, on stage, in front of that nasty audience.

I sat there and held my breath until Keeling blinked a few times in my direction.

"Keeling? You okay?" Reece asked.

She looked at the camera. The audience was eerily quiet, and she repeated her question.

"Keeling? Are you okay? Did you hear me? I said DNA revealed that you are not Keela's father," Reece repeated.

I wished I had super powers and was able to disappear in that instant. I grabbed the handles of the chair and braced myself for his reaction.

It happened so fast, I don't think anyone was prepared. One minute Keeling stared off into space like he didn't understand English, then the next minute, two bouncer guys pulled him off of me. For the life of me, I couldn't remember what all had happened in between.

His dark eyes spooked me. His strong hands felt rough as he clawed toward my neck. And the weight of his body made me start to hyperventilate.

The chair buckled under our weight, and I was beyond petrified. "Oh God! Oh God! Get him off me," I cried.

As I begged for my life, the stupid audience cheered. I heard people as they screamed and yelled all kinds of stuff.

"Get THOT!"

"Get her ass!"

"Snatch that weave outta her head!"

"Stomp that trick!"

"Die, bitch, die!"

Everything they yelled was directed at me. Some people even told the bouncers to let Keeling do his thing.

I felt like a warm pile of abandoned shit.

Finally, a couple of people came to try and help me. They helped me up off the stage, but I still felt like crap. One of my eyes felt like my fake lashes had been ripped from my eyelids. And my throat hurt. I recognized one of the producers who brought one of my shoes to me.

"Are you hurt?" she asked.

Unable to find my voice, I shook my head. I didn't want to find my voice. I was so embarrassed, I wanted to cry.

"You want something? You need something to drink?" another woman asked.

"Give that bitch some rat poison or anti-freeze!" someone from the audience yelled.

Laughter broke out and I felt even worse. It felt like they had all ganged up on me.

"Don't give her a damn thing. Let Keeling at her. Give the man ten minutes; that's all he needs!" another person yelled.

It was horrible. People actually wanted to see me get hurt and there was nothing I could do about it.

I snapped out of it when I heard a car horn honk. The light turned green and I sat there haunted by the past. When the horn sounded again, I smashed the pedal. When I turned onto my street, my mind started to race. Several people stood outside my house. I didn't need any more drama. Hell, I couldn't handle it.

"Oh, Jesus!" I muttered as I pulled up in front of the house. When I jumped out of the car, my mouth dropped to the ground.

"This foolishness needs to stop. Dani, look at this mess!" my mother, Charlene, whipped around and yelled at me. Normally, she was the calm, laid-back type. She was co-owner of a daycare business, and it worked out perfectly for me. But the minute something rubbed her wrong, she'd let loose like you wouldn't believe. Some of our neighbors stood and gawked, like they'd never seen anything out of order before.

"Who did this mess?" I asked the question aloud, but never really expected an answer.

"Ever since you went on that dumb show, I never know what to expect when I come home!" Charlene yelled. "I told you about doing dumb shit without thinking," she said.

"Chile, you know this generation always doin' stuff tryin' to get their own reality TV show," Ms. Howard, our elderly next door neighbor, said.

"Reality show, my behind! It's ridiculous! And I'm sick of it," Charlene spat.

I sucked my teeth at their comments. I already felt like shit. Going off on me, especially in front of nosey neighbors, didn't help. I was frustrated too. It felt like everywhere I went, people pointed at me like I was a circus freak. Who knew being on that show would've led to all of that?

Since my mother wanted to give everyone a show at my expense, I walked back to the car, grabbed my bags, and rushed into the house.

The words "lying bitch" was spray-painted in a bright, blood-red color across my mother's garage doors. I was hot, but the tongue lashing she gave me didn't help either.

Inside, I called my girl Niecy and gave her a play by play of my dreadful day.

"What did you say to the chicks at the store?" she asked.

"Girl, nothing. What could I say?" I asked.

"Yeah, I guess you were outnumbered, but still. What about the garage door?"

"They still out there, so what can I do about that? Staring at the words won't make them vanish," I said.

I looked out the window and noticed a few of the rubberneckers had left. It was about time.

"I don't wanna be nowhere near your house until this stuff dies down, Charlene. Not gonna go off on me, honey," Niecy joked. "Oh, and I know your mama must be tired. It's hard for her to go off, especially in front of people. Whew, chile, you got an epic problem on your hands!"

"Um. Yeah. Remind me not to put you on the encouragement committee."

"Well, I'm just keepin' it one hundred. Think about it, your mama, going off in front of the neighbors? Whoo-wee! Yeah, I'ma stay on this side of town 'til you work this one out," Niecy joked.

"Wait, that's my other line," I said to Niecy. "Hold on."

"Hello?" I clicked over and answered.

"Ms. Dani Patnett, please?" a voice that sounded proper said.

"This is she; may I ask who's calling and what business do you have with me?"

"Ms. Patnett, this is detective Chris Watt with the Houston Police Department. I'm calling to see when you can come down to the station for an interview," he said.

I nearly stopped breathing.

CHAPTER SIX

Arlene

"I don't know what I'm gonna do," I said as I looked at my mother from the kitchen table.

We had been in the midst of one of those conversations where I felt like I needed to remind her whose side she was supposed to be on.

I fidgeted at the table and tried to keep my thoughts straight. The kitchen was nothing fancy, just large enough for a few people to move around and not get in each other's way. But it was nothing like the grand kitchen I would've had in the house with Mark.

My mother stood at the sink with the water running, but turned her head, and looked over her shoulder to talk to me. After she gave me her two-cents that I'd never requested, she walked over to the stove.

"Cho...yo betta let that pickney go be wit eh pah," she added matter-of-factly as she stirred her beans.

I shrugged. "Ummph. That's what the law says I have to do, but..."

My mother spun on her heels and frowned at me.

"Look, ya gyal, anybody woulda giva wah arm an wah leg fo have de baby pah be wah part of de baby life. Yo betta get ovah dat an make da man be wit eh pickney!" she scolded.

I ignored her comment and focused on the clock. I knew my time was running out, and there was little I could do. But I wasn't about to sit and listen to my mom tell me that I had to do something she knew I didn't want to do. She sounded more like the stupid judge than my number one cheerleader.

"Yo got eh things ready?" she asked.

"I'ma get it together," I said.

She moved closer to the table and frowned down at me. "Yo need fo do de right thing. I know I me di raise yo betta dan dat."

My mama was old school, born and raised in Belize. So she didn't really understand, but I had no intentions of making anything easy for Mark. If he thought he could keep disrespecting me and I wouldn't do anything about it, he had another thing coming.

The only reason he got joint custody was because of his money. I already knew, I was nobody's fool, and by the time I was finished with Mark, he'd regret the way he had led me on.

The boom at the door came in what felt more like seconds, than minutes.

"Cho! I di tell yo fi get eh stuff ready. Now the people deh deyah and they haf fo wait," my mother complained. She sighed hard and loud.

I frowned and looked toward the door. This was not his dog-gone weekend and I didn't know anybody who banged on my door the way Mark did.

"Yo no gowen go get da door?" my mother asked. She used her hand to motion in the direction of the door.

If I thought she'd let me get away with pretending like no one was home, it would be a no-brainer. I knew if I didn't answer the door, she would. She'd probably pack my baby and shove her out the door and into that monster's arms.

Monster?

A thought rushed through my mind and I wanted to slap myself for not thinking about it before. I had always been resourceful, and if I didn't want Mark to be a part of my daughter's life, there was no reason I couldn't come up with a plan to block him for good. Monsters came in all shapes and sizes. You just had to pull back the covers and reveal their true identity. So what, this one had money.

With renewed energy, I got up from the chair and pranced out to the living room. If he knocked one more time like he was the law with a battering ram, I'd bust him upside his head.

I shook those thoughts from my head and pulled the door open.

"This is a court order that says if you don't let Markeesa come with me today, you're going to jail," Mark hissed.

Even when he was angry, his face twisted into a frown, he still looked good. He hadn't bothered to say hello. None of that mattered at the moment. However, if I thought I could ignore his piece of paper, the two officers who stood a couple of steps behind him, made me see that move wouldn't end well for me.

I pulled the door wider, flashed the officers and Mark a wicked smile and said, "Hi, fellas. It's hot. Would you guys like some lemonade or iced-tea?"

"No, thank you. We're here to retrieve the minor child," one of the officers said.

"This is a damn shame," Mark said. "It makes no sense that even after a court order that says you must turn her over, I still have to go to a judge for help," he muttered.

I really didn't give a damn what he thought was a shame. If he wanted to know the real shame, I could tell him. I hadn't heard from his buster ass in two weeks. I guess even with money, it took time for him to get his little paperwork together.

It was so hard to believe that he felt the need to bring the law to my front door. Something deep inside told me this was more Zaneda than Mark, but I held my tongue. By the time I was done with them, she'd learn to keep her nose out of our business.

"Was this really necessary?" I asked.

Mark shot me the evil eye, and stood off to the side as the two officers walked into my house.

"Where's the child?" one of them asked.

I rolled my eyes at Mark dramatically, and turned my attention to the officers.

"She's in her room. My mother will go and get her," I said.

My mother stood next to the kitchen, but she scurried off the second I told the officers she'd get my daughter.

Sleepy and somewhat disoriented, my daughter rushed to my arms and hugged me tightly.

"Mommy, what's wrong?" she asked.

As gently as I could, I eased her away from me and said, "Sweetie, I need you to be a big girl. I need you to go with your daddy."

Her little head whipped in Mark's direction, then back at me. I knew she was confused, but with the officers there, I had no choice.

"But, Mommy, you said you didn't want me to go back there," she muttered.

With all eyes on us, I took her little face into my hands and tried to reason with her. "Markeesa. A judge that Daddy probably paid off, says you have to go there. If it was up to me, I wouldn't force you, honey. But if you don't go, your daddy is going to send Mommy to jail."

"You have got to be kidding me!" Mark yelled.

CHAPTER SEVEN

Keeling

All kinds of crazy thoughts stayed on my mind. My head was messed up for sure. Every time I looked at something, all I saw was those damned DNA test results. When I opened the refrigerator door, I realized that my blood didn't match my daughter's.

Pouring juice made me see the similarities in our reflection, but that was confusing too. How could she look like me, but not be my daughter? How could Dani do some foul mess like that? Then my mind would race with memories, like how for all those years, she made me think that baby was mine, when she knew better. She had to know. Oh yeah, she knew, for sure.

"You okay?"

My mama's voice broke my train of thought. Naw. I wasn't okay. It was gonna be a long time before I would ever be okay again. I worked hard, and Dani took money from me. When I fell behind on my child support payments, she had my ass tossed in jail. My grand died while I was locked down, and the kid wasn't even mine?

"Oh. I'm good, Ma," I lied.

"You don't look good, baby," she said.

"Naw. I'm straight, for sure," I said, and shrugged.

My mama turned, glanced up, and looked me dead in my eyes,

then snickered. "Boy, I'm yo' mama. You can lie to yourself, but you can't lie to me, you understand?"

My eyes started to sting, and I swallowed a dry ball. I didn't wanna break down and cry, like a little kid, with my moms, but she wouldn't ease up. Ever since the show, she'd been hell-bent on finding a way to make Dani pay. My moms wanted to see her suffer. She seemed to think that if we could get Dani, it would somehow make up for some of what I had gone through.

"Listen to what I'm telling you. The people I got coming over this evening, they can help us," she said. "I finally found someone who's gonna help us."

The excitement in her eyes scared me, because I knew she was wasting her time, and theirs. The laws weren't set up for women like Dani, who could do all kinds of foul crap, then stroll away like their shit didn't stink.

"Ma! How come you can't listen to what I'm tryna tell you? Just let it go. There ain't nothing we can do to get my time back. I can't get my money back and what good is it gonna do to keep talking to her?"

My mother sucked her teeth, then turned away from me and went to the pantry. She pulled two bags of chips out and looked back at me. "You should let me handle this. You're too nice for that tramp. She needs somebody like me. By the time I'm done with that heifer, she'll wish like hell she had fingered some other man."

"Maaa, I can fight my own battles," I said.

It didn't sound as hard as I wanted, but I meant it. I didn't want my mama to get involved in this. I was pissed at Dani for sure, but I had already checked and there was nothing we could do about what she had done. I wanted my moms to let it go.

"Get those deviled eggs out," she said, and motioned toward the refrigerator.

"Ma. Is that what this meeting is about tonight?"

"Boy. Let me handle tonight." She dismissed my question with the wave of a hand. "You don't even have to be here. I'm having some people over and we're gonna talk about our options."

"Options?" My shoulders caved. "Ma. Please, just leave it alone." I had a feeling it didn't matter how much I begged and pleaded, her mind was made up. Her snacks were ready, and she wasn't about to change her mind or her plans.

My mother walked over, stood in front of me, and tilted her head back to look up into my eyes.

"Listen. This mess, what she did, it's gonna impact you for a very, very long time. I don't know how you're gonna trust another woman again, and because of that, because of the time she stole from us, I need to do everything in my power to see to it that she pays for what she did."

"But, Ma—"

"No, Son." She cut me off. "I ain't about to back off on this. I don't care how long it takes. I don't care how much money it costs. I won't take my last breath until I know that I have tried everything within my power to make her regret what she did to you, to us, to this family." Her voice cracked, and she choked up a little. "She lied. You lost a daughter. I lost a grandbaby. It ain't right."

The look in her eyes told me there was nothing I could say that would change her mind or her determination. I didn't want to think about what was ahead.

My mama might have only been five feet one inch tall, but she was bigger than most men, ten times her size, and I couldn't remember a time when I had seen her back down.

I knew first-hand that when she was determined to do something, she put her *all* into it, until she saw it all the way through. I didn't feel the least bit sorry for Dani, but I did feel like she really would wish she had fingered another guy after my mother was done with her.

The doorbell rang and my mother's vengeful eyes quickly got wide with excitement.

"Oh, thank God," she squealed. My mom grabbed me by the arm and led me out of the kitchen. "They're finally here. C'mon, Son. Let's go and see what we can do to make that bitch pay."

"Ma?" I frowned, and stopped.

She turned back and looked at me, "What?" She shrugged, then bolted toward the front door.

CHAPTER EIGHT

Mark

As I drove the family to dinner, the right side of my face felt like it was being scorched to a crisp. It felt like the heat penetrated my skin. That was how hard my wife stared at me, with murder in her eyes.

My focus remained straight ahead and my eyes glued to the road. I knew she was pissed, but there was nothing I could do.

"You know it was her," Zaneda said. "Who else would pull some mess like that? I hate her! I hate that you did what you did, and basically made her a part of our lives for the next ten years," she hissed.

Everything she said was correct. It was my fault; all of it was my fault. There was nothing for me to say. I made a mistake. I screwed up and Markeesa was a constant reminder of what I had done. But she was my child too and none of it was her fault. Zaneda and I survived the mistake, but when Arlene pulled the kind of stunts she pulled, it was like my wife was reminded of my betrayal all over again.

We had been through this before and I knew not to feed into Zaneda's anger. If I said something, I'd be accused of defending Arlene. So I let Zaneda get it out of her system, and I drove in silence.

"She must think we're stupid!"

"What did the lawyer say?" I finally asked.

"That's not the point. You know, and I know she did this," Zaneda said.

I glanced into the rearview mirror and watched the kids who all sat with headphones on. They were mesmerized by the movie the boys had selected.

"Can we talk about this later?" I asked. I turned to look over my shoulder to let her know the conversation was too much for the kids.

Zaneda pulled her crossed arms up to her chest. She was in a foul mood, and that wasn't good for the rest of our day.

"Doesn't it bother you that we are now in the middle of a stupid investigation because of her? It's like she's going to try and do anything in her power to make our lives miserable," she hissed.

Zaneda hated Arlene and the two of them would probably kill each other if ever given the opportunity.

At a stoplight, I looked over at Zaneda and asked, "Is this how we are going to be for the rest of the night? We're about to go out to dinner. Let's talk about her later and enjoy our family outing for now."

There was no way I wanted to let Arlene ruin our night. Our attorney was going to deal with the Child Protective Services complaint and I had to let him do his job. Us worrying about it would only cause more problems between us.

After we talked to our attorney and he told us what to do, we did it. It pissed Zaneda off even more, but his advice kept us out of trouble. I thought back to the look on Zaneda's face when I told her what our lawyer Timothy had said.

On that day, he had given us our marching orders. He had told us we needed to get the kids examined by our doctor.

Zaneda had balked at that. She frowned, cut her eyes at me and asked, "Why would we be going to the doctor's office?"

"Timothy said a doctor's report will prove there are no signs of abuse. Then all of the evidence we've submitted will prove that someone is trying to set us up," I said.

"Someone?" Zaneda snarled.

By the time we met with the CPS worker two days later, we were ready. Inside our attorney's office, a copy of the doctor's report sat on Timothy's desk for the case worker, Virginia, to see.

"My clients are the victims of a hateful and destructive false report," Timothy said. "We'd like to know who called to report the abuse because two days ago, both children were checked out and cleared by the family pediatrician," he said.

Zaneda picked up the report and passed it to the case worker. Virginia's pudgy fingers clutched the folder, then she opened it and read the paper inside.

After a few moments, she looked up and said, "We must look into each and every complaint we receive. None of this is anything personal."

"Yes, I get that. But I can assure you. We are good parents and our kids are not being abused," I said.

Virginia looked over at us and said, "All parents are potential child abusers. Children can really push you to your limit and if your patience is thin, anything is possible. But according to these reports, there are no present symptoms or signs of abuse. This is nothing personal, but I'm sure you'll agree, it's best to err on the side of caution."

But that was now all in the past.

My cell phone rang and brought me back to the present. I ignored the call and took off when the light turned green. It felt like I had driven all the way to Joe's Crab Shack on auto pilot. Once I parked, I hesitated before we got out of the car. I turned to Zaneda and asked, "Are you going to be okay? We can talk about all this later."

Her face looked like a sour taste was stuck in her mouth. I didn't say anything because it was obvious she wasn't about to let go of the CPS thing anytime soon.

Once they realized the car had stopped, the kids snatched off their headphones and started to free themselves from the seatbelts in the backseat.

"Oh. We're here!" Mark Junior said. He turned to his sister. "Markeesa, we're at your favorite restaurant."

"I know. I can't wait to have some crab legs. Daddy, you and Ms. Zaneda are sad. What's wrong?"

My daughter's question really made me upset with Zaneda. She needed to pull it together. I didn't want Markeesa to go back and report anything negative to her mother. Zaneda knew better, but she wouldn't let up.

The look I gave her must've told her exactly how I felt because Zaneda seemed to snap out of it all of a sudden. She whipped around in her seat and smiled at the kids.

"Oh no! Nobody's sad," Zaneda said, and flashed a fake, but massive Kool-Aid smile.

CHAPTER NINE

Dani

"What would you do if you were me?" I looked up in the mirror while Niecy flat-ironed my weave.

"I'd go to the home of the fifty-dollar, full head, sew-in," she said.

I jerked my head away from her hands.

"Oh. I see you got jokes, huh?" I wasn't in a joking mood.

"Girl! Quit, I nearly burned you." She tugged on my hair. "C'mon now and stop playing. You know I'm only messin' with you. Besides, I told you, we need to hurry. After ten, we gotta pay to get in and a cover charge ain't nowhere in my budget."

Niecy, Lulu and I did almost everything together. We all met in the eighth grade and have been tight ever since. You name it, and we've probably done it, almost always together. Even the stuff nobody was supposed to know about.

"But for real though," she said as she took a clump of my hair and tried to straighten it with the flat-iron. "I dunno what you should do. I mean, you playing with the law now, and I don't think that's a good look. I mean, what they calling you in for anyway?" she asked.

I shrugged. I hadn't slept good since I got that call. I was so nervous that I didn't even bother asking what I was gonna be questioned about. I just agreed to the date and time and started to think the worst.

"What y'all been doing?" Lulu asked as she walked into the bathroom. She was already dressed in a pair of liquid tights and a skimpy crop top. Her face was fully made up, and she sported a fierce short wig. She flicked her wrist and glanced down dramatically. "We not gonna make it," said Lulu.

I sucked my teeth. "We are. Don't trip."

"While y'all sitting here in counseling, y'all need to put a rush on it 'cause I ain't paying twenty dollars to get into no club. I don't care whose birthday it is. That don't even make any sense. I can't stand people who are *ghettwah*—you don't invite folks to your birthday party and make *them* pay. Hell, that's like me giving you a party!" Lulu complained.

"She got a point there," I said.

"Yeah, but I heard it's supposed to be some ballers there, tonight, so I really wanna go, but I feel you about paying twenty to get in," Niecy chimed in.

"Man, Dani, what's up with your weave? It looks like a rug. Maybe we need to pool our money and let you go to the fifty-dollar spot. How we gonna catch some ballers with your *ish* looking like that?"

The two of them broke out laughing. When they fist-bumped each other, I'd had enough. I jerked away from Niecy and got up.

"You know what, how about I just stay here and y'all go to the club without me?" I said.

"Why you getting all sensitive and stuff? You know we only playing," Niecy said. "Besides, I'm almost done; sit down so we can go, girl!"

Reluctantly, I eased back into the chair and looked at my reflection in the large mirror. I knew my weave was jacked up, I needed my nails and stuff done too, but money was tight and since I didn't have any extra money coming in, I was really messed up. I hated living life like a refugee with no means of support.

"So, I heard y'all talking about the police interview," Lulu said. "What happened when you went to talk to them and what did they want anyway?"

"I didn't go," I said.

Lulu's eyeballs grew wide. "Whatchu' mean you didn't go?"

"Girl, I wasn't about to go strolling up in no police station to talk to nobody when I had no idea what they wanted. You've seen how people get railroaded by the police. Hell, I watch *The First 48* all the time," I said.

Niecy frowned. "Dani, I didn't think you ignored the law! Girl, what's wrong with you?"

"Ain't nothing wrong with me. What they want me to come down there for? I ain't did nothing wrong to nobody, so I figured there wasn't no use in me going to talk to them." I shrugged. "Besides, if they wanted to talk to me that bad, they know where to find me. I ain't gonna make their job easy. Why go walk in there so they could pin whatever they want on me?"

My friends looked at each other and exchanged knowing glances. I didn't care what they thought. I wasn't going to no damn police station to talk to the law because I ain't did nothing wrong to nobody and nobody was gonna make me. We wrapped up and rushed to the car.

We got to the club and to the front door with two minutes to spare. I was relived because I only had $17.45 to my name and the last thing I wanted to do was spend it on somebody's cover charge for a birthday party at a club.

Nox's was packed and popping by the time we strolled through the doors. I liked the spot because it was big and spacious enough to hold tons of people. If one spot wasn't crunk, all you had to do was move around and it was like being in a whole new environment, all under the same roof.

My hair might not have been on point, but the little bandage dress that hugged my curvy frame was everything. The Nuccas would be on me something vicious. Because my body was the tightest, whenever we went clubbing, we walked in a straight line, with me at the front. Niecy and Lulu were on point too, but I pulled the most attention, and the overflow shine extended to them as we moved. It had worked for us like that for years and that's how we rolled.

I stopped and we posted up near the bar. This dude was all over Lulu so I leaned over and whispered to Niecy, "Girl, it's thick up in here tonight."

"Yup! Just the way I like it. I need to pull me a baller or a few, tonight," Niecy said.

"I feel you, girl, me too, 'cause the struggle is real!" We glanced around the packed place and scoped out who was doing what. There were several sections where dudes posted up got bottle service, while they puffed on cigars.

"That's where we need to be," I said, as I motioned to the far-right corner. "It looks like they doing big things over there."

Niecy turned her head in the direction that I had pointed.

"Oh, snap! Let's do it, girl!"

I glanced over my shoulder and said, "But wait. Lulu needs to come on. Get the digits and keep it moving! What is she doing?"

"I'ma go get her," Niecy said.

I stood off to the side as Niecy walked a few feet away and over to Lulu and the guy she was talking to. But suddenly these two dudes started to circle me. I loved it when dudes were creative with the approach, so I was eating it up.

It was all good, the way they put the spotlight on me. I knew after a bold introduction like that, somebody would be buying me and my girls a whole lotta drinks.

Suddenly, dude number one stopped in front of me and twisted his face. I didn't know if he was trying to act hard or what.

"Yeah, dawg, that's her, all right," he finally said.

His boy came and stood next to him. Now they both stood feet from my face, and threw shade. I started to get nervous.

"Shorty, that was all kinds of foul how you did ol' boy on that show," one of them said.

I rolled my eyes dramatically. Oh, shit! Here we go again.

"I dunno what you talking about; why don't y'all bounce?" I said, and tried to keep my cool.

At that very moment, the DJ lowered the volume on the music. It felt like every eye in the club was locked on me and the drama that was bound to come.

"Naw. Why you take my boy on national TV only to tell him the kid wasn't his?" the same guy repeated.

All of a sudden, other voices chimed in. It was like being on stage all over again.

"Told you that was her!"

"I'd get in that ass!"

"Trifling ho!"

"THOT!" another person yelled.

"She need to be under the jail cell."

Before I could defend myself, or even say a word, Niecy and Lulu rushed to my side.

"Girl, this ain't the business. We probably need to bounce," Lulu said. She looked more nervous than me.

"I'm not listening to these busters," I said, and tried to sidestep the two clowns. But Niecy stepped close to me and whispered in my ear.

"Ol' boy had Lulu hemmed up about the show too. That's what they was talking about. Let's just go. I ain't tryna be in the middle of no damn riot," she said.

I looked around the club and realized people either gawked in my direction, or whispered and pointed at me. My heart took a nosedive. I felt even worse when I had to follow Lulu through the crowd, while Niecy watched my back from behind.

CHAPTER TEN

Arlene

"Where you going, Ma?" I asked my mother as she came to the door with a weekend bag packed.

A horn honked outside the door and I really felt worthless.

"I tell yo this dah me weekend feh go da Louisiana with Carol and Betty."

I frowned.

"So you still going?" I asked.

My mother looked at me and threw her hand to her hip. "Weh make yo think I no gowein? I meh di pay for this trip long time. I wei come back Sunday," she said.

"But now that Markeesa is gone, what am I supposed to do?"

"Why yo no call Janet. Yo no see her all week," my mother said.

Before I could shoot that idea down, the horn honked again and my mother was out the door. I stood there lost. I didn't want a weekend of peace and quiet. Being alone for me was like being in an asylum. I knew it wouldn't be long before the memories crept back to the forefront of my mind and I'd spiral into depression.

Determined to beat that, I went into the living room and decided to watch TV. I clicked the on-demand button and scrolled through my options. Unfortunately, I was caught up on all of my shows and wasn't in the mood to start anything new.

I looked around the empty apartment and instantly felt bad. There was no way in hell I was supposed to be here. This was not supposed to be my life.

I grabbed my cell and called my best friend, Janet Grover. She answered by the fourth ring.

"Hey, lady," she greeted.

"Girl, what's up with you?"

"Nothing. Getting ready for date night," she said.

Janet was married to Bruce. For the most part, they were happy, but every now and then they had their moments. When things were good, Janet would vanish for days at a time with no contact. But when things were bad with them, she hung around like a bad cold that irritated the hell out of you. Her skills as a notary would come in handy, so I needed to shield her from the drama with Mark and me as much as possible.

"What are you and Markeesa doing this weekend?" she asked.

"Girl. She's with Mark," I said.

Silence.

"Uh, how did that happen?" Janet asked. "And so that means she's with Zaneda too, right?" The sudden sadness in her voice made me feel even worse.

"Yes, girl."

"Awww, how you doing over there? Why don't you and your mom go see a movie or something? You know, to take your mind off of it," she said.

"Mama went to Louisiana," I said.

"Shoot, Arlene. You gonna be okay?" Her voice was laced with concern.

I swallowed hard. This was so unfair. Mark messed up my life. If he had played his cards right, we'd be a family today. Instead he panicked, and screwed everything up.

"Yeah. You know I'm not used to me-time anymore, so it's kinda weird. But enough about me. I know you and Bruce are about to get out; maybe we can go have lunch tomorrow or something," I said.

"Okay, honey. Well, you hang in there, and I'll call to check on you later."

I settled on a rerun of *Scandal* and eased into the comfort of the sofa. As I watched Olivia Pope solve her client's problems, I started to wish I had a fixer in my own life. I didn't intend to fall in love with Mark. Everything with him just fell into place. That was probably what made me believe we were meant to be together.

It was hard to fathom I'd been going through this for more than seven years, but I had. I felt like a part of my life stopped when I realized he had gone back on his word and again moved in with his pathetic wife.

The day he told me, was one I will never forget. My swollen belly looked like it would pop at any moment. The pregnancy had been uncomfortable and very unpleasant. My neck was black; my nose had spread across my face from one side to the next; and I could barely walk because my ankles were so swollen.

But when Mark looked at me with those eyes of his, I felt like it was all worth it.

"You still beautiful to me, baby," he said.

Mark and I were in a condo he had rented while his new house was being remodeled. The house was way past schedule and he and Zaneda had fought over everything.

I felt so bad for him because he really was a good man. He wasn't ready for me and once I set out to get him, there really was nothing he could do.

Our story began nearly two years before we moved into the condo. I had been hired as the nanny. That's how I met the man I loved. His lazy, trifling, ungrateful wife hired me to look after her kids. Zaneda was the poster girl for the idea of looks being deceiving. When she first hired me, she was sweet and caring, but she changed in what felt like overnight.

"I don't want you to spoil the baby. It's okay to let him cry every once in a while," she told me.

"Oh, but it just hurts my heart to listen to him cry his little lungs out," I said.

Zaneda turned and looked at me. "Girl, please. A little crying never hurt anybody. Besides, it'll teach him that he can't always get what he wants."

Everything about their life seemed perfect, from the outside. Their big pretty house was filled with lots of expensive, flashy things. Mark played football for the Los Angeles Sea Lions and Zaneda spent his money. In the off-season, Houston was their home.

At that point, I had only been living with them for a few months before I realized something was very wrong. One afternoon, Mark came home as I fed the baby.

"Hey, Arlene. You heard from Zaneda? She's not answering her phone," he said.

I turned my head and was not prepared for what met my eyes.

Muscles.

Everywhere I looked, my eyes took in nice, taut, sweat-drenched muscles.

Warm embarrassment washed over me as I stumbled all over myself. I felt ashamed as I tried to shake naughty thoughts that ran through my mind.

"She's...uh, they left already," I said.

Mark frowned. On an average person that's what it would've been, but on Mark's handsome face, it looked just like his features readjusted themselves.

"Who is *they*? And what do you mean, they *left*?"

"Oh. She and her girlfriends; they went to the Bahamas," I said.

Mark pounded his fist onto the granite counter top. "You gotta be kidding me! I told Zaneda I needed her here. I've got an endorsement deal on the table and she was supposed to fix dinner for…"

"I can do it for you," I said, as I cut him off. I couldn't stand to see him suffer. He was visibly upset and I wanted to do whatever I could to fix his problem.

He looked at me, his head tilted slightly as if he was unsure that I was the solution. But I had the answers to his problem.

Four hours later, I had both kids bathed, asleep, and the house smelled better than a five-star restaurant.

Mark grinned from ear to ear. He had helped me with everything. It turned out that there were three guys and one woman and I put out such a spread, with drinks, and everything else that Mark worked his jelly and secured his new endorsement deal.

At one point in the evening, one of the guys even thought Mark and I were a couple. That was what brought the attraction to the surface.

CHAPTER ELEVEN

Keeling

"She said they was gonna do a show where they wanted to surprise some fathers who were trying to do the right thing. I ain't never heard of that show before, so when she told me I could make five hundred dollars, I was like, why not?" I said.

The little white man with the wire-rimmed glasses scribbled on his notepad just as fast as I talked. Or at least that was what it seemed like.

"Tell him how she got you arrested," my mother said.

I sighed. She wouldn't shut up. The last thing I wanted to do was sit up in an office with some scrawny-looking white man and tell him all my business. My mother nagged and nagged until I agreed to come to this meeting.

My mother wouldn't stop. I turned to her and said, "Ma. I told you. She didn't get me arrested."

She shook her head like she didn't know what she would do with me. "I told you. It might have been the attorney general who moved things along for the court order. But trust me, son, it all started with her."

"So, Mr. Lake. Tell me the details surrounding your arrest. Had you been given any warning prior to the warrant?"

I hunched my shoulders. I couldn't remember all that mess. All

I knew was I was on the job and my supervisor called me to the front of the building. I didn't even see the cops until I walked all the way into his office.

"Keeling, uh, these officers need to talk to you," my supervisor had said. He had looked nervous and that made me nervous.

Confused, I looked around like what the hell did the law want with me? I hadn't done a damn thing. I had been working at the auto body shop for almost a year and everything was gravy.

"You're Keeling Lake?" one of the officers asked.

I looked between the two of them and nodded. "Yeah, that's me. Why? What's up?" I asked.

"We have a warrant for your arrest."

My legs got all weak. Arrest? Me? Warrant? "I didn't do nothing!"

It was the first thing that came to my mind. Where I was from, people who went to jail went because they were out trying to rob somebody, or maybe they shot someone. I didn't do any of that so, I knew for sure there had to be some kind of mistake.

"Lemme call my moms," I said.

Before I could ask any questions, my mother was in my ear.

"What you mean you 'bout to go to jail?!" she screamed.

"Ma, chill. They just said they have a warrant for my arrest. I think you need to come and meet me at the station so I can get out."

"Ask them, Keeling. I wanna know what the hell you being arrested for, dammit!"

Like a puppet being pulled by a string, I turned to the officers. "My mama wants to know why I'm being arrested."

"Delinquent child support," one of the officers said. He seemed bored by the whole scene.

"Delinquent what? Nuh-uh, put him on the phone!" she screamed.

"Ma!"

"Keeling, I said put him on the phone. This is foolishness. So

Dani don' called and reported you because you fell behind on your payments? I thought you talked to her," she said.

"I did, Ma."

The officers looked at me and I said softly, "My mother wants to talk to one of you."

The one officer who shook his head like he was disgusted, reached for the phone. "Sergeant Eden here."

For a moment he didn't say anything, but he nodded, then he said, "Well, ma'am, you can get that information at the station, but we are taking him in."

As I walked through the body shop with the officers at my side, I was embarrassed. Even without handcuffs, everybody knew I was being arrested.

"We've gotta be able to do something here. He didn't deserve to be treated like that and I want her to know she can't get away with this," my mother said.

Her comment brought me back to the meeting. I didn't want to be there, I wanted to forget about all of this and get my life back on track. I felt like going after Dani wasn't gonna do us any good. It wasn't like she was gonna give back any of the money she made me pay for a kid that wasn't even mine. The only thing I was half-way interested in was getting them off my back.

I didn't think I should have to pay child support for Dani's kid, she needed to find the real father and hit his ass up. "Okay, okay. Here's what we're gonna do. First things first. I'm calling over to the AG's office so I can find out what they're saying. Then once you get another job, we will get the child support payments set up right away to avoid any future run-ins with the law."

My mother looked like she was about to have a stroke.

"You mean we're just gonna keep paying?" she asked.

"Mrs. Lake, we must keep paying. Until the attorney general

lifts this order, there is no question about whether or not we have to pay," he said.

"But the heifer lied!"

"I understand, but the law says your son must continue to pay until we work this thing out," the lawyer said.

"That's just not right. There's nothing right about that," she insisted. "Okay, so when does *she* go to jail?"

"Here's the thing," the man said. He paused. I think he was trying to figure out how to word everything just the right way. "I don't think she's going to jail. She hasn't broken the law."

"But she lied!" my mother screamed. "The little heifer knew my son was not that child's father and she lied and that lie led to him being thrown in jail!"

The man nodded. "Yes. Yes. I get all of that. Was it immoral? Absolutely. We know it was wrong, but the question of whether it was against the law is the issue."

"So she just gets to get away with this? Is that what you're telling me?"

"What I'm telling you is, we will see what, if anything we can do, but for now, she hasn't broken any laws." He settled back in his chair. "I know how you feel. I understand you want justice, but this is where we are."

I wasn't happy about what he said, but my mother, she looked like she was ready to kill, and a part of me was afraid that eventually, she would.

CHAPTER TWELVE

Mark

Zaneda burst into our bedroom and huffed as she stormed around the bed and onto her side.

"You need to go and talk to your daughter," Zaneda said as she kicked off her shoes. She flopped onto her side of the bed, picked up her cellphone, and let out a huge sigh.

"What's the matter now?" I asked. I hated when she referred to Markeesa as *my daughter*, instead of by her name.

"She won't take a bath and I don't have time to coddle her. My kids are all self-sufficient," she snapped. Zaneda ran her finger along the screen of her phone, then put it down, and picked up a copy of *Essence* magazine. She flipped through the pages as she talked. "It's not that I don't like her. She's innocent in all of this. But it's like Arlene fills her head with all this hateful stuff and I'm left to deal with it," she said, and rolled her eyes dramatically.

"I will talk to Arlene," I said.

Zaneda slapped the magazine closed and turned to me. "And speaking of talking to her, did you ask her about the call to CPS?"

"Timothy said to let him handle it. So, I'm doing what the attorney said. It's why we pay him." I tried to keep my tone as even as possible.

Zaneda sucked her teeth. "I don't care what you guys say. I know in my heart of hearts that she's behind it. I hate her. I swear, I curse the day I ever let that two-bit slut next to my family."

Unsure of whether I should stay and listen, or go see about my daughter, I was reluctant to leave. When Zaneda got on Arlene, it was hard to tell when she'd get enough and stop. If I left too soon, she'd go on the rampage and we'd end up in a war of words. I eased back onto the bed and tried to wait her out.

She looked over at me and frowned. "She's waiting on you."

"Oh. I thought you were just suggesting I go," I told her.

I walked down the hall and across to the other side of the house toward the kids' Jack and Jill bathroom.

After I knocked on my daughter's bedroom door and she didn't answer, I moved to the bathroom door.

"Markeesa, you in there, honey?"

"I wanna go home," she whined.

"Already?" I asked. "You just got here."

"I know. But Miss Zaneda don't like me. My mommy told me she didn't and she don't."

"Hey, why don't you open the door so we can talk?"

Slowly, the door opened and Markeesa's eyes peered through the crack. It looked like she'd been crying.

"Where is she?" my daughter asked.

"She's using the phone in our bedroom. Why don't you come out so we can talk? Zaneda loves you just like she loves the boys," I said. I knew that wasn't true, but after what we'd been through with CPS, the last thing I needed was to have my daughter feel uncomfortable in my home.

"Can I call my mommy?" she asked.

"Of course," I said. "Just come on out and I'll bring the phone so you can call."

If she called Arlene, things would go from bad to worse and I knew it. That phone call would raise a flag and Arlene would be on her way over here, probably with the police in tow.

As Markeesa eased out of the bathroom, MJ and Mason barreled down the hall. They laughed and horse-played, roughhousing all the way.

"Hey!" I yelled at the boys. "What's the matter with y'all? What y'all doing?"

"Mom said we can go night swimming!" MJ yelled.

All of a sudden, Markeesa's eyes lit up. She was still there with me physically, but mentally, she was right on her brothers' heels.

"You coming, Markeesa?" Mason asked over his shoulder.

She started to jump up and down.

"Can I go, Daddy, please? Can I go night swimming too?"

Instantly I was mad at Zaneda. She knew better than to let the boys go swimming alone, especially at night. But when I saw the immediate change in my daughter and she hadn't insisted on calling her mother anymore, I figured we'd all go night swimming.

"I'll tell you what. You go change into your swimsuit. I'm gonna put on my trunks and we can all go. How's that?"

"Yaaay!" she squealed in delight. I watched as she bolted to her room and closed the door.

By the time I made it back to our bedroom, Zaneda was yapping on the phone to one of her friends.

"So you were just gonna let the kids go swim at night by themselves?" I asked.

She pulled the phone from the side of her face, looked at me and frowned. "I was about to come out there, but my phone rang. Besides, I knew you'd go with them," she said. "It's not like they don't know how to swim," Zaneda muttered under her breath.

I ignored her comment. She went back to her call and I changed.

"You know how simple they are," Zaneda said into the phone.

"You and I both know she was behind the call. But what can we do? They just said it was an anonymous tip."

As tempted as I was to say something to her about putting our business out in the streets, I let it pass. I had too much to do and deal with. I knew it probably was Arlene who called CPS on us, but I couldn't prove it. And, if it wasn't her, but she knew about CPS showing up at our house, she never let on. Outside of that, I expected all kinds of drama when I went to get Markeesa and that was why I didn't go alone.

But to my astonishment, there was no drama. Arlene gave me the usual nasty glares, and stared like she wished she could kill with her eyes, but that was nothing out of the ordinary. I scooped up my daughter and left.

Thoughts of the CPS call stayed with me, but I wasn't going to worry about it. Timothy said he'd handle it, and that's what he'd been doing.

CHAPTER THIRTEEN

Dani

I t felt like relief would be waiting for me if only I could make it home. People hated me. They wanted to take it all out on me. I was everyone's enemy, and it was too much. Everywhere I went, people recognized me as that chick who lied about her baby daddy on national TV. I couldn't find anything but grief. I just knew the moment I got behind closed doors, I could relax with a drink and forget about all of 'em.

But the instant I walked into the house, I wanted to turn right around and leave.

It had taken nothing but a few months for my life to go from dusty to downright dirt.

"Why are the police looking for you?" my mother, Charlene, barked the moment she laid eyes on me.

As usual, I wasn't ready for her question and it caught me completely off guard. I knew I couldn't ignore her, because she'd get even more worked up and we'd start fighting again. I had hoped to be able to get some quiet time in before I had to pick up my kids. If I had known she was home, I would've gone around the corner and waited it out in the car.

"I dunno, Charlene," I said, defeated. I didn't have the energy required for a brawl with her. "They want to ask me some questions, but I have no idea what they wanna talk about so, I ain't been by there yet," I said.

She had followed me all the way to the room I shared with my three kids. When I turned and tried to close the door, she stood in the doorway with her hands on her hips.

If she had been a cartoon character, smoke would've been blowing outta her ears and her nose. She was ready to get down, but I was worn out and had nothing left. But that's how Charlene had been all my life. The moment she saw me down, she'd come for me with guns blazing.

"Dani, I got a feeling and I'm not happy about it," she said.

Unfortunately for me, she had followed me all the way into the room. She looked around and twisted her face so much it made mine hurt.

I trailed her eyes. Yes, there was a bunk bed on one side of the room, then my twin bed, and a couple of dressers in each corner. I also kept a small refrigerator in the opposite corner because Charlene would blow a gasket if I kept my cocktails in the kitchen.

The space was crowded and cramped, but I did my best to keep it clean. It wasn't easy to share a room with three kids, their clothes, toys, and on top of that, all of my stuff. But that was my life, for now.

As Charlene looked around the room, I felt so outta whack. I just knew she was hunting for something to fuss at me about. It was just a matter of time before she got on the topic of me and Keeling, and I wasn't really in the mood. There had been enough reminders about him.

Lately, it was like everybody looked for a reason to lash out at me, and there was only so much more I could take, before they'd start to feel my wrath.

I watched as Charlene walked over to the kids' bunk bed. I leaned up against one of the dressers and waited for her to finish her little inspection. She took a stuffed animal from the top bunk, and stared at it like she needed to figure out what was wrong with it. That was part of her damn problem. She always inspected everything for imperfections.

A few seconds later, she looked at me and asked, "Where did I go wrong with you?" Her voice cracked slightly, like she was about to break down.

She couldn't be serious. Only she was.

It wasn't easy, but I bit my tongue, rolled my eyes, then swallowed hard before I answered. "You didn't go wrong at all. I just wanted something different outta life."

My mother slapped her forehead with the palm of her hand. I braced myself for the theatrics that were sure to follow. I really needed to get my *ish* together, because I was so sick and tired of her and all the drama.

I stood back, crossed my arms at my chest, and waited for her to bring it.

"I did it all the right way. I graduated high school, went to college, married my high school sweetheart, then conceived you out of love. We brought you into a two-parent household," Charlene said. "We worked our butts off to give you everything. And this is how you repaid me." She waved her arm around the room. "You had everything."

If I could get twenty frigging dollars for the number of times I had to sit and listen to that self-righteous speech of hers, I'd have enough money for my own damn place. Hell, I quoted parts of it in my sleep.

I shrugged. "You chose a different path. But look around! Look around, where's your husband now?!" I screamed.

Her face twisted. She eased back a bit, and looked like she wasn't sure about her next move, but I didn't let up.

"You always quick to look down your nose at me. Yeah, I got pregnant at sixteen, and six years later, I have three kids. I'm not married, have two different baby daddies, but that's me! I'm sorry I'm not the perfect daughter you always dreamed of while you were planning your perfect life, but it is what it is!" I shouted.

"Dani, you're missing my point," Charlene said. Her eyes were filled with tears, but I didn't give a damn. Her tone had softened a little, but I knew her well enough to know, she was only setting up so she could go for the jugular.

"That's a low blow and you know it," she hissed.

"Do you really wanna talk about low blows? You act like your life has been such a fairy-tale. Yes, you did everything the right way, as you say, and I didn't. But, Charlene, you ever ask yourself how did we both wind up in the very same place?"

She didn't have anything to say about that.

CHAPTER FOURTEEN

Arlene

I was reminiscing, remembering when everything with Mark had started.

"This would be wrong," Mark said. His hand brushed mine as we washed dishes together.

His touch electrified me. I literally felt a shiver rush through my body.

"Sometimes, good things can come from something wrong," I said. My voice was just above a whisper. I didn't know what made me say it, but I felt as if I had to think fast on my feet.

He turned to me and for the first time, I saw so much when I stared deep into his eyes. Mark was a beautiful man, but he was in pain. The sadness I saw in his eyes pulled me in like a strong magnet. Our lips found each other's and we eased into a long, sensual, and scrumptious kiss.

My body fell into his. He stumbled back into a nook near the refrigerator and the standing wine chiller. I hungrily attacked his body and he just as eagerly ravished mine. He felt good, and I wanted the bliss to continue. Moments later, when we separated, our chests heaved as we tried to pull ourselves together.

Suddenly, he extended his hand, and I accepted. Mark led me through the hall near the back of the kitchen and down the three steps that lead to my part of the house. My legs followed blindly, like I was on auto-pilot. At the door, we kissed again. I was drunk with anticipation. The intensity between us was so raw, like once finally unleashed, it couldn't be tamed.

We stumbled over to the bed. My heart thudded in my chest, I quivered all over. Clothes flew into the air. His shirt was pulled over his head and flung across the room. Mark's body was a sight to behold. His washboard abs rippled along his lean, muscled torso. He hopped on one foot, removed one leg from his pants, then the other. The pants were shoved off to the corner. My fingers trembled as I unbuttoned my shirt. Bra, panties, and jeans fell like raindrops during a wicked thunderstorm.

I was in awe once his boxer briefs came off. His body had been magnificent, but when I took him into my palm, his girth prevented me from closing my hand.

"You're so beautiful," I said.

"No. That's you. Everything about you is beautiful, the way you take care of the kids, the house," he said, "and me," he added in a whisper.

That night, Mark and I made love over and over again. I intentionally screwed him on the chaise lounge, the wing chair in front of a large mirror, and over the ottoman. In the past, I had overheard him and Zaneda fight because she never wanted to do anything other than the missionary position in bed. I was determined not to make the same mistake. He couldn't get enough of me, and I was happy to let him get his fill.

Three weeks later, Zaneda and her girlfriends went on another trip. Again, while she was gone, I took care of her kids and her husband. We were in bliss, like a real family.

The night Zaneda came back home, I thought for sure Mark and I had been busted. It wasn't even ten minutes after I'd fucked

Mark and left their shower in the master suite, that I walked through the kitchen and found Zaneda on the phone near the pantry. She smiled as I approached and ended her call. "Girl, let me holler at you in the morning. I'm worn out," she said into the phone.

She hung up the phone and turned her attention to me. "I was looking for you," she said.

At times she talked to me like I was a girlfriend more than an employee.

My heart raced with pure adrenaline, and my eyes widened in fear. I wasn't sure how to respond. Did she smell Mark on me? Or maybe she smelled the fresh-washed fragrance from her shower. I was a nervous wreck. I was especially nervous because all I had on was a robe and a pair of slippers, but apparently my outfit didn't bother her.

"How long have the kids been asleep?" she asked, as she fidgeted with her cell phone and dropped it into her designer bag.

Zaneda looked like walking money. Her expensive weave was freshly done, and the St. John pants suit she rocked looked like it cost a mint. Her silver accessories dripped with sparkling diamonds. I wanted everything she had. I wanted her life.

"Oh, I put them down earlier," I said. "Why do you ask?"

She sighed. "I wanted to make sure they were asleep before I came barging in. If they see me, it's going to be hours before I get rest. I'm tired and I don't feel like being bothered tonight."

"You're tired? I thought you just got back from the Bahamas," I said, as I pulled the top part of my robe closed.

Zaneda rolled her eyes. "Girl, that was last month. We went to the Keys this time, and yes. I'm exhausted."

"Umph. Well, exhaustion looks good on you."

She moved closer and lowered her voice, "Where's Mark? I'm sure he'll want some tonight," she muttered, with so much disdain.

I wanted to tell her Mark was fine and he'd soon be sleeping like a baby if he wasn't already.

"Oh, he's down too," I said.

When her skillfully arched brow went upward, I thought for sure a slap was coming to my cheek. But instead, Zaneda sighed hard, like she was relieved, and said, "Thank God! I really need to get some rest tonight."

But before she let me go, her eyes started at my feet, then rolled up my body and stopped at my face. She tilted her head ever so slightly, and frowned.

"So, if everyone's sleeping, how come you weren't in your room?"

"Oh, I thought I heard Junior, so I got up to check on him. I know how you don't like to be disturbed after the kids have gone to bed."

It hadn't dawned on her or me that the kids' rooms were on the opposite side of the house. I was sure the split floor plan must've been her idea.

The mess didn't sound right to me, but she bought it and waved a dismissive arm. "You are so good with the kids. I don't know what we'd do without you," she said, then yawned and didn't even cover her mouth.

Once she finished, she picked up her large Gucci bag from the counter and continued to sing my praises. "It's not just me either. Mark was kind of reluctant to hire a live-in at first, but you have completely restored his faith in finding good help," she said.

Good help?

I nearly laughed out loud at her description of me, but there was no use. She had already started to make her way down the path I'd just left, toward her master suite.

Ringing sounds peppered the air and pulled me back from that painful memory. I grabbed the phone when I realized it was Janet.

"You okay over there?" she asked when I answered.

"I am. Just wish I could stop thinking about his worthless, ignorant ass," I said.

Janet laughed and that made me laugh too.

CHAPTER FIFTEEN

Keeling

"Ma, I want you to leave it alone. I'm sick of this crap. I wanna focus on getting my life together. I ain't got time to be wasting behind Dani and what she's doing."

I dipped my head down and shoved the spoon into my mouth. Why couldn't she let me enjoy my cereal in peace? My moms had just walked in after work, busted through the door with a foul attitude and a stank tone.

"You haven't heard nothing from the attorney?"

That was the question that set me off. I didn't want to hear from the attorney. I wanted to forget all the stuff with Dani and I was mad my moms couldn't let it go.

"Naw," I said.

"My coworker told me about another plan. I think we need to take matters into our own hands."

I saw no point in telling her to forget about it. It was obvious she was determined to ride this thing 'til the wheels exploded. She was more hardheaded than me.

She moved around to the table and placed a bucket of chicken in front of me.

"Cereal, Keeling? Really?" "I was hungry."

"I told you I was bringing food."

"I know, but after looking for a job all day, I needed something when I came in. Don't worry, I'm still gonna tear up that chicken too."

Moments later, we ate the Kentucky Fried Chicken she'd brought home; then I got up and helped her clean the kitchen. As we cleaned up, my moms turned to me and asked, "Son, I'm not trying to blame any of this on you, and I know you don't like to talk about it, but there's just one question that's been burning me."

"Whassup, Ma?" I folded the dish rag.

"Did it ever cross your mind that maybe that baby might not be yours?" she asked.

"Ma."

"I know, Son. I know. But I'm just asking. I know you guys like the girls who are easy and will give it up in a heartbeat, but you gotta think, if she's so quick to give it to you, she's probably giving it to everybody else too.".

I sighed. I wasn't trying to get a lesson about women from my mom. But, I needed to let her say what was on her mind. Otherwise, I'd never get peace.

"Ma, ain't no point in going back in the past. It's not gonna change anything."

"I know, Son. But you gotta have some respect…"

While my moms yapped about everything that I needed to do to make my life right, I thought back to when I first met Dani. My moms was right. Dani was raunchy and hot in every way possible, and I liked it. Back then, I wanted the baddest chick, and I thought that chick was Dani.

It was a mild summer evening in Houston. Humidity was low even though the temperature was high. We were at one of my boy Roger's infamous backyard bashes.

"Hey, Papi," Dani said, as she strolled up to us and popped her gum in rhythm. I had never heard a woman pop gum like that, especially not chicks her age. "You must be new 'cause I ain't never seen you before."

My boy Roger spoke up real fast. Roger was my best friend. He was on the healthy side, but still had a way with the ladies.

"Oh, this my cousin Keeling," he said. Roger was light-skinned and still wore the high-top fade. He didn't care that the hairstyle had gone out in the early nineties. Roger also thought women liked family better than friends. So when we rolled up on the honeys, he was quick to say we were cousins.

Dani looked me and him up and down.

"Kee-ling?" she said, as she broke my name into two. "I ain't never heard a name like that before."

Dani had a big ol' booty with lots in the front and curves for days. Her body was tight. The tiny shorts she had on put everything on display and if her top was any smaller, she might as well not had one on.

She had long, bright-orange fingernails that curved and pointed at the tips, something I hadn't seen before. The little braids she wore made her hair look long and wavy. All I wanted to do was run my hands through it and snatch a few fists full.

The day party at Roger's house was like an institution. The only reason I had missed most of the ones in the past was because I always had to work.

But when I finally got a Saturday off, and he told me another one was around the corner, I was hyped. I used my entire check to get a new outfit. I bought a fresh pair of Jordans and put on a pair of starched shorts that came just below my knees with a crisp, new, white T-shirt. I was clean and I knew it. I wore my Raiders cap and a big diamond-encrusted medallion hung from a silver linked chain around my neck. Of course, the diamonds were crystals, but females didn't need to know that.

"I peeped you the moment you stepped through the gate," she admitted. My chest swelled.

"Right, right." I nodded.

When she stepped to me and I got a whiff of her Cashmere Mist fragrance, I was hooked. I felt like it was the sweetest scent that ever teased my nostrils. She looked good, and smelled even better.

"You know what, I might have to make you my new boo thang," she said, as she started to walk away.

Her boldness was the bomb. It was like she wasn't scared to say anything that came to her mind.

"I don't know if you can even hang with my cousin," Roger said to her.

Those words made her stop cold. She tilted her head, circled back, then came and stood right in front of me. Everybody in the yard stopped what they were doing and looked at us like they wanted to see what would happen next. I felt like some of her shine was covering me, and it felt good. She was so close, the rose tattoo across the top of her left breast looked like it moved every time she took a breath. I could smell the liquor on her warm breath.

"Why your cousin trying to gas you up like that?" she asked. She still popped her gum while she talked.

I shrugged. "Who says he's gassing me up? Maybe he don' heard something you don't know about," I said, as I played it cool.

Dani studied me.

"I'm drinking Henny," she said.

There was no way I could flinch in front of her, but I wanted to. She looked too small and too cute to handle such a manly drink. But, I realized she told me what she wanted as her way of telling me to go get her a drink.

For a second I didn't know whether I should go or stay. I didn't want her to get the impression that she could push me around. But, when her red luscious lips parted, and by the time the words slipped from her lips, "On the rocks, daddy," I nearly tripped over myself as I scrambled to get to the bar.

CHAPTER SIXTEEN

Mark

A few days later, Timothy called me in somewhat of a panic.

"Mark, you at home, buddy?" he asked when I answered.

"Yeah, what's up?"

"I'm a few minutes away. CPS has a case worker on her way there and I told them not to approach your door until I can meet them," he said.

"Them? Who's them?"

"They're bringing an officer again. It's just precautionary. Listen, buddy, I don't know who you've pissed off, but I thought for sure this would wrap up after our last conversation and the doctor's report."

Zaneda had just come home from the spa and I considered giving her my card to go shop at the mall. But then it dawned on me that she probably needed to be here.

Nearly an hour later, Timothy knocked at the door and told me to open up.

"Where are the boys?" he asked as he came into our house. It was moments after I'd told Zaneda what was going on. She had an attitude, but I told her we needed to play it cool and let them do what they needed.

"What's the use of having a damn attorney if we still have to be treated like we're a couple of losers?" she asked.

Minutes after Timothy finished briefing us, the knock came.

I looked in Timothy's direction. He nodded and I pulled the front door open.

"Mister Clyburn, I'm Virginia Cole." She flashed something that looked like a cross between a badge and an identification card. It was so fast I couldn't tell if she really was the person pictured on the card. "I'm here to see your children." She looked at the paper on her clipboard. "I need to see Mark Junior and Mason," she said.

Zaneda turned, went to the edge of the hall and yelled for our sons.

"Mason, MJ, come here, please."

"How long is this going to take?" Timothy asked.

"Not very long. We just need to look at the kids, look around and ask a few questions," she said.

As the boys hurried in our direction, they slowed as their eyes took in the police officer and the stranger who stood next to him.

MJ's eyes darted to me, then to his mother. Mason rushed to my side and grabbed me at the waist.

"It's okay, boys," I said.

"Can we have a moment alone with them?" Ms. Cole asked.

Timothy stepped forward. "That's not gonna happen. Any questions you ask, need to happen in our presence."

The lady looked at him, then smiled and looked at MJ. We watched as she inspected my children one by one, from head to toe. She used a small flashlight and aimed it at their body parts. Halfway through the process, Zaneda whipped around and walked off. She was angry, but I was so glad she walked away.

Once the inspection was done, Ms. Cole asked the kids a series of questions. Then she turned to me. "We need to look around. Where do they sleep?"

"In their bedrooms," I said.

I looked at Timothy.

"Let's show her where they sleep, around the house a bit," Timothy said.

"Is that the kitchen over there?" Ms. Cole asked.

We passed through and I stood back as she opened the cabinet doors, searched inside; then she moved to the refrigerator.

"We could've done all of this the first time," she said as she opened the door to the pantry.

It took a couple of hours for Zaneda to thaw out after Ms. Cole, the officer, and Timothy left. I wasn't sure whether she was mad at me or mad because of all we had gone through.

"Why did that lady look at us like that?" Mason asked.

Zaneda looked at me like she needed help with the answer.

"She was doing her job. Sometimes they want to make sure that kids are doing okay, that's all. But it's no biggie; it's over and we're all good," I said.

As I talked, Zaneda's expressions seemed to morph from pissed to evil.

The boys seemed a little skittish, but I didn't want to give in to their negative vibes. Zaneda had enough of those for everyone.

I hardly wanted to look at her sour expression.

"So, you're just gonna let this ride?" she asked.

"Hey, guys, why don't y'all go change and we can go to that paint ball place you like so much," I said.

My sons fell all over each other as they tried to get out of the room first. Once they were out of earshot, I turned to Zaneda. "You do know that we had to go through that, right?"

She sucked her teeth and threw her hands to her hips.

"Are you still gonna stand here and act like you don't know who did this to us? It's like you let her get away with every damn thing and I'm sick and tired of it!"

"Zaneda. Keep your voice down," I said.

"Don't tell me to keep my voice down. Tell me you're gonna go over there and confront that tramp for what she's doing to us. I'm tired of this. Man up!" she screamed, threw her hands up and bolted for the door.

I didn't have the energy to go after her.

When the boys came barreling in my direction, I was actually glad for the burst of energy.

"C'mon, Dad! It's about to go down!" MJ sang.

"Yeah. It's about to go down," Morgan repeated.

Everything Zaneda said stuck in my mind, but I didn't know what she wanted me to do. Timothy told us not to confront Arlene under any circumstances, but Zaneda acted like she didn't understand.

What would I look like saying something to Arlene about the CPS call? What if she really had nothing to do with it? There was no need to make the situation worse than it was already.

"Okay, okay. Let's go," I said to my sons.

They raced to the door and I rushed to keep up.

CHAPTER SEVENTEEN

Dani

"I don't get why you can't go out and get yourself a job."

Her thunderous voice was laced with disgust. Charlene made me want to strangle her sometimes. No, make that most times. I rolled my eyes at her so-called innocent comment. She'd been making them more frequently lately.

The refrigerator door was open wide, and her upper torso was buried deep inside. She had been cleaning the refrigerator for the past thirty minutes. Everything she did had to be detailed and meticulous, but even in deep concentration, she still ran her mouth.

"I mean, who cares if people are talking about you. It's what people do. You had to have known that was a possibility when you decided to go on that trashy talk show, and tell a bunch of strangers your business."

I pursed my lips and gnawed at the inside of my cheek, while I struggled to come up with a way to get from under her roof. It was a test in patience to listen to her comments. She always had something to say and I was tired of listening to what all I had done wrong, and how I couldn't get it right. I got it. I was a loser who hadn't lived up to her expectations and she knew for sure I never would. Blah, blah, blah, blah.

"Those kids, they need stability and they need to see you doing positive things," she continued.

Charlene glanced in my direction with pitiful eyes as she moved from the refrigerator to the bags that sat on the counter. Now, her back was to me as she put groceries away. When she stepped into the pantry, I used that as the perfect opportunity to ease out of the kitchen. If she wanted to beat up on somebody, she'd have to find another poor sucker. I'd had enough.

Once behind my bedroom door, I picked up the remote and started to flip through the channels. I wasn't looking for anything specific, but wanted a good movie so I could lose myself and try to figure out my next move.

Everyone treated me like I was a diseased circus freak. I needed to figure out what to do, and I needed to do it quickly. My cell phone rang and I glanced at the caller ID. "When is he gonna take a hint," I muttered, as I looked at the detective's phone number flash across my screen.

Her question came a few seconds later. "Why didn't you answer your cell phone?"

The sound of Charlene's voice made me jump. I pulled myself up on the bed and looked toward the door. I wanted to ask what she was doing in my room. But the truth was, every room in the house belonged to her. It was why she felt like she didn't have to knock before she barged in.

"What are you talking about?" I frowned. I really wanted to ask why she had pushed her way into my room without knocking on the damn door. It just reminded me more and more that I needed to get my own place. Being up under my mother was doing more harm than good. It was good to have help with the kids, but all the *ish* I had to take from her made me want to take my chances out on my own.

"Officer Watt says he's been calling you for an appointment and you keep avoiding his calls," Charlene said, like she was now his personal assistant.

She looked down at me like she wanted to whip my butt. I didn't understand why we had to have that conversation. If I didn't want to talk to the police, there was nothing she could do to make me.

"You told him to call me?" I asked.

"Of course. He kept calling here for you and I didn't understand why you wasn't answering your phone." She threw a hand to her hip. "So, what is it this time? What have you done?"

"Are you for real right now?" I couldn't stop my neck from snaking like it might slither off my shoulders.

"Dani, in all the years that you and your kids have been living here, we've never had a problem with the law, until—"

"Until after I went on that trashy talk show," I finished the sentence for her. I was sick and tired of Charlene. She reminded me every chance she got of the poor choice I had made when I decided to go on the show, and the absolute mess it had made of my life.

She nodded. "Yeah, that's right."

"Listen, I'm tired of hearing about how stupid it was for me to go on that show. I did it. There's nothing we can do about it now. I went, I talked, and that's all there is to it."

"Well, you might think it's that simple, but it's not. The last thing I want is to be under police scrutiny because your hot little behind don' went out there and stirred up some problems."

Rage tore through me, but there was little I could do. I sat and tried to remind myself to stay calm. If I blew up at Charlene, it wouldn't do me any good.

I tilted my head in her direction, but I didn't say anything else. I waited to see what she was going to do.

"Well?" she hissed.

I shrugged and twisted my face slightly.

"Well what?"

"Call him back," she said.

"Call who? I'm not calling no doggon' police! For what? I know I didn't do anything wrong. I ain't got nothing to say to anybody in uniform."

Charlene stared at me like she needed to figure out whether I'd been switched at birth. The look was all too familiar.

When she leaned against the door and pulled her arms up to her chest, I knew we'd be in for a long, drawn-out standoff.

"You don't get it. I wasn't asking you. I'm telling you. Call that officer now, before I dial his number for you," Charlene threatened.

I got comfortable on the bed, leaned my back against the wall for support, and pulled my legs up underneath my body. If it was a staring contest she wanted, she was in luck because I was planted, and had no intentions of moving.

"Roll your eyes at me again and I'll slap them back up into your damn head. Now I'm tired of you and your antics. Call the officer right now!"

CHAPTER EIGHTEEN

Arlene

I was tired as I sat and held the phone. I didn't have much time and I had no idea what took so long. I provided all of the necessary information and we still weren't finished.

"Ma'am, you still there?" he asked.

"Yes." I sighed. I looked down at the information I'd scribbled on the legal pad. It didn't take long for me to gather the information, but it seemed like the hardest part was getting up the nerve to go through with it. Everything was there—make, model, price, phone number, and address. I just needed the man to take care of everything. A quick glance at my watch told me I needed to wrap things up. I'd been on for more than an hour.

"I think we've got it all," the man finally said. "Okay, are you sure about this price?" he asked.

He worked my nerves. What the hell difference did it make? The customer was supposed to be right all the time. Of course I was sure about the price. That would be the very best part.

"For the last time, the price is right. Like I said, five thousand," I repeated, with much attitude.

"Okay, hold on for me again."

Before I could protest, he was gone. Who knew something so simple would be so cumbersome and so time-consuming? I waited because I had no other choice.

"Okay, thanks for your patience. I think it all looks good on this end," he said, when he came back to the line.

I was glad to hear that. Once I paid, with a pre-paid gift card, we finally wrapped up the call. I looked at the burner phone I had purchased for the project and smiled inwardly. I couldn't wait for that bitch's world to get flipped upside down. There was nothing left to do, so I sat back and waited for my daughter to be dropped off.

As I sat on the sofa, all kinds of thoughts ran through my mind. What if she mistreated my child? How long was Mark gonna pretend like he was happy? If only I could see the look on that wench's face. There was no way I could, so I decided to go see what my mom was doing.

Just my luck, the moment I made it down the hall, the doorbell rang. Since it was Mark, I rushed to the large mirror that leaned against the wall in the living room. I reviewed my reflection. It all checked out, so I snatched lipstick from my purse and painted my lips.

The doorbell rang again.

"Coming!" I yelled.

By then, my mother had made her way into the living room.

"I never sure if ya hear the doorbell da ring," she said. She glanced around like she needed to search to see what had prevented me from answering the door.

"Yeah. I got it, Ma," I said, and moved toward the front door. I tucked the lipstick tube down my shirt and prepared myself.

When I opened the door, Mark stood there with my daughter and one of his other kids. He looked straight ahead like it was a struggle for his eyes to connect with mine.

"Hi, Ms. Arlene," Mark Junior said.

He had been my favorite when I took care of the family. The boy looked so much like his father, it was wild. He had grown so much since the last time I'd seen him.

"Hey, MJ, you doing okay?" I asked.

"Yes, ma'am," he replied.

Mark passed Markeesa's rolling backpack to me, and our daughter turned to give him a hug. My eyebrow went up. I didn't like the loving exchange between them. I didn't want her to like Mark and I damn sure didn't want her to get used to spending time with him and Zaneda.

"See you next time, MJ," she sang at her half-brother before she walked into the house.

"Please have her ready week after next," Mark said to me. I didn't say anything. I rolled my eyes and waited for them to leave.

Later, after a bath and a story, I talked to my daughter about her time at her father and Zaneda's. It had been worse than I suspected. I'd have to step up my game, because they played dirty.

"What did they feed you?" I asked Markeesa as I tried to inspect her without causing her to become alarmed.

"I had everything, Mom! They had ice cream, cake, all of my favorites," she said excitedly. "We had so much fun. Ms. Zaneda let us play dress-up with all of her pretty clothes," my daughter said.

Her little words stabbed at my heart. I didn't want her to have any kind of fun with Zaneda and Mark. I wanted her to hate them being together as much as I hated to let her go.

"What about everything I told you?" I asked.

My daughter's features twisted. She tilted her head to the side and looked at me with wide, innocent eyes.

"Momma, Ms. Zaneda wasn't mean at all. Daddy said they liked having me around because I get to play with my brothers and I'm their only sister."

"Okay, but remember how I told you, you have to watch out for tricks. This is a trick. They're really nice to you now, sweet pea, but that's only so they can get you to leave your mommy and Grams," I said.

My daughter's eyes filled quickly and she looked like she was confused. "But Ms. Zaneda said I'm lucky because I'm part of two families."

That burned me up. How dare she tell my child some mess like that? Zaneda knew good and well every time she looked at my child, she was reminded of what went down with Mark and me.

I pulled my daughter into my arms and hugged her. "You and me, that's the only family you need. You understand me?"

"Yes, Mommy, but Ms. Zaneda said…"

"I don't care what she said," I cut her off. "I don't care what your daddy said. They can give you all of the cake and cookies they want, but you and me, we're the only real family. Okay?"

"What about Grams?" she pulled back and asked.

"Yes, me, you and Grams."

"Go day a bed and Grams go come get ya directly," my mother said.

I didn't know how long she'd been in the room, and I had no idea how much she'd heard.

My mother craned her neck to look after my daughter as she walked down the hallway. Suddenly, she turned her attention to me. "No do dat to de baby," she said.

"What?" I frowned.

"Make da pickney have a relationship with eh pah. I warn ya from the beginning dat yo da play wit fire. Now make da pickeny have a relationship wit eh pah, ya hear me?"

It wasn't very often that my mother pissed me off, but when she did, it was by incredible proportions. Mark would never have a relationship with my daughter and I'd die before I allowed it.

CHAPTER NINETEEN

Keeling

When we first started, me and Dani felt right. That afternoon at Roger's turned into a late night in his second bedroom. She had her Henny, and I was hard.

"It's something about you," she said. I didn't even mind that she slurred a little. She'd been drinking Hennessy on the rocks all afternoon, and I had never known a female who could do that. Everything about Dani impressed me.

"Yeah, I'm digging you too," I said.

She looked around the room, then back at me. At first, I felt crazy being up in Roger's place, since I knew what was about to go down. When he first moved into the apartment, the room was gonna be his gym. It had a bench set, and an old school boom box, and that was pretty much it. Roger used an old sheet as a curtain for the window and we had spent many hours in there shooting the shit and chilling. At first, I thought Dani was gonna complain, but she hadn't uttered a word about the surroundings. She wasn't like those prissy girls that acted like everything had to be perfect.

There wasn't a bed in the room, but the old ratty futon worked just as good.

"Why don't you come and sit over here, next to me," I said.

Dani drained the glass. Then she walked over and straddled me. That was the moment I knew for sure she'd be my girl. She wasn't for all of the fancy, get-to-know-you stuff. She moved fast and that's what I liked.

"You want me?" she asked.

The smell of liquor was so hot on her breath. Her breasts were all up in my face and I only had one thing on my mind.

"What's up with you?" I asked.

"You, daddy," she said. Her voice was raspy, and she sounded sexy to me.

Dani didn't wait for me to say anything. We smashed faces and sucked each other's tongues real hard. There was nothing soft and delicate about her. She liked it rough and rugged. After we kissed for a few minutes, her hand was down into my crotch.

Everything she did to me felt good. I wanted to flip her over and get at it, but I kinda liked the way she took the lead, so I let her do it how she wanted.

When she got up, I didn't know what to expect. That was when she turned it up. Without any warning, she broke into this sexy striptease-like dance, and all I could do was sit there with my mouth hung open.

"You want some of me, don't you?" she asked. That voice of hers turned me on. I nodded. There was no way I could find the words.

Dani stripped down to her matching purple bra and lace thong. I thought I'd lose my mind. She came closer and allowed me to palm that ass.

"You like what you see?" she asked.

"Hell, yeah!" As she peeled away at my clothes, she moaned and whimpered. Every sound she made was like my favorite rap song stuck on repeat in my mind.

When she dropped to her knees and spread my legs wide, I knew

I had died and gone straight to heaven. She fumbled with my zipper and got through to what she really wanted.

Nearly two hours, and several sexual positions later, Dani was in my arms, and breathing hard. We were both wet with each other's sweat. It felt like we had gone to another place. We were in our own little world and I liked it.

The faint sound of a phone as it vibrated reminded me that we were in Roger's extra bedroom and there was probably still traces of his party going on, on the other side of the door.

"Oh snap, is that me?" I asked, as I searched for my phone beneath the pile of clothes nearby.

"Naw. I think that's mine," she said.

She reached over and grabbed her cell. She frowned as she looked at the screen. "Oh. I gotta take that."

It didn't bother me. We were all good as far as I was concerned, or at least that's what I thought until Dani answered the phone.

"Hey, Big Daddy," she sang.

My eyebrows went up. I didn't want to be *that* dude, but she had just sexed me thoroughly, and now she sat on the phone and sweet-talked another man?

I cleared my throat loudly, but that didn't stop the conversation so I eased forward. Dani got up and moved away.

"C'mon now, Big Daddy," she cooed into the phone. Then she whined, "Bernard, why you trippin'?"

Unable to help myself, I tapped her on the shoulder and waited for her to turn to me.

When she did, to my surprise, she shrugged and frowned as if to ask me what was up.

"I'ma do that for you, Daddy, you know I will. But first, I need to make sure you're gonna handle that bill for me. It's only three hundred fifty," she said, as she looked at me. "Uh-huh," she continued.

"Who you talking to?" I asked.

Her expression changed and she looked baffled. It wasn't a look that said she didn't know the answer, but one that questioned why I had even asked.

"Whoa! Hold up a sec, Big Daddy. I'ma have to holler at you later," she said.

"Yeah, talk to that fool later," I said.

"No. Nothing. Just give me an hour. I'ma circle back around to you," she said.

When she got off the phone, she looked at me like I had morphed into a three-headed monster. "Um. What's really going on?"

"Hell, that's what I wanted to know. After all of that, you're gonna sit up on the phone with some other dude? And right in front of my face, like it ain't nothing?" I asked.

"I was handling business," Dani said.

"Business? What kind of business you in that you gotta be sweet-talking dudes on the phone? Calling him Big Daddy and shit. What's up with that?"

"Oh. You got me twisted," she said. Dani jumped up and snatched pieces of her clothes from the bench and the floor. "You act like you got papers on me or something."

"What if that's what I want?" I asked.

That stopped her cold.

CHAPTER TWENTY

Mark

Lately, Zaneda's sour attitude had been wearing me down. It was hard to walk around my own house like the other shoe might drop at any moment. I probably wouldn't admit it to her, but her 'tude had started to impact our relationship. It was especially bad because anytime I tried to talk to her about it, the discussion would end in an argument.

She was mad because she said I let Arlene get away with murder, and it somehow meant I must've still had feelings for her. I had no control over Arlene and what she did. I tried to be civil with her, because she had my daughter, but Zaneda never wanted to hear that logic. Women were so clueless at times. Once again, we were at a standoff in the kitchen.

"So, what are you gonna do about this?" she asked nastily.

After the last time she demanded that I man up, I didn't want to give her another opportunity to question my manhood. I was tired of explaining myself every time she felt like Arlene had gotten the upper hand.

As she stared at my face like that might help the answer to her question come faster, I wondered whether I should call Nebo and some of the guys to go out. I didn't need this shit.

Her cell rang.

She looked at the screen and frowned, then snatched the phone. "Who is this?"

I didn't say anything as she took the call.

"This is Zaneda," she answered. Seconds later, her face contorted even more as she listened to the caller.

"Oh, no. You definitely have the wrong number," she said.

Her eyebrows nearly touched in the middle of her face, as she listened.

"Yes, that's my number, and yes, that's my car, but I'm telling you, you've got the wrong number, because we are not selling a car."

She turned, looked at me, and shrugged. As she shook her head and wrapped up the call, I could see the anger that had settled deep into her features. I was tired of looking at that expression on her face.

Once she ended the call, she turned her attention to me. "Guess who that was?"

I shrugged. How the hell was I supposed to know?

"That was someone calling about the Bentley I have for sale," she said sarcastically. Her neck snaked as she threw accusatory words in my direction. She behaved like I was in cahoots with someone.

My eyebrows shot up. "What do you mean?"

Zaneda slapped her palm on the counter top to emphasize her words. "It's like the seventh call I've gotten today. At first, I thought they had the wrong number, so I'd cut them off before they could get started," she said. "But obviously something is going on."

A few minutes later, when her phone rang again, she looked down at it, then back up at me, and twisted her lips to the side.

"See, this is probably another one. Go ahead, answer it," she said, and shoved the phone in my direction.

I grabbed it and answered.

"Yo, Bruh. Lemme holler at Zaneda," a male voice said.

"Um. Who is this?" I asked.

She rushed to my side and motioned for me to hold the phone so she could hear. I put the caller on speaker.

"Hey, my name is Jackson and I'm calling about the Bentley for sale," the caller said.

"The Bentley for sale?" I asked.

"Man. Is Zaneda there or not? I'm trying to buy the car she has for sale."

"Yeah, about that. This is her husband and we're not selling her car, dude," I said.

"Then what y'all put an ad on Craigslist for? I knew that shit was too good to be true. Who in their right mind sells a 2015 Bentley for five thousand dollars?" the caller hissed.

"Five thousand dollars?!" Zaneda screamed. She walked from one end of the island counter to the next and held her forehead in her palm.

I tried to ignore her.

"So you say there's an ad on Craigslist?" I asked.

"That's why I've been getting all these damn calls," Zaneda snarled.

"Shush," I said in her direction. The caller continued.

"Yeah. Says Zaneda is having some mess called a love hangover sale. Her ex bought the car and she wanted to get rid of it as soon as possible."

I grabbed a pen and wrote down everything the caller told me.

"Hold up," the caller said. "So you trying to say y'all didn't place the ad?"

"Naw, man. We're not selling her car. As a matter of fact, we're not selling anything. And we wouldn't be trying to sell on Craigslist either," I said.

"Aw, man! That's some jacked-up shit. Somebody must really hate y'all asses to pull a stunt like that," he said. When he laughed a bit, I was pissed I hadn't cut him off sooner.

The look Zaneda gave me said it all before she fired her sharp words in my direction.

I scribbled down as much information as I could from the caller, and dreaded the conversation I'd have to have with my wife.

Before I could end the call completely, Zaneda had gone on the attack.

"Now if this doesn't prove that your stupid-ass baby mama don' gone and lost her mind, I don't know what will. I mean seriously! Do you think this is all a coincidence? First an anonymous person reports us to CPS, then my phone is ringing off the hook because someone put an ad on Craigslist? C'mon, Mark, what's it gonna take for you to open your eyes?"

It wasn't that I didn't believe Zaneda's accusations; it was just that I knew unless we could prove Arlene had done these things, it would look as if I was just trying to attack her.

Zaneda didn't care. She moved closer to me. "If you don't say something to that low-down trick, I will. And trust me when I tell you, I won't be nice."

CHAPTER TWENTY-ONE

Dani

It took three pairs of pantyhose for me to get it right. My nail kept poking a hole through them, and I would have to start all over again. Who even wore this crap anymore? I was real nervous, but I needed to ace this so I could take the steps I needed to get my own place.

My car barely had enough gas, but I made it on time to the address Lulu had given me. I was relieved, because I couldn't afford to get anything wrong. I pulled into the garage, and parked, then said a little prayer. I wasn't religious in any way at all, but I figured it wouldn't hurt to try prayer.

When I got out of the car, I pulled my skirt down on each side and grabbed the folder Lulu told me to take. There was nothing in the folder, but she said it would help make me look more like a professional. And I needed all the help I could get.

The skirt and jacket I wore didn't really match, but they were close enough in color that you could barely tell. I was glad because the jacket covered up the tattoos on my breasts, and my upper arm. I didn't need anyone judging me based on my tats.

"Hi, I'm Dani Patnett, and I have a ten-fifteen appointment with Ms. Granger," I said, once inside the cool office building. I tried to talk as properly as I could, and I made sure I smiled.

"Oh yes, Ms. Patnett. Have a seat and she'll be with you in a few," the receptionist said. She was nice enough, but she looked kind of sloppy. Her hair was all over the place, and her clothes looked wrinkled. All I could think was, if they'd hire someone who looked like that, maybe I had a real chance.

She showed me to the waiting area and I took a seat.

"Oh, there are magazines for you to enjoy while you wait, and help yourself to coffee or water," she said.

"Okay. Thank you," I said.

All of the smiling I had to do made my cheeks hurt. I wasn't used to wearing dress skirts, so I had to remind myself to keep my legs closed. I tried to cross them at the ankles like I saw ladies do on TV talk shows, but that felt too awkward.

Right when I got somewhat comfortable, this sharply dressed black lady came to the edge of the hallway and stopped. She glanced down at a clipboard and said, "Dani Patnett, ten-fifteen."

She looked up after she called my name, and I smiled.

I got up from the chair, and walked over to her. "Hi, I'm Dani Patnett."

I accepted the hand she held out to me and shook it.

"Dani, it's good to meet you," she said. "I'm Savannah Granger. Come with me."

Savannah Granger was just as sharp as she looked. Her office was small, but it was nicely decorated with pictures of her and other smiling women. There were pictures of her in different cities, and it looked like she had a happy life.

"So, Dani, what brings you in today?" she asked.

I had to pull my eyes away from all of the little trinkets and pictures in her office.

"Um. I need a job."

Savannah glanced down at a piece of paper in front of her, then back up at me.

"Well, you've come to the right place because it's our business to put people in jobs," she said.

Her words made me scream on the inside. I sat there and struggled to hold a straight face as she talked. I was really excited, until she suddenly squinted her eyes and tilted her head. She frowned.

"Wait, I've seen you somewhere before," she said.

My heart quickly sank to the bottom of my feet. This was the turn most of my interviews would take.

"Where did you go to school?" she asked.

I frowned at that. Savannah was fashionable and very nice-looking in a Plain Jane kind of way, but if she thought we could've gone to school together, I hated to be the one to burst that bubble. She was way older than me and I didn't know any kind way to break that to her.

"Um. I went to Madison," I said slowly.

"Hm. Okay. That's not it. We don't do outreach at that school. You know what, it'll come to me." She quickly turned back into interview mode. "So what type of skills do you have, Dani Patnett?"

I struggled to remember what Lulu told me to say. We had done a few fake interviews just so I'd feel comfortable, but as I sat across from Savannah, my mind had gone blank.

"I have a very pleasant telephone voice. I'm very organized, and I'm always on time for everything," I said.

"Okay, that's great," Savannah said, and she wrote something down on the piece of paper. She looked up. "But what about computer skills? Which programs are you most familiar with?"

"Huh?"

"Computer skills?" she asked again.

Before I could answer, she snapped her fingers.

"I've got it! Where do you go to church?" she asked. Her eyes were bright, like she was relieved.

I wish I knew where she went so I could lie, but I didn't. After I sat there with a blank stare across my face, she must've gotten the hint.

"No, it's not from church either," she said.

This time when she looked up from her paper, she hit me with another question. "What about ten-key?"

I had no clue what she meant. What the hell was a ten-key and why were there ten of them?

"I'm always early for everything and my friends always joke about it, and I am really good with customer service," I said.

I felt like the biggest fool around. There was no way these people would be able to put me in anyone's job and I knew it.

"Hmm," Savannah said.

I watched closely as she flipped through her pages and made marks on a piece of paper. I wanted the misery to end. There was no doubt in my mind that the minute I walked out, Savannah Granger and her co-workers would talk about me like a dog.

How did I let Lulu talk me into doing something so stupid? I had no skills, could hardly work a computer, didn't know what ten-key was, and could barely string two sentences together.

When Savannah got up from her desk, I just knew it was so she could personally throw me out of her office.

Instead, she walked past me and closed her office door. She came back around the desk and took her seat. I was confused when she closed the folder on her desk.

"Normally, I wouldn't do this. We are a temp agency and we get paid based on the number of skilled workers we place into jobs. Honey, I don't know what you've been doing, but it hasn't been working. I'm not sure what's going on with you, but you keep saying how punctual you are, and if that's true, then I'll find some kind of work for you," she said.

"Oh, my God! Thank you."

It was a real struggle not to cry. No one had ever done anything so nice for me. I wanted to tell Savannah that, but figured that would've definitely crossed the line.

"I promise if you give me a chance, I will not let you down," I said. I didn't know what else to tell her.

"Okay, let me see if I can find a placement for you right now."

Savannah got on the computer and I marveled at how her fingers glided over the keyboard. It was like she didn't have to look at what she was typing. The only time I saw people do that was on TV.

"Here, let me have you sign this, and we can get you officially into the system. Once we've created a profile for you, we can start sending you out on jobs."

In my mind, I questioned whether she really knew what she was doing because it looked like she had hired me. But the desperate part of me said to go with the flow and play stupid. Maybe they wouldn't find out until after I was on a job.

Suddenly, she stopped typing, turned to me and said, "Wait a minute, you were on that show, *DNA Revealed*, huh?"

I wanted desperately to lie.

CHAPTER TWENTY-TWO

Arlene

"I understand what you're saying, but things are different now, than back when you were dating," I said to my mother.

We were at the park on a bench while Markeesa ran around on the playground.

My mother looked at me. "Look ya, Gal. Anything weh yo weh do, I don don dat. Whey I de tell yo da no jus fo yo, but fo me precious granpickney too."

"I just wish he would've kept his word, Mama," I said.

"Arlene, yo do no de firs for pick up de pieces after wah man lie to yo, an yo no weh be de las."

She started on her soapbox and I thought about how Mark was supposed to be different. Instantly, my mind went back to my time with Mark. We were in their family room.

"You've gotta tell her," I said.

Mark sighed hard. He dry-rubbed his face with his palms and made a noise that expressed his frustration. Our love affair was still hot, but once I found out I was pregnant, I wanted Mark to do the right thing. I was on him daily and I didn't plan to let up. I wanted him to end things with Zaneda for the right reasons.

"I don't wanna keep talking about this," he said.

Our conversation was tense and uncomfortable, but it was one that had to take place. Mark didn't know I was pregnant yet, but he told me it made no sense for him and Zaneda to stay together.

I thought that meant he would get rid of her and we could start our life together.

"You don't have to keep talking about it, babe," I said. I made sure to speak to him with a soft and easy tone. I didn't want to be anything like Zaneda.

She was rude and completely disrespectful to him, in my opinion.

"I just want you to know that the kids and I are ready for us to become a family," I said.

Mark turned to face me. For a long time, he stared at me like he was deep in thought. I hoped his thoughts involved the way he was going to break the news to Zaneda. She needed to know because I was tired of the charade.

Unexpectedly, the door swung open and she walked in. I thought she was out of town with her friends as usual. Zaneda looked at Mark, then at me and said, "What's wrong in here?"

"Oh, nothing. I was asking Mark what you guys would want for dinner," I stammered.

Zaneda looked at her husband, then back at me. The expression on her face said she didn't believe we'd been talking about dinner.

She walked all the way into the house, but not before she tossed a dirty look in my direction.

"Mark, can I talk to you in the room?" she asked. "Oh, and, Arlene, make some spaghetti, then you can have the rest of the evening off."

Mark's eyes looked everywhere except near me. I didn't want to press the issue, but I needed him to step up and end things with Zaneda.

After she left, he turned and walked toward their bedroom. I pulled pots from the cabinets, and ran the water at the sink, but all that crowded my mind was what they could've been talking about.

My gut feeling told me they were talking about me. Lately, I'd felt as if Zaneda suspected something. I didn't think she knew Mark and I were in love with each other, but I felt as if he needed to come clean so we could all move on with our lives.

I threw a pot of water on the stove and rushed to their bedroom door. Quietly, I eased up next to it, pressed my ear against the door, and struggled to hear their conversation.

"Mark, you'd better get it together!" Zaneda screamed.

"What's it to you? Every time I turn around, you're gone. It's not like you're handling business. You're out partying with your girlfriends. Zaneda, you need to decide whether you still want to be a part of this family."

"What are you saying, baby?" she asked. I noticed the instant change in her tone.

I hoped Mark wasn't gonna fall for that. All of a sudden, Zaneda wanted to be sweet. She had ignored her husband and her family for a very long time and Mark never said a word. But the minute he gave her an ultimatum, she obviously came to her senses.

The change in her tone made me worry. I liked Zaneda when she behaved recklessly, and left her family to figure things out alone. But when she turned on the charm, Mark would fall for whatever she wanted. He was gullible like that at times.

When he walked out of the room, he couldn't even look me in the eyes.

"What happened in there?" I whispered.

She hadn't come out and I wasn't sure what that meant.

"We'll talk later," he said. Mark spoke as if he didn't want it to be obvious he had spoken to me.

"When are you gonna tell her?" I whispered.

Mark looked at me with sad eyes. Because of the way I took care of him, the kids, and the house, I think he could've carried on the way we were with no problems. His wife was hardly ever home anyway.

But I couldn't do it. I wanted more. I wanted what Zaneda had, especially since it looked to me as if she didn't want it.

I finished dinner, but I took my sweet time. The entire time that I cooked, Zaneda never left their room. I wasn't sure if I should go knock on the door, or act like I didn't notice there was an issue.

"Dinner's ready," I sang, a few minutes after I couldn't figure out any other way to stall.

When the door creaked open, I held my breath as I waited to see what would happen next. Zaneda strolled out slowly as the kids made a dash for the table. Mark hadn't come back, and I wasn't sure whether I should call out to him again.

"Arlene, I told you that after you cooked, you could have the rest of the night off," Zaneda said.

I turned to her. "Oh. You don't want me to clean up after you guys eat?"

Zaneda shook her head and said no. She looked at me with cold eyes, but I ignored her. I wanted her to go back on vacation with her other ungrateful girlfriends.

"No. You can go. We will be fine," she said.

A quick glance at her eyes made me think she may have been high on drugs or something.

I dropped the pasta spoon and walked out of the kitchen.

"Where you goin'?" one of the kids asked.

"Oh, I'm gonna let your mommy and daddy spend some alone time with you guys," I said.

Zaneda didn't say anything else as I walked to the back, and closed the door to my room.

Alone inside my room, I felt like crap. I was angry and bitter because a few feet away, the man I loved, the father of my unborn child, played house with a woman who clearly didn't want him.

Even though I was a live-in, I still had a place I shared with my mom. I didn't feel like going home, but Zaneda had made it clear that she wanted me gone. I hated that Mark didn't speak up and say anything to keep me there, but what could I do?

After I changed and grabbed my purse, I walked out and through the family room to avoid the happy couple and their kids. I heard laughter and chatter as I pulled the front door open and walked out.

Two hours later, my cell rang and Mark was on the other end. I was excited that he had called, and thought maybe he had come to his senses.

"I knew you would call to see about me," I said.

"Arlene. Ummm. The reason I'm calling is because Zaneda says you can take the rest of the week off."

"What? Why?" Panic rushed through my veins.

"She wants to try and do things differently," he said. "But don't worry, I'll still pay you. It's just, while she's in the mood, I want to give her a chance, so thanks for understanding." His words hurt so much I could hardly focus.

"Mark?"

"Yeah," he said.

"Why don't you tell her it's over? You're not happy with her, and you and the kids are better off with me."

"Arlene. This is not the time to have this discussion." His voice was so cold and uncaring.

He talked to me as if there was no connection between us. I felt like I needed to do something to get his attention.

"Mark, I'm pregnant," I blurted out.

The sound of him as he breathed into the phone let me know he was still there.

CHAPTER TWENTY-THREE

Keeling

"Man, I just knew you were gonna get the job," Roger said.

"Yeah, me too," I said, and sighed into the phone. I was pissed off. I felt discouraged and defeated.

"But hang in there, playboy. Don't give up; we'll find something for you to do."

"I'm starting to feel like that shit ain't never gonna happen. I mean, you knew the supervisor and he told you it was all good, so what changed between then and when I went in to meet him in person?"

"You think it's got anything to do with the child support crap?" Roger asked.

The child support crap was like the burden that wouldn't go away. I was frustrated because it seemed like people didn't want me to explain a damn thing. Once they saw a child support order, it was like I was this deadbeat who didn't want to step up.

"I know it does, but what's a brotha to do? I still gotta pay for this kid, while she sits there and spends my money on clothes, nails, and hair weaves," I said. It burned me up when I thought about it. Dani robbed me blind and nobody cared.

"Look, man, I got this other dude who works for the Budweiser Company. They deliver beer, a few bottled drinks and other stuff.

If I remember correctly, I think he told me a few of them caught DWI cases and stuff like that. As a matter of fact, I'm about to holler at him now. I'll get back with you later," Roger said.

"Good looking out, Bruh," I said.

There was no way I'd tell him not to try, but deep down, I kinda felt like somebody with a prison record a mile long would get a job before they'd give me a shot.

I got up and walked into the kitchen. A stack of envelopes sat on the counter and I wondered how my moms had left them sitting there. Her hawk-like eyes rarely missed a thing.

A letter from the attorney general's office made me do a double-take. I snatched it up, but my hand started to shake uncontrollably.

What if they were trying to send me back to jail? It wasn't fair how this mess had screwed up my life, but life was still lovely for Dani.

"Oh, I meant to read that. What they want now?" my mother asked.

I didn't even hear when she walked in.

"I didn't open it," I said.

My mother walked around to look me in the face. "Son, what's wrong? Open the damn letter. Also, I wanted to tell you about this man I met. I think he can really help us."

That made me put the envelope down. I had no idea what it was gonna take for her to get the message.

"Ma, when are you gonna get tired of this? You keep dragging all these people into my business and nothing ever happens. Let it go."

She shook her head and picked up the envelope I had just put down. She never said another word to me, but ripped the letter open and started to read.

Her expression told me everything I needed to know.

"Like hell!" she screamed.

I didn't even ask. I was worn-out. The situation made me mad all the time and it took too much energy to keep up the happy façade.

"Oh, but no! I'm not about to sit back and let this foolishness happen all over again. If this little hooker thinks she's about to sit back and keep getting paid from you, for a kid that's not yours., I've got news for her little trashy behind."

I closed my eyes and pulled in a deep breath. I could only imagine what had set her off, this time.

"We're calling this man right now!" she yelled.

"Ma, what man? What did the letter say?" I asked. When I reached for the letter, she snatched it away.

"They're talking about sending you back to jail! Again!" she yelled. Fire burned in my mother's eyes.

"Hold up a sec!" I reached for the letter again. This time she gave it to me.

My moms was breathing flames and I couldn't blame her. After I read that mess, I couldn't believe it myself.

Before I could react to the letter, she had rushed over to the phone and started to dial. I wanted to go and ring Dani's neck with my own two hands. I couldn't believe that she didn't go and tell those people that the kid wasn't mine. So she just thought it was cool to keep taking my money?

I grabbed my cell and dialed her number. When her voicemail kicked on, that pissed me off even more. I ended the call and redialed her again. Her voicemail picked up almost immediately. I wanted to throw the phone against the wall until I heard my mother's conversation.

"Yes, my co-worker told me that you spent time in jail for not paying child support and said I needed to call you about my son."

I turned my head and listened to what she said to the caller on the phone.

"Yes. Just like you, he went to jail over child support. Then come to find out, the kid isn't his and now we just got a letter saying that he could go back to jail again," she said.

"I have the letter right here. Okay. Don't Force Fatherhood," my mother said. "No, I never heard of it before. Okay, I'll look it up. But do you think you can help us?"

I walked closer to her.

"Okay. Yes, Mr. Redman. He's right here," my mother said. Soon, she shoved the phone in my direction.

I took the phone, cleared my throat and said, "Hello?"

"Hey, is this Keeling Lake?" a man's voice asked.

"Yeah. It's me."

"Listen. Your mother told me a little about what's going on with you. I'm already interested in your situation. And since you just got this letter, there are a few things we need to do first," he said.

"Uh. Okay."

"I need you guys to come to the office so we can take care of this. I know some people over there at the AG's office, but first I need to know, when did you take a DNA test?"

"Um. We took it to get on the show."

"The show? What show?"

"She convinced me to get on this new talk show called *DNA Revealed*, and the test showed that the kid ain't mine," I said.

"Okay, what happened after the show?"

I thought for a moment. I wasn't sure what was supposed to happen.

"Nothing, I guess," I said.

"Did she go to court, sign an affidavit? What did you guys do?"

"Ah, man. We ain't did nothing like that. She went on national TV and said she lied to me, but since then, I ain't talked with her again and she hasn't said nothing else to me."

"Well, no wonder the AG wants its money."

What he said made sense, but I wasn't about to go back to jail for nobody.

"So, let's do this. You and your mother need to come by so we can talk and I'll put a call through to the AG's office. I'd also like to talk to the young lady too."

I was with him until he said that. Why did we need to drag Dani's lying behind into this? If it was up to her, I'd be broke and paying until the end of time.

CHAPTER TWENTY-FOUR

Mark

Zaneda didn't understand my situation. I was stuck in a real hard place. If I pissed Arlene off, she'd keep my daughter away from me. It was that simple.

That was the hold Arlene had on me! And she knew it was my weakness. I could never share that with Zaneda because she wouldn't get it. Deep down, she probably would like it if Arlene kept Markeesa away. But I wasn't having it!

I simply needed to figure out how to beat Arlene at her own game. That's what ran through my mind as I listened to Timothy tell me what I needed to do. Zaneda and the boys waited for me as I wrapped up the phone call.

Timothy had some logical ideas about how we should handle Arlene in light of the CPS investigation. I tried my best to get Zaneda on board, but she was still pissed.

He said if Arlene never complained or said a word, I needed to behave as if everything was normal. He even suggested we plan a family vacation. Timothy said if we displayed a strong family unit at all times, it would help offset the false complaints.

About an hour after my phone conversation, I called Zaneda and the boys into my office.

"What's up, Dad?" MJ asked.

"Yeah. What's up?" Mason repeated.

Zaneda was the last one to stagger in. Everything about her demeanor said she was reluctant to hear anything I might have to say. She had been pissed because she felt as if Timothy hadn't done enough to protect us, but I explained to her that he had.

Both of our boys were still at home. The investigation wasn't going to find anything, so when it was all said and done, we had nothing to worry about, but it felt like she wanted to remain miserable.

"How about we go on a Disney Cruise?" I said excitedly. Her expression remained stuck on sour.

The boys' eyes grew to the size of basketballs. A large, silly grin spread across their faces, and soon, they broke out into wild laughter.

"We going on a cruise?" MJ asked.

I nodded.

"We going on a cruise!" Mason said. "Yes we are. Markeesa is going too."

As I watched them dance around, I couldn't help but notice that Zaneda hadn't reacted at all to my news. She stood off to the side, arms crossed at her chest, and her face twisted. The kids were beyond excited.

"Do you really think a family vacation is going to change anything? You know good and well, she's not gonna let Markeesa go anywhere with us, especially out of the country," Zaneda snarled. Even her words sounded nasty.

"All I can do is ask. Who knows? Maybe she'll surprise us all and say yes," I said. I tried to remain optimistic.

Initially, Zaneda didn't protest, but I felt like she tossed the idea around in her mind and started to add up everything that was wrong with my plan.

"And of all things, a Disney Cruise?" she asked, like I'd tried to pull a fast one.

"I figured we'd go someplace where the kids would enjoy themselves too," I said. "Besides, I know you like the Bahamas."

My tone was even, and I never came off like I wanted conflict. I was tired of us being at odds with each other.

For a second she didn't say anything else, and I figured she wanted to warm up to the idea even if she disagreed. The boys had come up with their own celebratory dance routine and couldn't hide their excitement.

My eyes focused on the kids, because Zaneda acted like I'd told her we'd all inhale carbon monoxide and die in our sleep. It seemed like nothing made her happy anymore.

"Go look for the clothes you want to take on the cruise ship," she finally said to them.

We watched as the boys took off and raced toward their bedroom. The moment they were gone, Zaneda turned to me and said, "So, this is your answer?"

I shrugged.

"Mark. Are you really not gonna confront her about all the bullshit that's been going on around our house?" she asked.

"Timothy says we need to hold off until we know for sure," I said. It was not an argument I wanted to have, but she wouldn't let up.

Zaneda smirked. She looked at me like I was the simplest man on the face of the earth. And still, I was prepared to ignore it all. I didn't want to fight with her. My focus had shifted to more constructive things. I wanted to figure out how we could convince Arlene to let Markeesa go on the cruise.

Sometimes I wondered why Zaneda didn't realize we were better off if we worked together.

"What are you gonna do when she says no?" she asked.

I got why she assumed Arlene would say no, and I figured, she would, but Zaneda's question pointed toward the fact that she was negative about everything. It wasn't the best time to point it out, so I remained quiet, and made a mental note to chat with her about it, later.

"If she says no, we'll wait a little while, then ask again. Eventually, she'll realize that we want Markeesa to be a part of our family too."

Zaneda suddenly turned and walked back out of my office. She didn't say another word. Left alone, I decided to move forward with plans for the cruise. There was no doubt the kids would all be happy, but I needed to figure out a way to make Zaneda happy as well.

I jumped on the computer and searched for the cruise. Once that was done, I sat and thought about the things I might need to say or do to get Arlene on board.

Despite how I racked my brain, I never came up with anything that sounded convincing. If she knew this was a family trip, I felt like she'd work that much harder to keep my daughter away.

Most of the time, I felt trapped between two angry black women. Both were angry, but for different reasons. I wished they knew the kind of energy and time they wasted being mad all the damn time.

CHAPTER TWENTY-FIVE

Dani

I wanted to dance on my way out of Savannah Granger's office. But I couldn't do that. It wouldn't have been professional. She was honest with me and said it would take a little longer for her to push my name through to her partner, because of the show, but she was certain she could.

So, even though I didn't have the job just yet, I left her office with a feeling that I would real soon. As promised, I called Lulu the minute I got out of there.

"Didn't I tell you she was cool as hell?" Lulu asked.

I was so happy, I wanted to offer Lulu drinks on me, but because I was broke, that would have to wait.

"Yeah, but, girl, she really is. I mean, where'd you meet her? And when she asked me about being on the show, you know I wanted to lie, but I broke down and told her how it had ruined my life. I was so glad I told her the truth. I feel like that's what encouraged her to help me," I said.

"So did you get a start date yet?" she asked.

"Not yet. She told me she has to work some things out with her partner first," I said.

I expected Lulu to tell me I was crazy because I had fallen for the okey-doke, but instead she said, "If she told you that, then you're just as good as working. She's mad cool, and totally down-to-earth. You know how some people act all stuck up once they got theirs? Savannah ain't nothing like that," Lulu said.

When I heard that, I was happy because it helped to reinforce what I thought I had felt about Savannah. She kept it one-hundred and that meant she'd do what she said she would.

"Well, needless to say she's got me over here feeling like I need to celebrate. I'm so happy I could cry," I said.

"Girl, I'm glad it worked out. Listen, I need to go, so let's chat later," Lulu said.

Her timing couldn't have been better because I was close to the house anyway. I told myself that nothing my mother said would mess with my good mood. Savannah was gonna give me a job, and that meant I was steps away from leaving Charlene's house. All I had to do was be patient, and keep my mouth closed.

I turned onto our street and noticed something strange almost right away. I had no clue what worried me more: the TV van that sat in front of the house or the police cruiser that was parked in the driveway?

It was hard to ignore the urge to keep driving. I didn't know whether my mother was dead or what had happened. There was no doubt I needed to find out, even though I didn't really want to.

Cautiously, I parked across the street and got out of the car. From the outside, nothing looked out of place, except for the odd vehicles that didn't belong there.

I walked up and opened the front door. When I did, three strangers turned and looked at me. I was confused. Charlene came from the kitchen with a tray that held glasses of lemonade. She looked like one of those housewives from a bad 1950s sitcom. I rolled my eyes at her role play and stepped all the way into the living room.

"Oh, you're finally here," Charlene said. Her smile was so fake,

I wondered whether someone had promised her some money or something.

"Who are these people and why are they here?" I asked.

The Hispanic lady looked familiar, but I didn't remember her name. The big, burly guy who stood next to her had a large camera in one hand and a tripod in the other. Those two didn't bother me as much as the officer who sat in the wing chair like he belonged in our house.

"Oh, this is Rita Sanchez from Channel Two and remember I told you that the officer…"

I saw red and couldn't make out anything else she had said.

Was my mother really that crazy? What made her think I wanted any of those people there?

"Rita is doing a special report about child support and she had so many questions, I told her it would be easier to come on over. I knew you'd be willing to help."

My eyebrows went up. She couldn't be serious. This was the same woman who continuously insulted and harassed me about going on TV and telling all my business. Then she had the nerve to bring the media to our house? Charlene was more than a trip.

"And Officer Watt was tired of not getting you on the phone so I told him he should just come on by too," she said.

She had to have lost her mind.

"Uh. Can I talk to you back here for a minute?" I said to my mother.

"Oh. Okay," Charlene said. She passed out glasses of lemonade to her guests, and looked at me like she was bothered.

"I'll be right back," she said to them.

In my bedroom, I struggled to keep my tone even and my voice low. There was no point in blowing up at her. "Why would you have these people over here like this?"

"What?" My mother shrugged. "I know how much you like going on TV, so when they called, I didn't think twice. It was a coincidence that Officer Watt happened to come at the same time," she said innocently.

I wouldn't be surprised if she didn't set the whole thing up just to try and make me look bad.

"Well, you need to go and tell Rita I don't want to talk to her or anyone else. I'm sick of all this mess about child support."

"Oh, so now you wanna act all shy? I think you should do the interview," Charlene said.

"Well, I don't care what you think. You need to go and tell them I'm not talking to anyone and I mean it."

She tossed her hands to her hips, and looked at me like she wanted me to die right where I stood. I didn't care.

"So you expect me to go out there and tell them you're not talking after I all but promised them you would?"

"I don't care what you tell them. I'm telling you I'm not doing it. I've had enough of being on TV. Tell Rita she's gonna have to find someone else."

My mother was pissed and I got that, but I was closer to being able to pull my life together than I had ever been before. There was no way in hell I was about to go back on TV and stir things up again.

CHAPTER TWENTY-SIX

Arlene

The nerve of Mark. "You know the court says you're supposed to give me at least two weeks' notice, Mark," I barked into the phone.

He made me so sick. Now, after all Zaneda had put him through, he was making a fool of himself by trying to act like they were one big happy family. The thought made me want to throw up in my mouth.

"We want to take all of the kids and it wouldn't be right if Markeesa couldn't come," he said.

As Mark pled his case about why I should let him take our daughter on a week-long Disney Cruise next week, I wished there was a way I could ruin the trip for them. My mind raced with all of the things I could do to make it a miserable experience, but none of them seemed practical.

"It's not two weeks, but we're not leaving for a whole 'nother week, so can't you work with me, Arlene?"

"Oh, work with you, like the way you worked with me?" I asked.

He didn't respond or react. I hadn't heard any fallout from the last stunt I pulled, but with them planning a week-long vacation, that gave me another idea.

"She's my child too, and you should know that as her father, I want her to experience just as much as my other children," Mark explained.

The more he talked, the harder my brain worked to piece an idea together. So far, nothing I had done worked. He and Zaneda were still going strong and that irked me to no end. It wasn't fair to me that they should be happy, even if, as I suspected, they were just fronting.

"So, how long will you guys be gone exactly?" I asked.

"We'd leave Sunday and come back the following Monday morning," Mark said.

"That's more than a week."

"Arlene, think about our daughter. You know she would enjoy herself."

Little did he know, I planned to let them take Markeesa on that cruise, not because of the reasons he said, but because I didn't want anything to mess with the plans I had in store for them.

"So, what time should I have her ready on Sunday?" I asked.

"Arlene, we want to pick her up Friday evening, the cruise is Sunday, but we need to do some things Saturday to get ready, and it's best if we're all together because we leave before daybreak Sunday to go to Galveston," he said.

"Um. You think taking her on vacation is gonna make this sham of a marriage work out?"

"Arlene, you and I are only supposed to discuss Markeesa and what's best for her. My marriage is off limits and you know that," he said.

"I can talk about anything I want. If my child is gonna be there with the two of you, I deserve to know what's happening in that house."

"So, does this mean we can take Markeesa on the cruise?"

"I'll let you know," I said. "I need to think about it."

"Arlene," he said.

"If you keep pushing me, y'all not taking her anywhere, dammit! Now, I said I'd think about it and let you know. What else do you want from me?"

"Okay, Arlene, I'll wait to hear from you. But can you please let us know by Wednesday at the very latest?"

I hung up the phone. Mark was nothing but a spineless punk. He let Zaneda do whatever she wanted, then he wanted to come and try to bully me.

My mother walked into the room right when I got off the phone. I wasn't in the mood for whatever she was about to say. She must've read my vibe because she smiled, then moved closer to me.

"I de make stew chicken, with rice and beans for dinner," she said.

"Okay, that sounds real good," I said.

I felt she wanted to say more. The look on her face told me she probably wanted to go in on me about Mark and the vacation. My mother ear-hustled so much it was hard to keep her out of my business. But since she didn't bring up the cruise, I wasn't about to either.

Later, as my mother cooked in the kitchen and my daughter watched a movie, I decided to get started. But as I picked up the phone, a call came through. It was Mark again.

"What do you want?" I answered.

"Listen, we've been getting some strange calls and visits, lately. Did you do something you wanna tell me about?" Mark asked.

I hated when he tried to *handle* me. It was like he thought he could sweet-talk me when he wanted and I'd fold like cheap patio furniture.

"What the hell are you talking about?"

"I'm just trying to figure some stuff out," he said. "We're eventually gonna piece this all together, Arlene."

Mark tried to talk like he ran something, but I didn't care. His bravado didn't scare me because I knew the truth about him. I felt like Zaneda had put him up to the call, but I knew he wouldn't admit it if I asked. He needed a favor from me. It wasn't the other way around.

"Someone put Zaneda's car up for sale on Craigslist. Our phone's been ringing like crazy and people keep popping up. Did you do it?" he asked.

"Zaneda gets around. I'm sure she's pissed many people off. I don't know anything about her car or Craigslist. Knowing her, she probably did it herself just to get some attention."

"Stop playing, Arlene. If I find out you did this…" he threatened.

I laughed at him.

"Mark, get real. You don't scare me. We both know you have no balls. That's why your wife runs around on you and you sit there and take it. You have no backbone," I said.

"What, Arlene?" he cut me off, "if I had a backbone or some balls I'd be with you instead of Zaneda?" he asked with a huff.

"I wouldn't take you back if you begged me. You showed me what kind of man you really are, so I'm good. Now, if you don't quit harassing me, I may feel uncomfortable with you taking my daughter on vacation."

"That's cold, Arlene. Like I said, I was calling just to see if you knew anything about all the strange calls we've been getting. We're not selling Zaneda's car, but I guess when we talk to the people over at Craigslist, they'll be able to help straighten this out."

"Okay, well, go talk to them, and quit messing with me. Besides, if strange people are popping up at your front door, I don't know if that's a safe environment for my daughter."

"Arlene, you said you didn't place the ad. I've moved on. I guess I'll wait to hear from you about the cruise."

CHAPTER TWENTY-SEVEN

Keeling

My appointment with Parker Redman made my mother so happy I wanted to kiss the dude myself. But I'm not like that. Parker was sharper than sharp. I liked him because he knew exactly what I'd gone through since he'd literally been there before, and he was determined to try and help us make things right.

His office was sleek with modern furniture, and pictures of him with lawmakers and celebrities all over the place. The dude was important for sure.

"Here's what should've happened. The minute she recanted, we needed to get that information over to the AG's office. Just because she was on a national talk show and she came clean there, the law has no way of knowing that," Parker said.

"I told him we needed to press charges or something," my mother said. She was so hyped I was tempted to tell her to calm down.

Parker shook his head. "I'm not talking about the police. The first thing we need to do is protect your son and his rights. We can't worry about her and what happens to her. Our focus is to get the AG out of his pockets," he said.

It made me feel good to hear him say that. It had been nearly three months since I'd gotten out of jail, and Parker was the first person who made me feel like he was interested in helping me.

"Now, we need to set up a time for DNA testing," Parker said.

"But we already took a test; that's why we went on the talk show," I said.

"I get that, but the AG's office is going to require another test. Listen, if we want to do this right, believe me, we've got to do it all by the rules."

"Okay. What do I say to her?" I asked.

"You don't need to say anything to her. I'd like for you to tell the police how she lied to you and how she got you to go on that stupid show when she knew all along she was screwing some other sucker," my mother said. Her face was twisted like a pretzel. My mother's hatred for Dani was always on display.

"We will reach out to her and let her know that we need to do the testing again. If she doesn't respond, we can get the AG's office to threaten to withhold payments."

"You have that kind of power?" my mother asked.

"Well, luckily for you, Keeling, the laws have changed here in Texas. Now that we know the child isn't yours, the agency wants to free you and find out who the actual father is, so that he can pay."

"But nothing happens to her?" my mother asked again.

Parker shook his head and said no.

"Unfortunately, the laws haven't caught up to technology. What she did is morally wrong, and she should be embarrassed with the whole going on TV and telling everyone, but other than that, we need to focus on clearing your son's name."

I saw the disappointment on my mother's face. I knew if she could, she'd kill Dani herself.

When we walked out of Parker's office, I finally felt like progress was being made.

"Can you believe what happened to him?" I asked my mother as I opened the car door to let her in.

"Son, that could've been you. I have always had a bad feeling about that girl. The way she let you go on that national TV show and didn't warn you about the ambush? Who does that kind of crap?"

She didn't really expect an answer and I didn't want to give her one, because that would only prolong the conversation.

"Hopefully, we can get this mess cleared up and I'll be able to find a decent job. I'm tired of being seen as a deadbeat especially since I'm innocent," I said.

During the drive home, my mother talked about Parker and everything she liked about him. I listened and didn't add too much, but my mind thought about all of the people she had gone through before she found him. In the end, most people lost interest in my case and simply moved on.

When we made it to the house, I called and brought Roger up to speed on the meeting with Parker.

"Man. I swear, I curse the day you picked her up at my place. THOT, if I knew how drama-filled she was, needless to say, she would've never been invited to my place."

"It's all good, dawg. How could we have known Dani was cray-cray like that?"

"Yeah, that's true, but honestly though, cray-cray shouldn't come in such a pretty package. How you gon' look good but be rotten to the core?" Roger said.

We laughed at the comment. The truth was, Dani didn't even look as good as I thought she did back in the day. When I looked back on it, everything about her screamed trouble, but back then, I thought that was what I wanted in a woman.

"Man, I'll be glad when this is all over, and believe me when I say a brother feels good knowing I don't have to worry about the threat of jail again."

"That's what's up!" Roger said.

"Keeling!"

My mother's scream caught me off guard.

"Hey, lemme see what Moms wants. I was just calling to tell you what had happened."

Roger and I ended the call and I went to see what my mother was making noise about.

"It's on again!" she screamed.

"Ma, quit watching that mess. This show must be really short on episodes because I swear it feels like they show this every week," I said.

"I wanna watch it."

I heard her, but I didn't listen. I went and turned off the TV because the reruns made it feel like I was going through the mess all over again. Besides, the last thing I needed was a reason for my mother to feel like she needed to go to Dani's house and exact her own vigilante justice.

"Why'd you turn it off? I told you I wanted to see it again," she said.

"Yeah, I heard you, but we've seen that enough. Let's get ready to move on. Like Parker said, we need to focus our attention on the AG's office. If we watch that show every time it comes on, all we're gonna do is stay stuck, and I'm tired of being stuck, Ma."

She looked up at me and I wasn't sure what she would say, but after a few seconds, she nodded. "You know what, you're right, Son. Let's clear your name first; then once we're done with that, I can focus my efforts on Ms. Dani herself."

"Ma," I whined like a two-year-old. She cut her eyes at me and I knew she meant what she said.

CHAPTER TWENTY-EIGHT

Mark

"I have had this number for nearly twenty years! Why should I have to change it because you can't control your baby mama?" A menacing glare wrinkled Zaneda's face, and her lips were pursed together. "I'm so sick of her and her shit!" she hollered. I was sick of both of them, but I didn't say it.

Zaneda was angry, as usual lately.

"Let's get ready for a relaxing vacation. We don't have to talk about the number, Craigslist, CPS, or any of that. Let's go on vacation and have a wonderful time with the kids. I'll let Timothy deal with Arlene. Okay, babe?"

I pulled Zaneda into my arms and tried to share an intimate moment with her. Her body stiffened as I wrapped my arms around her. I hated that she wanted to hang on to the anger.

"It was just a suggestion. I didn't say you had to change your number, but I know how irritating it is to get all of those phone calls. Babe, I was trying to come up with an immediate solution."

"But why does the solution always have to mean an inconvenience for me, for us, for our family?" Zaneda said, toward my neck.

At least she hadn't pulled away from me.

"The best way for us to get back at her is to go and have a great time with the kids. Think about it; these stunts are designed to rip our family apart. If we ignore her and them, she'll get the message and realize that she's wasting her time."

When our embrace broke up, she stared into my eyes like she hoped to find some sign that I knew what I was talking about.

"I'm so tired of her," Zaneda said. She sighed hard.

"Me too, babe, me too. But we can't let her, or her stunts, get the best of us. If we do, she wins," I said.

"But don't you get tired?"

I gave her an empathetic nod.

"Did she say she was letting us take Markeesa?" Zaneda asked.

"Not yet. She said she'd think about it, so we'll have to wait and see."

Zaneda's eyes glazed over with disbelief. Our intimate moment was over. It had been short-lived.

"So when will her majesty let us know whether we can take her child?" Zaneda asked sarcastically.

"Babe, I'm not gonna worry about it. I've asked her, and she said she'll think about it. All we can do is wait and see what she decides to do."

Good moods never lasted long around our house anymore. I felt Zaneda's frustration, but she needed to realize we were on the same team. Instead, when she got mad at Arlene, she took it out on me.

"Why don't you go and do some shopping for you and the kids?" I suggested. "They could probably use new swimsuits and beach shoes."

At first, she didn't even crack a smile. Her features were touched with concern. But I could see faint hints of a smile.

"Wait," Zaneda said. She eyed the black card I held out to her. "What's the matter? You got something you need to tell me?" she asked.

"C'mon, babe, I'm trying to help you feel better, that's all," I said.

Zaneda snatched the card, and looked at me again.

"I sure hope I'm not being set up for a serious fall later," she said. "I've had about as much as I could take with Arlene, CPS, and this Craigslist bullshit."

That's why I gave Zaneda the benefit of the doubt. I knew it was all a lot. Most other women would've probably left me a long time ago. But when she forgave me for what happened with Arlene and me years ago, I promised her and myself that I'd spend the rest of our time together trying to be a better father, husband, and man.

"I know you have, babe," I said. "And every single day, I'm grateful that you decided to give our family another chance. I won't let you down. I know it feels like it's taking forever, but believe me when I tell you, Arlene is gonna make a mistake, and when she does, she's gonna pay," I said.

A skillfully arched brow rose on her face. She pursed her lips and looked at me like she wasn't sure she should believe me.

"I'm gonna hold you to that, and I mean it," Zaneda said as she turned to leave. "Besides, somebody has to pay," she added.

Her cell phone rang and we both froze.

The message across her face was vividly clear. She looked down at the screen and instantly, her features softened.

"It's a real call," Zaneda said as she pulled the phone to her ear and walked out.

If I had to admit it myself, I was excited about the cruise too. During the off-season, my only real goal involved getting stronger for the next season. I worked hard to keep my body in shape and gear up for what was ahead.

It had been a long time since Zaneda and I had taken the kids on a real family vacation. She probably didn't want to admit it, but it was clear, she was excited about it, too.

With Zaneda and the boys headed out, I got up and decided I needed to do some packing of my own. I had purposely avoided it because Arlene still hadn't called to say whether or not we could take Markeesa.

I thought about the times I let her take my daughter to Belize, her mother's country. I never gave her a hard time. I told her as long as I could pick up the phone and call, it was all good. She acted like I was being unreasonable because I wanted to take my entire family on vacation.

In the kitchen, I opened the refrigerator and grabbed a sports drink.

The house phone rang.

I put the bottle down and rushed across the room to get the cordless. It was Timothy.

"Hey, Mark. What's up, buddy?" he greeted me.

"Nothing much. You got news for us?" I asked.

"What's up with your cell phone? I tried you there first, but didn't get an answer. I thought you guys had already left for vacation," he said.

"No, not until Sunday."

"I wish I had better news, but none of the stuff leads back to Arlene," Timothy said.

His news crushed me like a ton of bricks hitting a plate glass window.

"Nothing?" I asked.

"Nope. If she's behind it, she did a great job of covering her tracks," Timothy said.

"I get the CPS complaint. I read up on that and it said anyone can report you and they don't have to give their names, but the

Craigslist ad? Someone has to have some kind of information on file," I said.

"Yeah. I get where you're going with that too. But if she used a false name, a pre-paid card, you see where I'm going with that, right?"

My heart sank. There was no way I could tell Zaneda that. If I did, our vacation plans would sink.

We ended the call and I sulked back to my office. Behind my desk, I tried to think of ways to outsmart Arlene. If there was nothing to tie her back to the antics, that meant she'd get away with the harassment she'd launched against my family. And Zaneda would soon be on a warpath.

CHAPTER TWENTY-NINE

Dani

It only took a mid-morning trip to Walmart to figure out what had happened, again. I was pissed at myself because I decided to run out in my pajamas since I was running to Walgreens real quick. When Walgreens didn't have what I needed, that forced me to go to Walmart. That was an epic mistake.

I needed two things and I figured I'd be in and out real fast.

Once I parked, I high-tailed it into the market part of the store where food was sold. I rushed to the aisle and found the first item I needed.

As I stood and looked for the smallest bottle of vinegar I felt a couple of people as they stared at me. It tripped me out how people had no shame.

"Is there something wrong?" I turned my head and asked. My tone was nasty, but I didn't care.

"Who you talking to?" the trashy-looking woman asked me. Both of her bony arms were covered with tattoos and her eyebrow, nostril, and lip were pierced.

"Just wondering why y'all staring at me," I said.

I wasn't about to back down. She and her friend started it, and I was tired.

"Ain't nobody staring at you. You blocking the section," she said and waved one of her arms.

I turned to see what she meant, and realized she was right. "Oh. My bad," I said, and moved to the side.

The odd glances I got could've been from the pajamas I had on, or at least that was what I wanted to believe. But by the time I left that aisle and made it to the spice section, I knew for sure something else was up.

People pointed, and covered their mouths as they laughed and gawked at me. It made me feel even more like a circus freak. And I knew it had nothing to do with the pajamas.

"I swear that's her," I heard a voice whisper loudly.

"Girl, bye!" the other voice replied.

From the corner of my eye, I saw them approach. There were three of them and I prayed they were looking for sugar or seasoning salt.

I grabbed the alum powder I needed and turned to leave.

"Aye, that was you on *DNA Revealed*, huh?" a big woman, who looked like a man, asked.

My eyebrows twisted, and dipped into a frown. She was massive and didn't seem friendly. I was not in the mood for a fight, especially one I knew I'd loose.

"Naw, that wasn't me," I said, and pushed past her, then headed for the checkout lines.

On my way, a few people pointed in my direction, but I didn't care anymore. I just wanted to get back to the house. I was so over people who wanted to make themselves feel better, so they felt the need to judge me.

"I told you that was her!" a different voice said.

I rolled my eyes and snatched my bags. On my way out of the store, a woman bumped into me so hard, I dropped my bag.

"Damn! Watch where the hell you going. What's wrong with you?" I snapped. "You didn't see me coming?" I asked, as I bent down and picked up the bag.

"Oh, my bad. Didn't know you was there, just like you didn't know dude *wasn't* your baby's daddy," she quipped. The two females with her cracked up with laughter.

I rolled my eyes. It was all too damn much! It didn't matter whether I missed the rerun; all I had to do was go to the store and I'd know instantly whether the stupid episode had aired again. I wanted to call or write a letter to the network. How come they didn't have another episode to run? It seemed like once every couple of weeks they aired the episode with me and Keeling. I was sick of it.

My plan had been to call and follow up with Savannah, but since I realized the episode just aired again, I decided against that. I'd wait for that to die down.

Back home, as I was about to mix up the alum powder and vinegar, my phone rang. I rolled my eyes. If I hadn't been nosey, I would've focused on my prep instead of the phone call, but I didn't recognize the number and got curious.

"Hello?" I answered.

"May I speak to Dani Patnett?" a real professional voice asked.

My heart went wild. Maybe it was Savannah's partner. I didn't expect it to be a man, but whatever. I just needed him to tell me I had the job. Instantly, I felt bad about the way I had answered the phone. I told Savannah I was pleasant on the phone and there I was snapping.

"Hold on," I said, and rubbed the phone against the dish towel. I figured if nothing else, I could act like someone else had answered my phone.

"Hi, this is Dani Patnett," I said cheerfully when I returned to the phone.

"Ms. Patnett, my name is Parker Redman," the man said.

Was that Savannah's partner? I didn't know anybody named Parker, so I figured I'd play along to see what he wanted.

"Hi, Mr. Redman," I said. "How can I help you?"

"I wasn't sure if you were expecting my call."

"Yes, I thought you'd be calling. I'm glad you did." Excitement rushed through my body as I spoke to him.

"Okay, well, can you come down to my office, I'd really like to meet you and talk face to face," he said. That had to be a good sign. He wouldn't want to meet if I wasn't hired.

"Oh. Of course," I said. "Are you in the same office?"

But I asked right when he started to say something.

"I'm sorry, Mr. Redman," I said.

"No problem. Do you have a pen?"

"Hold on a second. Let me get one," I tried to talk slowly and softly. There was a part of me that was glad Savannah's partner was a man. If convincing him that I could do the job was all I needed to do, I felt like the job was as good as mine.

After I took down his address, I jumped up and tried to figure out what I should wear. I wanted to be sexy since he was a man, but not too much since I was supposed to be professional.

I tried to call Lulu to tell her the great news about my second interview, but she didn't answer. Since I had less than two hours, I showered, changed and tried to pull together an outfit.

In the end, I decided to go with a plain black dress. I grabbed a scarf from Charlene's closet and picked up the folder I took when I met with Savannah.

Since it had given me luck on that interview, there was no point in leaving it at home. Unfortunately, one side of it was stained with something and a piece was torn off. I figured all I needed to do was remember to hold it on the good side and I'd be okay. Ready, I darted out of the house and made my way to the address Parker had given me.

"I'm so confused," I muttered as I looked up at the name on the building. I looked down at the address I had written down and couldn't make sense of it.

I decided to call Lulu. She got hired so she'd know what the heck was happening.

Lulu's voicemail came on and I was pissed.

"Hey, girl, it's me. I just pulled up at Mr. Redman's office for my second interview, but I'm confused. It's the right address, but the name on the place says DDF. Anyway, call me when you get this," I said and ended the call.

Maybe I needed to go inside and ask for directions. I was so baffled. I got out of the car and walked into the building.

"You must be Ms. Patnett," a tall and handsome man said before he grabbed my hand to shake it.

I frowned. How did he know my name? So, I was at the right place after all.

"Uh, is Savannah here?" I asked.

There were pictures of the man with lots of famous people. I didn't see any of him with Savannah, but I figured since she wasn't famous, he probably didn't want to put her on blast.

"Please have a seat," he said.

That's when I realized the folder was still in the car. I thought I was in the wrong damn place. I wasn't sure how I felt about that, but there was little I could do. I sat where he told me to and braced myself.

He walked around to his side of the desk and took a seat. "I'm glad you agreed to come in and talk about this. I understand you've admitted that Keeling is not the father of your youngest child, so now, I think we both know what's next."

I frowned. What the hell? I wanted to talk about my new job, not old tired baby-daddy drama. Oh, snap!

CHAPTER THIRTY

Arlene

I pulled up in front of the store to get the yard signs I'd ordered. "I'm here to pick up my signs," I said, once I walked into the small store front, and up to the counter.

"Name, please?" the clerk asked.

"Zaneda," I said.

The clerk stopped typing, and looked up at me briefly.

"Z-a-n-e-d-a," I said slowly.

"Last name, please," he said. I was glad he focused on the computer monitor and not my face. That meant it would be a challenge if he ever had to try and describe me.

"It's only under my first name," I said.

"Okay. I see it here." He typed faster. "Twenty-five signs; they're ready."

I placed a one hundred-dollar bill on the counter and waited for my order. Once the clerk rang me up and printed a receipt, he reached under the counter and pulled out my order.

"Please take a look and make sure everything is correct. Then, if it's all good, sign here, and initial here," he said.

The signs were simple, white with black text, small eighteen-by-twelve inches with the stakes. I scanned the words on the sign and nodded my approval.

"Yup, it all looks right," I said.

I signed the papers, careful not to use my own name and was soon on my way.

Once I pulled the car around the corner, I parked, got out and removed the signs from the backseat. I needed to put them into the trunk and under a blanket and several bags so my mother wouldn't see them and try to talk me out of it. I would need to lay low for a few days, then work out the other part of my plan.

Back at the house, I tried to figure out how my mother would feel about leaving to go back home.

"You didn't have to cook again," I said. "There were more than enough leftovers."

"Chow mein." My mother sucked her teeth and focused on the pot she hovered over, at the stove.

I had only one day before I needed to let Mark know my decision. Since our last conversation, I had been busy, so there was no doubt that I'd let Markeesa go with them.

As my mother cooked, I decided to let her in on the news.

"I think I'm letting Markeesa go on vacation with Mark and his family," I said somberly.

At first, my mother didn't respond or react to what I had said.

"Gyal mek di pickny go," she said.

I figured she'd tell me to let her go, so it was no surprise when she said it.

I sighed and looked at my mother. She knew how much I hated to let Mark win.

"It's not fair. He gets to impress Markeesa with all his money and fancy gifts, and what do I have?"

"Dat da lone rass," she said, and sucked her teeth again.

My mother had never been shy when it came to how she felt about the way I handled Markeesa and Mark. We disagreed on it, but I couldn't go ballistic on my own mother. I especially couldn't trip because later, I would need her support if I expected to pull things off smoothly and get Mark out of our lives for good.

Since I sensed my mother was in one of her moods, I decided to leave her to the dinner she was fixing. I got up from my chair and made my way into my room.

I picked up the phone and called Mark. He sounded surprised to hear from me. "Hi, Arlene," he said.

"I was calling to let you know I've decided to let Markeesa go with you guys."

"Oh, that's great news," Mark said. "I can't wait to tell the boys. They'll be really happy and so am I. Thank you, Arlene."

When he talked sweet to me, or used a friendly tone, it always made me think about where we would be today if he had done what he was supposed to do.

"Well, I need to know what to send for her," I said.

Regardless of what my mouth said, I was not happy about Mark taking his family on vacation. Everything good he did with them, made me feel like I had missed out even more.

When my burner phone rang, I quickly wrapped up the conversation with Mark so that I could focus.

"Hi," I said as I answered the secret phone.

"Ma'am, I'm trying to confirm your order," he said.

I double-checked the address, and all of the related details. Once everything was done and paid for, all I had to do was sit back and wait for the happy family to leave for their seven-day Disney Cruise.

If I couldn't be with Mark, and obviously I couldn't, I didn't want him being free to play house with Zaneda. Even if she was on her best behavior now, that was still a challenge for her. I didn't worry because it was nothing but a matter of time before she'd fall back into her old ways. Why Mark couldn't see that, was so crazy to me, but that's what it was.

The risks I took were serious and I understood that. It was why I didn't tell anyone, not even Janet. There was no point in dragging her into my drama.

I opened the note pad I kept in my nightstand drawer, and looked up the number for the temp agency.

"Hi, Savannah, this is Penelope Jones, and I'm following up with you about that assistant I said I'd need for the day."

"Oh, I haven't forgotten," Savannah said. "I think I've got the perfect person for that assignment."

"Okay, great," I said. "What will I need to do?"

"Nothing really. You send us the address and time she needs to be there. Also, if there's a possibility that this assignment will run longer than the time you ordered, simply let the assistant know before she leaves at the end of the day."

It looked like everything had fallen into place. There was nothing left for me to do but sit back and wait for the happy family to head out on their vacay.

CHAPTER THIRTY-ONE

Keeling

I straightened the tie around my neck and looked at my dapper reflection in the full-length mirror in my mom's room. I felt good and confident, like I might really have a chance this time. I hadn't worn a suit in years; I was shocked that the only one I had, still fit. My life looked completely different since Parker Redman started to help. One minute, it felt like my name might have been mud for good. Then days later, I got a call from the Budweiser Company. I couldn't believe it.

Roger had been trying everything he could to get me an interview and things moved slowly. But Parker asked what he could do while he helped work on the situation with Dani. At first, I didn't feel comfortable saying anything. But I told him how I was having a hard time finding a job and he asked where I had looked.

That dude knew everybody. When I told him my boy Roger was trying to get me in over at the Budweiser Company, Parker picked up the phone, and within minutes, I had an interview. If I hadn't seen him do it myself, I still wouldn't believe he had made it happen.

"I helped a few of the supervisors over there," he said.

Parker was all right by me. He didn't even brag or carry it like someone who had lots of power. My man was cool and that was what made it so easy to like him.

Days later, as I walked out of the supervisor's office, I felt good. I couldn't remember a time when I had felt like I had aced an interview.

It seemed like I had a good answer for all of his questions, and after we talked, he even showed me around the place and introduced me to a few of the workers.

Back in the office, when it was time to wrap up, he smiled at me and looked over his paperwork once again. Finally, he stood, looked up at me and said, "Mister Lake, you can expect to hear from us really soon." Then, he shook my hand.

It felt good to be wanted.

"Thank you, Mr. Bradshaw. I look forward to hearing from you."

Behind the wheel of my mom's car, I felt better than good. I wanted to go and tell Roger the good news, but he was at work. I barely turned the corner before my cell phone rang. I thought for sure it would be my moms, but it wasn't.

Instantly I wondered whether I had forgotten something at the interview. I answered the phone and prayed nothing had gone wrong in the time since I had left the office.

"Mr. Lake, this is Corey Bradshaw. Listen, I told you, you would hear from us, and although I didn't expect it to be this soon, there's no point in waiting. What I'm trying to say is I want to offer you the job," he said.

I was so happy, I wanted to cry.

"Uh, yes, Sir. Thank you, Sir," I said. "Thank you."

He gave me information about my start date and where I needed to go to take the drug test. He said pending everything coming back clean, I could begin training at the beginning of the next week.

"Welcome to the team," he said, before we ended our call.

I called Parker next.

When his secretary told me he was with a client, I left a message and asked her to tell him to call me.

The next call was to my moms.

The phone barely rang once before she answered excitedly.

"How'd it go?" she asked.

"Dang! Anxious, aren't we?" I joked.

"Boy, don't play with me," she warned.

"Listen here, lady, you don't tell a working man when he can and cannot play."

My mother squealed so loudly, the sound nearly pierced my eardrum. She was more hyped than I'd expected.

"Oh, baby, I'm so proud and happy for you!" she screamed loudly.

"Thanks, Mom."

"We have got to celebrate."

"Well, it won't be official until the drug test comes back," I said.

"Shoot, boy! I'm not worried about no doggone drug test! I know I didn't raise no weed head. That job is as good as yours."

I laughed at my moms. She was right about that. I didn't mess with any drugs, so the job was as good as mine, finally.

Later at home, I started to undress while I looked for food.

The phone rang, and I was hyped when I saw it was Parker.

"Keeling! What's up, my man?"

"Oh, Parker. You the man, dude," I said.

"I take it you're now among the employed," Parker said.

"I can't ever thank you enough," I said, and I meant it from the heart.

"No need, no need. I understand what you've been through, and I wish I could help solve all of your problems that easily."

That instantly wiped the smile right off of my face. That was when I realized something was wrong.

"What happened? The AG's office ain't budging?" I asked. My

heart felt heavy. I wanted to go back to work. I was excited about the thought of making money again, but I didn't want to make money and have to pay to support a kid that wasn't mine. My hope deflated that quickly.

"No. It's not the AG's office," Parker said.

I should've known what he was going to say next and it really shouldn't have taken me by surprise. But it did.

"It's Dani. I don't think she's gonna play ball, and that's gonna make things harder than I like. I didn't say impossible, but harder," he said. "Listen, this isn't anything I want you to worry about. You focus on the new job and putting your life back on track. Let me handle this," he said.

"Parker, man, I don't know how to thank you, but I do know that I'm always gonna worry about this, at least until the day we get the green light that it's finally cleared up."

"That's understandable," he said. "But at least shift your focus to the new job. I want that to be a good experience for you. Let me handle Dani and I'll keep you and your mother posted."

That comment made me chuckle a little. Parker wouldn't get any rest until something was resolved. My moms only knew how to go hard. I just hoped she wouldn't frustrate the man and chase away the first real person who had been willing to help us.

We ended the call and I changed clothes. I was hyped about my new job. I decided to take Parker's advice and let him handle the situation with Dani. There was no need to create more problems right when things looked like they were taking a turn for me.

From the bathroom, I thought I heard my cell phone, but figured it must've been Roger. It wasn't until I got out and the phone rang again that I saw it was Dani. She had called three times.

What the hell did she want?

CHAPTER THIRTY-TWO

Mark

Arlene's call and decision to let Markeesa go with us made me consider the possibility that maybe she wasn't behind the drama, after all.

It was a fleeting thought because if Arlene wasn't behind the antics, that meant we had suddenly become the unluckiest people on earth.

However, during that phone call, there hadn't been a single cross word between us, no bickering, no fighting, and that was strange enough.

For a change, when Arlene talked to me, her tone was calm and gentle, like it used to be back in the day. In the beginning, Arlene was sweet and compassionate. That kindness she showed me left me in a state of confusion. Back then, Zaneda seemed more interested in globe-trotting with her friends than taking care of her family, and Arlene was the opposite; she was there. She was different. She didn't mind doing anything she thought might make me happy. I loved that about her.

I loved my wife, but back then, Zaneda acted like we were nothing more than roommates. With Arlene's constant attention and meticulous care for the kids and me, I started to feel like there might have been something real between us. She was everything a wife should've been. Unfortunately, one thing led to another, I crossed the line, and got caught up.

At a time when I was ignored by my wife, sex with Arlene was everything it wasn't with Zaneda. It didn't matter what I wanted her to do, she'd do it. She never complained, and was always willing to please.

By the time I found out that she was pregnant, my marriage was completely on the rocks. Zaneda had been out doing her own thing and I found evidence that those trips with her girlfriends weren't as innocent as she claimed. It became the fuel that fed my infidelity.

I moved out and our family was in complete shambles. Regardless of how vicious the fights became with Zaneda and me, Arlene was there with comforting words.

"She doesn't deserve you," Arlene would say.

"A man like you needs someone who knows how to take care of her husband," she would remind me.

Everything she whispered in my ear seemed to make sense. I knew there were hundreds of women who would've jumped at the chance to take Zaneda's place. But I didn't have to look far. Arlene was capable and willing.

After arguments with Zaneda, Arlene helped ease my frustration and let me know that once the baby was born, we could be the kind of family I never had with Zaneda. The great thing about Arlene was, she loved the boys, so to her, taking care of us all, was already a given.

As I tried to figure out what to do about the marriage and Zaneda, Arlene and her mother completely took over. The house was clean and quiet, hot dinners were always on the table, and it looked like Arlene and I were headed for a solid future together.

But I didn't move fast enough for her. She wanted Zaneda to know about us and about the baby.

"You need to tell her," she said.

The problem was, Arlene pushed continuously. In between taking care of everything she said she would, she kept reminding me that I needed to do right by her and our unborn child.

After my daughter was born, I had convinced myself that my future would be with Arlene instead of Zaneda. Arlene and her mother made me feel like I was a part of a close-knit family. Her mother's accent was hard at first, but the more time I spent with them and the kids, the more it all seemed to make sense.

"What are you doing in here? Daydreaming?" Zaneda asked.

I snapped out of those thoughts and smiled at her. I got up and met her near the door.

"Did everything go okay?" I asked.

"Yes. We're all set," she said. "Oh, do we know what's up with Markeesa?"

"Yes. Arlene called and said we can take her," I replied.

I searched her face for any signs or reaction to that news.

"The boys will be glad to know she's coming," Zaneda said.

I pulled her close to me. "Yeah, but what about you? Are you happy?"

She frowned. That was nothing unusual.

"Yeah. You know how I feel about Markeesa. I can't stand her mother, but that little girl loves being around you and the boys, so yeah. I'm glad she's coming with us."

Her answer made me feel better. Because Arlene took her time to get back to me, we were pressed for time. It didn't matter that we needed to make sure Markeesa had what she needed. I was determined to work with what we had.

In the family room, I walked up behind Zaneda and started to rub her shoulders.

"That feels good," she said. She adjusted her neck and leaned back. "I'm tired."

I was careful not to rub too hard.

"Oh, I was hoping you'd feel like doing some more shopping," I said.

Zaneda craned her neck and looked back up at me. "What's going on?"

"Arlene is letting us take Markeesa on the cruise. I'm thinking she might need some new clothes too," I said.

Zaneda rolled her eyes. I didn't know what to expect when she opened her mouth again.

"Babe, I already bought clothes for her when I got all of our stuff for the cruise." For the first time in a while, something she said finally made me happy.

"That's a relief. I didn't wanna say anything to Arlene about it, but I didn't want Markeesa to feel left out if the boys had a bunch of new stuff and she didn't."

I moved away from the back of the sofa and was about to sit down.

"Oh no, buddy," Zaneda said. "Your work is far from over here. Get back here and do some more work on my shoulders."

As I moved to finish what I'd started, I wondered whether I'd make it after an entire week on a cruise ship with Zaneda and the kids.

CHAPTER THIRTY-THREE

Dani

Thoughts of how to get away with murder stayed fresh on my mind. If Keeling and his mama thought they could sic some old dude on me and that would make me run, they had another thing coming.

I had to figure out what to do because that guy seemed like he knew his stuff and I didn't want to get caught slipping. There was no way I could survive without the money from Keeling. It wasn't gonna happen, plain and simple.

"You going out tonight?" Niecy asked me.

"Naw, I gotta put in some work," I said.

"I'll be glad when you start your real job because that shit is not the business," she said.

"Girl, who you telling? But I need some paper and I don't know of anybody who's willing to give it up the way he does."

Niecy and I were talking about this older dude named Bernard Franklin. He was real cool and would lace me with a few c-notes every now and then. The only thing was, I had him believing that he was the only man in my life. I told him since I already had three kids and lived with my mother, she was mad strict and didn't allow me to do anything except watch my kids so she wouldn't have to.

"Y'all going somewhere tonight or kicking it at the house?" Niecy asked.

"You know I don't like going out with him. People be acting all foul like they've never seen an older man with a young female, so I told him to order some Mexican food, and have some drinks ready," I said.

"Well, when you rolling through?" she asked.

"As soon as you finish my hair. Why? You wanna come?"

"I dunno. I ain't trying to give Bernard false hopes of a possible threesome," she said.

I rolled my eyes. "Girl, please! Even if we begged him, he wouldn't know what to do with all this youngness."

We both laughed.

"I might come with you. I mean, it wouldn't hurt to go have a few drinks before I figure out what to get into later," she said.

"Yeah, if you go, that's less work for me."

Niecy looked at me. "Sounds to me like I deserve a cut, at least ten to fifteen percent." She laughed at her own lame joke.

"Bernard ain't dropping enough paper for me to share with anybody, girl. You know that."

It was obvious she was joking. We listened to music while she finished up my hair. I watched in the mirror as she picked up swatches of hair and clamped them into the flat-iron. Niecy wasn't a professional stylist, but she could do some hair. Lulu and I always told her she needed to make hair her side hustle.

More than an hour later, I liked my hair and the little skimpy dress I had slithered into. There was no doubt that Bernard would like it too.

"You need to ask him if it's cool for me to roll," Niecy asked as she put away all of her equipment.

I looked at her sideways and smirked. "Girl, please. Bernard is always thrilled to have my company. I could bring along a billy goat and he wouldn't mind. Besides, what straight man in his right mind wouldn't want to spend an evening with two fine young thangs?"

Niecy put her palm up for a high-five. "Dig that," she said, as we slapped palms.

We were about to leave when I realized I didn't have the alum powder. I rushed back in and grabbed the bag I was about to leave at Niecy's house. I had to dress a lot less fabulous in order to get away from Charlene at night. If she thought I was going out to have even a little bit of fun, she'd start to run her mouth and threaten not to watch the kids.

"You got everything?" she asked.

"Yeah, but I need you to make sure you leave the key so I can get back in and change before I go back to Charlene's."

Now, Niecy looked at me side-eyed. "How long we been doing this?"

She had a point there.

"I nearly forgot my magic potion," I said as I walked behind her.

"Girl, you still use that stuff?" she asked, with her face twisted.

"Oh, and you know it! I swear by that stuff and I will use it for the rest of my life. You should too."

Niecy started to laugh. "I can't believe nobody has ever caught on," she said, and laughed some more. She stopped when her phone rang and pulled a finger to her pursed lips to hush me.

"Hey, Boo," she answered.

I walked over to my car and watched as she climbed into hers. I was so glad she was coming to Bernard's with me. Most times he bored me to tears. But a girl had to do what she had to do, so I pretended like he was all that and stroked his ego among other things, for the few dollars he'd give up.

Later, at Bernard's, Niecy and I had eaten and gotten full. Bernard ordered my favorite Mexican food from Cheuy's and he had a bar filled with Henny, Patrón, Grey Goose, and Crown. I was in heaven, and from the look on Niecy's face, I could tell she was, too.

He left the living room and she leaned over to me and whispered, "I don't see how you do it to him. He's all fat and sloppy-looking."

I raised my glass in her direction. "After a few more of these, it won't matter how fat he is."

"Oh, I believe that because I'm feeling quite nice right about now," she said. "A cross-eyed midget could get it tonight," she joked.

Bernard came back into the living room and Niecy sprang up from the sofa like a Jack-in-the-Box. "Well, you guys, thanks for the hospitality, but I need to run."

"Aw. Already?" Bernard whined. "And here I thought you two would kiss before you go," he said.

Niecy threw her hand to her hip, but I waved off his comment and said, "Bernard you don't really wanna go there, do you?" My eyebrow was raised as I waited on his answer.

"You know I'm joking," he confessed.

That's what I thought. I turned and followed Niecy to the door. "I'll be right back. Lemme walk her out and check in on the kids," I said.

Once outside, I asked Niecy to hold up a second while I tried Keeling again.

The moment he answered, I lit into his simple behind.

"You should be ashamed of yourself! Did you and your mama think y'all could scare me with this dude? You're such a sorry loser! You will always be a pathetic mommy's boy! I swear you make me so damn sick!" I yelled.

"Girl!" Niecy spun around. "Be quiet before you wake the dead out here with all that yelling."

I lowered my voice.

"If you try to stop paying child support for Keela, I'm warning you right now, I will have your ass thrown back under the jail," I said.

When I hung up the phone and turned back to Niecy, she had a strange look on her face.

"What?" I snapped.

"Um. Dani. I'm confused. How you gonna try and make that man pay for a kid that's not his after you went on national TV and told the world he was not the father?"

I sucked my teeth. "Girl, I'm not thinking about that show. And it's not me that's making him do anything. The law is! He's the fool who signed the birth certificate, so he's still the father whether he wants to pay or not. And besides, I need that money."

I ignored her when she cut her eyes at me.

CHAPTER THIRTY-FOUR

Arlene

The day I had waited on finally arrived. My mother fussed around the house as she helped me get Markeesa's things packed for her week-long vacation with Mark and his family. I had everything set and ready to go, and we were close to having Markeesa's stuff together too.

I tried my best to think sad thoughts because I didn't want to give any hints that I was planning something. It was amazing to me that Mark was simple enough to think that just because I agreed to let Markeesa vacation with them, all was well between us, but that was what I wanted him to think. He could be so simple.

It didn't take much time for me to get the ball rolling and put everything in place, so I needed him and Zaneda to think everything was kosher. I was careful to be extra sweet the last time we talked. I knew he'd fall for it, and run to tell his wife. They were both stupid if you asked me.

"Ma, she doesn't need another item," I said.

My mother acted like the girl was going away for a month instead of a week.

She meant well, but I felt like Zaneda would have something to say about any little thing I did. I didn't need that idiot to think she could have my child.

This time, when Mark came to pick our daughter up, he had enough sense to come to the door alone, for a change. He still looked good and despite how hard I tried, his good looks continued to have an impact on me. But not enough of an impact that I didn't want to go through with my plan.

"Mommy, are you sure you don't want to come on the cruise with us?" my daughter asked as Mark wheeled her adult-sized suitcase out of the front door.

Mark's sons waved excitedly at me from their seats inside the Range Rover. I still missed them and was always stunned by their growth.

"Thanks again for doing this," Mark said after he put Markeesa's luggage into the truck. "She's really going to have a great time and we're real happy that you let her come. I know it wasn't easy for you."

His words didn't mean much to me. After all this time, I still felt like any sincerity on his part could have been proven if he had done the right thing.

When I came back inside, my mother was waiting near the kitchen.

"Ya wah be alright?" she asked.

"Oh, yeah. I'm gonna be more than okay," I said. When the grin made its way to my face, she looked suspiciously at me and put a hand on her hip.

I shrugged. "What?"

"Weh ya de do?"

I turned quickly and started to move toward the back. Too much time with my mother would force me to make some confessions and I wasn't ready to do that.

"Arlene!" she yelled after me.

Over my shoulder, I told her the quickest lie I could muster up.

"We need to get ready to go. Janet is gonna be here soon," I said.

The truth was, Janet wouldn't be by until later, but if my mother stayed on me, I'd spill the beans and tell her everything, and I didn't want to be talked out of it.

Once behind my bedroom door, I turned on the TV, took a seat next to the window and pulled out the new burner I'd bought.

"Yes. This is Penelope Jones. I'm calling to check on my project," I said.

"Hi, Ms. Jones. Yes, everything is in place. We have Dani Patnett scheduled to arrive at the site at eight sharp Monday morning. Dani is punctual and she's very clear on what she's expected to do," Savannah said.

"That's great. But I may need her to do something on Saturday as well. I know you guys don't work weekends, but this would be a few hours out of the day. I need her to pick up some flyers and drop them off at four locations in the area. Is that something she'd be able to do?"

"We can handle all of your business needs. If Dani is not available, I'm sure we can hire a courier to take care of that," Savannah said.

"Yeah. Um, I don't think a courier will do for this. I'd really prefer the same person who will be at the site on Monday."

"Well, I'll tell you what. Let me reach out to her and I'll call you right back to confirm. If she's not available, we'll work to find someone who can get it done."

"Thank you, Savannah," I said.

"No. It's our pleasure. We appreciate your business."

True to her word, less than thirty minutes later, Savannah called me back.

"Ms. Jones. Everything is set. Dani will pick up the flyers and deliver them to the four businesses."

"Great!"

I was glad to hear this. I told Savannah exactly where the flyers would be located, and where Dani could find the key Monday morning. I had a couple of minor things to handle and we'd be all set.

My next call was to the two neighborhood magazines and the Green Sheet for the area. I didn't want to do Craigslist again. Not that I thought they'd remember me, but there was no need to take unnecessary chances.

Once I made sure the ads would run when they were supposed to, I called the hair shops, and the two spas to remind them about Saturday's delivery.

Something happened when I opened my bedroom door to walk out. My mother jumped back. The startled look on her face confirmed that she knew she'd been caught.

I was pissed.

"So you're eavesdropping now?" I asked.

"Arlene, weh ya de do?" she asked. "Ya deh do something whe yo do got no business fe do!"

"Ma. I need you to stay out of my business."

"Yo dah fe me business. Yo, and Markeesa," she said.

I sighed and walked past her. An argument wasn't on my agenda. I had entirely too much to do.

My real cell phone rang and it was Janet. I was glad for the distraction. I realized a while back that my mom snuck around and listened to my calls and conversations, but I had never caught her in the act before. Since we were about to go out of town for a few days, there was no need in being salty.

"Girl, I am so glad you suggested this trip. I really need the time away," Janet said when I answered the phone.

"Good, when are you coming?"

"I'm on my way now," she said.

That surprised me because I thought we were leaving later to try and avoid rush-hour traffic on I-10.

"What time are we getting on the road?" I asked.

"I figured we could leave around two. That way we'll bypass Houston traffic, but we'll get there while it's still early," Janet said.

"Hmm. Okay." My mind raced. I needed us to leave later because I still had to drop off the flyers for the shops. And I had to do it without my mother being all up in my business. "So, you were heading over here now?"

"Arlene. What's going on? What are you trying to do?" Janet asked. She was always able to see right through me. "And how much trouble will we get in behind it?"

"Nothing much. But did you notarize that letter for me?"

"Umm. You mean, the blank page," Janet said. "If I go to jail…"

I cut her off, thanked her, and ended the call.

CHAPTER THIRTY-FIVE

Keeling

Training at work was easier than I thought it would be and I liked it. Basically I rode on a large truck with a driver and helped him unload Budweiser products. What I liked most was how the customers treated him. Every time we stopped at a new place, to make a delivery, people were nice and very excited to see him.

"Malcolm, we're glad to see you, buddy," a store manager said as we walked into his business. "We need everything today. I hope that truck is full."

Malcolm was real cool. He treated me like we were close friends from the neighborhood. While we sat in traffic, we talked and discovered we knew some of the same people.

By the third day of training, Malcolm had told me all about his baby-mama drama and how he worked so hard only to pay his kids' mothers. He had three kids by three different women and he said each woman's drama was enough to make him want to commit bloody murder. I never bothered to tell him my own drama-filled story. I was sure Dani and what she had put me through was enough to put all of his drama to shame.

Another reason I decided not to add anything to that story was, because most of the times when I did, people didn't get it anyway.

"So, how do you like it so far?" Malcolm asked after we wrapped up our last stop.

"Man. I love it! I can't wait to get my own route; everybody back at the warehouse seemed real cool and I'm hyped," I said. He released a little chuckle.

"Yeah, I remember when I was hyped like that too," Malcolm said.

Every job had its pitfalls and no place was perfect, but if he knew how hard it was for me to find a job, he'd understand my excitement. I was still very new, so I didn't want to share my personal business. Malcolm seemed real cool and he had already opened up and told me all of his, but I didn't get down like that.

My cell phone rang again. All morning, Dani had been blowing me up, but since I was at work, I ignored her calls.

"Damn, Dawg, somebody's been hunting you down," Malcolm said. I snatched my phone from the holder at my waist and looked down at my screen. It was Parker's number.

"Damn. Actually, I need to take this," I said.

"Oh, go ahead, man. You don't need my permission. It's all good out here. We're on our own."

"Hey, Parker. What's up?" I didn't even try to hide the enthusiasm in my voice. I was so glad to finally have a job and there was no question that he was solely responsible for it.

"Keeling. How's the job going?"

"It's good, real good. Thanks again," I said.

"I wrote a note to remind myself to follow up with you today. Have you heard anything from Dani?"

"Yeah, I did. She called yapping and carrying on about how if I turn her in and she loses the child support money, it's not gonna be good for me. She's hot, says I tried to trick her by sending you after her."

I caught myself before I said too much. I was still in the truck with Malcolm and I didn't want him all in my business. I didn't know him like that, and being new to the job, I still wasn't sure whom I could trust.

"She's not going to make this easy on us, that's for sure. But I've dealt with her type before. It's gonna take a little longer than we'd like, but we'll take care of this. So you like the job so far?" Parker asked.

"Oh yeah, it's all good. I'm working now. We're about to take a lunch break before we finish out the route for the day. Man, I can't thank you enough."

"Don't thank me yet. When I get Dani to do the right thing, then you can thank me all you want," he said.

"Okay. Bet that."

"I'm gonna let you get back to it. I was checking in on you. Remember, if you need anything at all, I'm a phone call away."

"Thanks, Parker, man. Thanks."

Malcolm drove a few more minutes before he turned to me. "Is everything okay?"

I nodded. I didn't want to bring him up to speed on my situation with Dani. I hoped he wouldn't ask since I didn't volunteer the information.

"Yeah, man. It's all good on my end. I'm eager to learn, so I can be successful on this job," I said.

"Oh, you got this man, I can tell. Trust me. I've trained many during my eighteen years and I can usually tell by day two whether we've got a winner. I see that in you. You're gonna do real good on this job. Don't even sweat it."

That made me feel good. I needed the job so I wanted to make a good impression every chance I got.

"I appreciate that, bro, I really do. It took me a while to get this job and I just wanna make sure I get through my probation period and maybe hang around at least half as long as you."

"Just stick with me and you'll be straight. I haven't lost a trainee yet."

When Malcolm's phone rang, that gave me the break I needed. The last thing I wanted him to do was start asking questions about child support and who was hemming me up.

"Sup?" I heard him say.

That's when I realized I was hungry. Once we pulled up at a Popeyes, I was glad to get out of the truck.

"Yo. You need to take that up with them and not me. I did my part. I ain't dropping no more cash, so if that's what this call is about, you might as well hang up now!" he barked into his cell phone.

When I jumped out of the truck, he was still yelling into the phone.

The minute I finished my order, my cell rang. I turned and saw Malcolm as he walked into the restaurant.

It was Dani.

"Hey, what's up?" I answered.

"You are Keela's father! I don't give a damn what any DNA test says. And if you try to change that, you are abandoning us and you said you never would."

"Dani, look, you need to go find her real father. I ain't about to be stuck paying child support for no damn kid that's not mine," I said.

"Well, the law says you have to. You signed the birth certificate. Nobody twisted your arm! You can't go back now, years later and try to renege."

"I'm not about to do this with you. You know what, how about I need you to lose my number! Don't call me anymore. If you keep calling me, I'm gonna report you for harassment," I said.

"I am the mother of your child!" she screamed. "You need to listen to what I'm trying to tell you."

"Listen, the gravy train is about to end soon, Dani. I suggest you go out and find a real J-O-B!" I said and pressed the END button on my phone.

When I turned, Malcolm stood and stared at me. The look on his face was one of stunned confusion.

"Did you just say Dani? As in Dani Patnett?" he asked with a deep frown. My heart sank.

CHAPTER THIRTY-SIX

Mark

We were able to pick Markeesa up without incident and for that, I was grateful. Arlene was actually pleasant, and that made me think again about whether she was capable of some of the things we'd been through. I told myself to put that on the back burner, at least until we got back from vacation.

The day before our vacation, my house erupted into straight chaos. But the craziness was all good. The kids ran around trying to find last-minute toys and swim trunks. It was good to see Markeesa as she ran around behind her brothers. They were happy, all of them, and that made me happy.

The night before the cruise, the kids were so excited it was hard to get them settled and into bed. Despite all of the horsing around, and the bouncing off the walls, I was excited too. It was special to me because everyone in the house was eager for the cruise, even Zaneda.

She had tons of new clothes and shoes she needed to go through and clear for the trip. I didn't mind because I couldn't remember a time I had seen Zaneda that engaged in anything that had to do with our family.

"Do you think this is too much for a Disney Cruise?" she asked, as she twirled in front of the full-length mirror.

She wore a floor-length dress that was low-cut in the front and the back. I liked everything I saw, and didn't care about whether she wore it on the cruise. At that moment, I only wanted to see the dress on the floor.

After I eased up behind her, I hoped she was able to feel my excitement. I held her tightly and grinded my hips into her plump behind.

She wiggled away from me. "Mark. Quit." She swatted in my direction. "I'm trying to get my wardrobe together."

I rolled my eyes. "Babe, you'll look good in anything you wear. Let's do something now, that we won't be able to do for the next seven days because we'll be on a cruise ship with the kids in close quarters," I whined.

Zaneda threw her hand onto her hip and whipped around to face me.

"Um, didn't you get us a suite?" she asked.

"I did. We're in a concierge suite, but the kids are gonna be a little scared about sleeping in a strange place; don't you think?"

She cut her eyes at me and frowned. "They'll be fine." She turned back to her reflection in the mirror. "The kids will be so hyped they won't care where they sleep."

I considered what she said and sat back to watch as she changed from one outfit to the next. After a while, they all started to look the same to me, but I didn't dare say so.

Early the next day, we headed out to our cruise ship. We boarded the ship early, because we had a concierge suite, and the kids were already having a ball. When a man dressed in a starched white uniform with sailor's hat met us and escorted us onto the boat, the kids really got giddy.

"I'm Karim Blair. I'll be your personal concierge for the duration of your Disney Cruise," the gentleman said.

I was glad Timothy suggested a family vacation. Markeesa's eyes lit up the moment we stepped onto the ship. It actually looked like a magical place.

In addition to the ever-so-present Disney theme, which was everywhere, the ship's interior was elegant and classic with lots of polished wood mixed in with gold and earth-tone colors. Disney recorded music could be heard all over. I hoped I'd be able to get the songs out of my head, at the end of the cruise.

"You know you're gonna have to put that thing down, right?" I said to Zaneda. She'd been on the phone since we got on the transfer bus that took us to the cruise terminal.

Since we were so early, we headed up to the ship's buffet for some lunch. The food selection was incredible; there were rib-eye steaks, sautéed mushrooms, grilled asparagus, jumbo shrimp, and crab legs in addition to the regular buffet selections. And we hadn't even left port yet.

"Can we take a picture with Minnie? Please, Daddy, please?" Markeesa whined.

"Yes. We can."

I liked the idea of several Disney characters roaming around the ship for pictures and autographs. The boys behaved like they were too cool for pictures with the characters, but Markeesa was happy to smile and pose.

"You need to tell her we can go to our cabin. She wants to wait for Goofy," Zaneda whispered in my ear.

It was thrilling to see my daughter having a great time. I didn't want her to feel less than nor left out of anything the boys experienced.

"We are going to have a wonderful time on this cruise," I said to Markeesa.

"I know, Daddy. I'm so excited. I can't wait to tell Mommy. She said I had to be careful because you guys might get tired of having me around."

I frowned.

"What did you say?" I stooped down to meet my daughter at eye level.

"Mommy said since it's my first time being with you and Miss Zaneda for such a long time, I should be careful not to make you all mad because…"

"Markeesa," I cut her off. "I don't want you to think about anything like that ever again. You're my daughter and I love you. You don't have to ever worry about a thing when you're with us. This is your family too," I said.

Her big bright eyes locked in on me and I felt as if I had gotten through to her. I could strangle Arlene for trying to brainwash my child. I needed to push those thoughts from my mind because there was nothing I could do about it now.

"We are about to have the time of our lives. Let's have a great time and not worry about anything your mommy said, okay?"

She nodded.

Initially, I wanted to race to the room and tell Zaneda what Markeesa had told me. But I thought about it. Zaneda was already upset because we couldn't link Arlene to the car for sale or the CPS investigation. On second thought, I decided it was best to keep Arlene's comments to Markeesa to myself.

"We can go check out our cabin and see where we'll be living for the next seven days," I said to my daughter.

Our dinner seating was late, at 9:40. Our first night, we ate in our room. Since we were "concierge," we were able to have food delivered and served in the room.

As we enjoyed our food, the fact that Arlene still tried to ruin our trip despite that she was hundreds of miles away, ate at me. But I suffered in silence.

CHAPTER THIRTY-SEVEN

Dani

My job came in right on time. The little money I had gotten from my date with Bernard was enough to hold me over for a hot second, until Keeling's child support came through. But that money felt different. It felt like the harder I tried to hang on to it, the harder it would be to keep it.

Every time I thought about the possibility of losing that money, it made me want to beat the crap out of Keeling. I'd be willing to bet good money, his nosey-ass mama was behind whatever he was trying to do with that Parker dude.

When I saw Savannah's number pop up on my cell phone, I took a deep breath and closed my eyes. I tried to sound calm and relaxed when I answered.

"Dani Patnett," I said. I heard one of those executive administrative assistants answer the phone like that in a movie and was dying to try it out.

"Hi, Dani. This is Savannah. How are you?" she asked.

She always sounded so professional, like she didn't have any problems at all.

"Savannah. I'm good. I'm glad to hear from you," I said.

If I could do cartwheels while I talked to her, I would. But the last thing I wanted was to let her know how desperate I was for the phone call.

"Well. Like I told you before. This is a temporary gig, but if you do well with this, I know for sure we will be able to place you in other jobs really soon."

I got all of the information I needed from Savannah. It seemed a little strange to me at first, but when I realized the bonus I was about to make for a few hours of work on a Saturday, I was down for whatever.

Saturday afternoon arrived quickly.

"Charlene!" I yelled. "Charlene! Where are you? I told you I needed to go and take care of something."

My heart was beating out of control as I ran from room to room in search of my mother. I just knew she wasn't about to mess this up for me. I told Savannah I could handle it and at the last minute, my mother was M-I-A!

"What's wrong with you?" Charlene asked as she rounded the corner from the kitchen. "Why you yelling like a silly banshee?"

"I didn't know where you were and I need to go to an orientation for my new job."

"I'm outside with *your* kids," she said. She eyed me up and down. "You look nice. I hope you do well with this job."

"Thanks," I said as I balanced myself on one foot and hopped to put my other shoe on.

By the time I got behind the wheel, I was a complete mess. I couldn't remember the address where I needed to pick up the flyers.

For a second, I pulled in a deep breath and told myself to calm down.

I picked up my phone and searched email. Thank God, Savannah had sent everything by email. She had the pickup place, with the address, then drop-off locations, all with addresses and Map-Quest directions.

Relieved, I cranked up my car and rushed to my first stop.

I looked at the flyers and my heart raced like an out-of-control Ferrari. I could hardly believe what I read.

"Estate sale. Top designer clothes, shoes, and accessories from name brands you love: Gucci, Kate Spade, Michael Kors, St. John, and much more. All for ten dollars."

Could my eyes be playing tricks on me?

"Everything for ten dollars. First come, first serve." I read the words aloud and still couldn't believe what I read.

I pulled up at the very first stop and asked for the person I was told was expecting me.

"Hi, I'm Dani Patnett and I'm here to see Heather," I said.

Women in various stages of the beauty process sat in chairs, under dryers, and at shampoo bowls.

"Oh, you can pass them out if you want," the receptionist said. Although Savannah didn't say I was supposed to pass anything out, I didn't mind.

I walked around and handed each woman one of the flyers.

"Hi, there's an estate sale going on. Everything for ten dollars," I said.

A woman snatched the hooded dryer from her head and looked at the flyer.

"Everything for ten dollars?!" she yelled.

"Yes. Just like the flyer says," I said.

"Gucci? Michael Kors? Oh, where is this again?" she asked as she looked at the flyer, then back at me.

"Oh. The address is right there, at the bottom. It's in the Memorial area."

I tried my best to sound as professional as possible. The truth was, I couldn't believe it my damn self! I couldn't wait to make some calls and let my girls know what was what.

By the time I finished my last stop, I was mad because I couldn't find Niecy or Lulu. I knew I'd hear from them within the hour, but I needed to run this entire situation by them so we could try and figure it all out.

When my phone rang, I answered eagerly, until I realized who was on the other end.

"Keeling, what the hell do you want?"

"Dani, I really need you to go and take the test," he said.

"Did I ask you what you needed from me? I got way too much shit on my plate right now and I don't have time to be sitting up here worrying about what you need me to do."

"Dani. This is not gonna end well for you. You have to go and take the test. If you don't go on your own and take Keela, it's gonna be worse when a judge makes you go."

I listened to him and his overdramatic plea.

"Listen, boo, I'm busy and I ain't got time for this call. It's like I told you the other day. You are Keela's father. It's what her birth certificate says and it's what the law says. Now, I got other shit to do, so buh-bye!"

Before he could say another word, I ended the call. It was right on time too, because my phone rang again and it was Lulu.

"Girl, where are you? We need to talk something serious and we need to do it ASAP!"

CHAPTER THIRTY-EIGHT

Arlene

By the time I pulled up in front of the house, my heart sank at the sight of Janet's car. Since it was empty, there was no way to tell how long she'd been waiting. Either way, I knew I'd walk in to a barrage of questions. I tried to prepare myself for it, but knew I could never predict what all she would ask.

Earlier, it was all I could do to get off the phone with her, without confessing the full details of what I was about to do. I pulled down the visor mirror, and checked my eyes. My reflection didn't scream guilt or nervousness and that was a great sign.

I got out of my car, rushed up the walkway, and opened the front door. When I walked in, I faced three women who looked like they had grown tired of waiting for me, a while ago.

"It's about time," Janet huffed. "Where've you been anyway?"

"Oh, I had to go run an errand before we head out," I said.

My eyes shifted from her to my mother and the other women. The last time I checked, the trip was for three, not five. My mother had managed to highjack our trip and brought her entourage to boot.

"Hi, Miss Betty. Hi, Miss Carol," I said, as I looked at my mother's friends.

"Hey, baby," Miss Carol, a tall, portly woman with a short silver Afro said. "We sure hope you don't mind. But when your mama said y'all was going to Louisiana, we asked if we could tag along."

I cut my eyes at Janet, and she shrugged. I shook my head slowly. How did she let them take over like that?

"Sure, why not," I said. "I guess it's not gonna hurt to pile two more people into Janet's big ol' SUV."

"I need to talk to you," Janet said as I rushed past the crowd and headed toward my bedroom.

"I'll be ready in about ten," I said over my shoulder, as I rushed to get away from her.

"Not so fast," Janet said. She raced to catch up to me. "Where have you been and why was your phone turned off?" she asked. "You knew I'd be calling. What kind of errand did you have to run?"

Oh the questions.

Janet was right on my heels. I walked into my room and she was right behind me like a shadow. "Aren't Mark and his family gone?"

I whipped around and frowned. "Yeah. But what's that got to do with anything? I told you, I had errands to take care of since we're gonna be gone for a couple of days."

"Errands or an errand? And, on a Saturday?" she asked. It was clear she didn't believe a word I'd said. She had every right to be suspicious. If she knew what I had done, I was sure she'd be filled with every lecture point imaginable.

"Yes, an errand. If you must know, I had an ingrown toenail. You wanna take a closer look at it?"

"Eww," Janet said. She frowned and feigned disgust. But that at least got her to move away from me for a bit.

"Well, come on. You're holding us up. You know those little old ladies are eager to get on the road."

"Okay. I'm coming. I'm already packed so I just wanted to change. It's gonna take me five minutes and I'll be good to go," I said.

Janet gave me a look that told me she knew there was more to the story, but she didn't have time to dig. I was glad for the reprieve. She finally left the room.

Once I changed, I grabbed my bags, and bolted out to the living room. "Okay, I'm ready to hit the road!" I yelled, with lots of enthusiasm.

My mother and her friends sprang from their seats and nearly ran over each other to get to the front door. I let them go outside and pulled the door closed to stop Janet.

"Ten minutes. I was ten minutes late, and I come back and we've got a whole convoy of old biddies tagging along to Louisiana," I said. "What the hell happened?"

Janet broke out in laughter.

"You'd better hush before they hear you," she said.

"I don't care if they hear me. It's the truth. Now we're about to sit on the road for the next five hours with Miss Carol complaining about her arthritis, my mother giving her every old Belizean herbal solution, and Miss Betty nodding off to sleep and snoring! Lord, help us!"

"Stop being mean. What was I supposed to say when they showed up with their weekend bags packed and their bank envelopes stuffed with cash?" Janet asked. "See, if you were here, you could've stopped the madness. Too late now. You can't complain. Let's get on down the road before we hit rush-hour traffic!"

The first three times I called Mark's cell and there was no answer, I told myself not to trip. I figured with all the craziness of getting on the ship and finding their cabin, he might have missed my call.

I told myself I'd give him until late tonight to check in with me and let me know everything was okay with Markeesa.

There was no doubt that them being away was best for us all, but I didn't need him to act like he had gone and lost his mind because they were heading out of the country.

Four hours into our road trip and I was ready to take back everything I had said about the old ladies. They'd actually made the trip seem shorter.

Miss Carol talked about her four husbands and how back in her day she didn't mind having a man take care of her.

"Yes, ma'am, that's just you new millennium women who think you should do it all by yourselves! Back in my day, we understood that God put man and woman together on this earth for a good reason."

Janet and I stayed quiet as the old ladies schooled us on all we'd done wrong or were doing wrong.

Even though I had planned to wait until later, I decided to try Mark's phone again. When his voicemail kicked in again, I was really pissed.

"This is why I didn't want to let him take my daughter out of the country! How come he's not answering his cell?"

"Chile, let that man have some time with his child. I'm sure everything is okay and everyone is fine. You need to enjoy yourself and stop worrying," Miss Carol said.

"I me di tell ah, let that man be good to fe he pickney," my mother said.

Janet looked at me and frowned. My mother's broken English and thick accent were still a challenge for her after all our years of friendship.

"She's saying I need to let Mark be a father to his daughter," I translated.

"Oh. I feel her there, no doubt," Janet said.

I sucked my teeth and looked out the window. My mind raced with thoughts of why I hadn't heard from Mark and none of them were good. I was pissed at him and started to question whether I had made the right decision.

CHAPTER THIRTY-NINE

Keeling

"Well, I'm telling you. That ain't his baby and I don't understand why we gotta keep taking money out of his check!"

My mother's voice boomed loudly before I made it in the front door. I had no idea why she had to scream and yell at the top of her lungs. I've told her you get more done with sugar than salt, but she never listened.

"Y'all need to do your damn job! If he gotta tell those people he's got a child support order, they might fire him. I'm sick of this! How come y'all not going after that little tramp that fingered him for a kid that's not even his!"

She saw me, but it wasn't like my mother to pump the brakes once she was on a roll.

"Well, yeah, he signed the birth certificate, but that was because she told him the baby was his. Since then, she went all over national TV and bragged about how the baby wasn't his!" she screamed. "I don't get why that don't count for something!"

"Ma," I tried to interrupt.

She waved me off, and turned her back to me.

"You're not listening to me. I told you. She went on that show *DNA Revealed*. The little heifer told everybody that the baby ain't his! Don't y'all watch TV?" She rolled her eyes dramatically.

I walked around to face her. "Ma, hang up. Please!" I begged.

My mother put her hand over the mouthpiece on the phone, like that would mute what she was about to say to me.

"I'm sick of this attorney general's office. I don't want them trying to take any money from this new job. Son, listen when I tell you, when your new boss sees that you have to pay back child support, they immediately make judgment calls about your character. I don't want that to happen to you."

"Ma. Hang up. Please let Parker handle this. Let me at least tell you the latest. Please."

"But I'm waiting to speak to a supervisor," she said.

My mother meant well with everything she did for me. When I was little and trouble broke out on the playground, she rushed to my rescue. She even threatened to fight a bigger kid who she thought was bullying me. If a teacher said I wasn't working to my potential, she explained the mistake they had obviously made. During sports, when the coaches made me stay on the bench, she gave them a piece of her mind. She always meant well, but things hardly ever worked out the way she wanted.

Reluctantly, she went back to her phone call.

"Listen. I'm gonna talk to my son. Then I'll call back. This ain't over," she said.

She put the phone down, then turned her attention to me. "I have full confidence in Parker. I really believe he's gonna be able to help us, but Son, he's not moving fast enough. I don't want anything to mess up this new job for you."

"Okay, Ma. I get it and I appreciate everything you do for me. But Parker really is on it. He's the reason I got the job in the first place. And besides, he's already set up for a new DNA test. He already talked to my supervisor about it, so I'm gonna go take the test, then meet my driver at his third stop."

Her eyebrows went up. She crossed her arms over her chest and eyed me up and down, like she needed to make sure I hadn't lost my mind.

"He arranged all of that?" she asked. The skepticism in her voice was in full effect.

"Yeah. That's what I'm trying to tell you. He said it's gonna take a while because he doesn't think Dani is gonna agree to the test, but there's a chance she'll shock us all and show up."

"Boy, if you and Parker think that hood rat is going to do something that might cut off her cash-flow, both of you are plum crazy!"

I threw my hands up in the air. "Okay, Ma. Okay. She might show, she might not. All we can do is try."

"I can't stand her!" my mother spat out.

She cut her eyes at me.

"I know. I know. But for now, we need to let Parker handle this. You calling and going off on folks ain't gonna do us any good and it's not gonna get us anywhere."

"So you don't care if they start taking money out of your check for child support?" she asked sheepishly.

"Naw. I'm good, Ma. Parker is gonna handle it." Before she said something else, I turned to leave. I needed to change clothes.

In my room, guilt ate at me. I shouldn't have lied to my moms about Parker setting up the DNA test. But I felt like I had little choice in the matter. I only told her so she would stop badgering people.

Most times, she didn't even know if she was talking to the right agency. For all we knew, the attorney general's office has a special procedure to follow in cases like mine, but you couldn't tell that to my moms.

More than an hour later, after I changed clothes, I planned to chill in my room for the rest of the night and listen to music, but

I couldn't. My mind went back to the moment when Malcolm realized he knew Dani too.

Did you just say Dani? As in Dani Patnett?

"Yeah," I said. My interest was piqued by his question. "Why? You know her?"

"On the real, I wish I knew you the moment you met her, because I would've told you, that one wasn't nothing nice," Malcolm added with a wink and a chuckle.

"Is that right? What's up, dawg?"

Malcolm shook his head. "Oh, naw, I didn't hit it or nothing like that, but one of my boys used to hook up with her friend Lulu. Well, back then and this was a couple of years ago, we crashed a retirement party for his uncle. Lulu brought a couple of her friends and remember, this was a family thing, so it was mostly older heads there."

I listened, and expected the worst.

"So, it's all gravy. We thought we'd get juiced up with the old heads then take Lulu and her friends to this little hole in the wall. Well, before we could, a fight broke out. Seems my boy's uncle's wife learned the jump-off showed up at the party not knowing who the guest of honor was. Well, that jump-off was none other than your girl, Dani."

"Whaaaat?" I asked.

"Yeah, dawg, looked like LuLu and your girl and their other girl used to play with the geriatrics for a portion of their social security checks," he said.

"Dayaum," I said.

"Yeah, but that day, she got that ass tapped. It was wild. Talk about being in the wrong place at the wrong time. They had no idea what they were walking into."

We cracked up at the story. Later, when I thought about it, I knew the story was true. I remembered when I met Dani, she was romancing some dude on the phone. I didn't know he was old, but the tired-ass lines she used on him made me feel like he couldn't be our age.

"Keeling!" My mother's voice pulled me back to the present.

"Whassup, Ma?"

"Boy! Dinner is ready, where are you?"

I jumped up from the bed and walked out to the scent of tantalizing aromas. My moms might have been many things I didn't like, but her skills in the kitchen were second to none.

"Dang, what all did you make?" I asked.

My stomach growled so hard and loud, I was nearly embarrassed.

"Your favorite, smothered chicken, baked macaroni and cheese, green beans, and hot water cornbread," she said. The smile on her face was wide and bright.

My cell rang, and without a second thought, I answered.

"The law says you're the father! Tell that man to stop calling me or else! I'm serious, Keeling. I ain't taking no damn test and neither is Keela!"

She ended the call.

"Who was that?" my mother asked.

I didn't even bother to answer.

CHAPTER FORTY

Mark

By day two of our cruise, I was glad I'd made the decision to bring the kids along. We were all having a blast. The first day, the kids were with us for the entire day. We hung out by the pool, played games, enjoyed music from the live band, ate, and drank. It was awesome.

The ship itself was incredible. I saw something that said it was more than 15,000 square feet. Nearly an entire deck was devoted to activities for the kids, which was cool because that meant there was always something to do. They had everything: the children's activity centers, outdoor activity areas, and two swimming pools.

"Wanna go see a movie?" Zaneda asked.

The theaters seemed to cater to family entertainment with lots of large-scale production shows, movies, and even lively interactive game shows. There was so much to do on the ship, it was hard to settle on any one thing.

"Tonight we should go and check out some of the adults-only places," I suggested, in a wicked whisper.

Zaneda grinned. She leaned over in her lawn chair and snuggled closer to me.

"What kind of adults-only places?" she asked. Her tone was a little flirtatious too.

"Get your mind out of the gutter," I teased. "It's a few themed bars, and lounges."

"Oh. Where are those located?"

"There are a few near the area in front of the lobby atrium. There's also the Promenade Lounge. That's near the elevator lobby and Cove Café, which is a quiet spot near the adult pool. They've got coffee, Internet access, or just a quiet place if you wanna read," I said.

"You sure seem to know a lot about this cruise ship."

"I started reading up on it as soon as we decided to come. Besides, it may be a wonderful world, but I wanted to make sure there were options for us too."

Zaneda looked at me with a cheesy expression.

"Really? A wonderful world, huh?"

She reached over and swiped my beer. "How many of these have you had?" she joked.

We laughed.

I felt like our short time on the boat helped bring us closer. I hadn't see Zaneda so happy and carefree in a long time. It seemed like the fresh air allowed her to relax and enjoy the moment.

"Is that your cell?"

The laughter stopped abruptly. I frowned. Did I have my phone?

We looked around and Zaneda picked up her beach bag.

"No. I think that's your phone," I said. I grabbed my beer bottle and leaned back in my chair.

Her original stunned expression faded from her face as she dug through the bag. She pulled the phone out and frowned as she looked at the screen.

"What the hell is she doing calling my phone?" Zaneda snarled.

That made me focus on her phone too.

"Who?"

"Who else? Your nasty-ass baby-mama," she snapped.

In that instant, playful, funny Zaneda was replaced by the old reliable, sour, bitter Zaneda.

"What the hell do you want?" she said into the phone.

A few seconds later, she passed her phone to me. The sour expression looked as if it would be etched into her features for a very long time.

"Hello?" I tried to keep my cool and remain calm.

"What the hell is your problem? You take my daughter, and it's been three whole days since I've heard from you!"

"Arlene, calm down," I said.

"Don't tell me what the hell to do! Where's my daughter?" she asked.

"Uh. The kids are at an activity center," I stammered.

"What? What the hell are you talking about?!" she screamed. "So you took my daughter on a family vacation so you can dump her off on some baby sitters?"

"Arlene, it's not like that," I said.

But Arlene wouldn't listen to me.

"You take my child on a damn cruise ship, only to dump her on a group of strangers? What kind of bull is that?"

I closed my eyes, then opened them. Zaneda watched my every move. The last thing I needed was for her to think I couldn't handle Arlene.

"Arlene, that's customary on cruises. We are with the kids most of the time, but there are activities designed specifically for kids. It's not the way you make it sound." I tried my best to watch my tone. But she kept pushing my buttons.

"That's why I didn't want her to go in the first damn place! If I knew this was what you two had up your sleeve, I would've made her stay at home!"

"You're making a big deal out of nothing."

"See! That's what the hell I'm talking about! Now she's nothing?"

"Arlene," I said.

"Don't Arlene me! When were you gonna let her call home?" she asked.

But before I could answer, she answered the question for me.

"Probably once y'all made it back home, huh?!" she screamed.

I moved the phone from my ear and allowed her voice to yap in the wind. There was no way in the world I was about to argue with her. We were on vacation. The stress she tried to bring was not only unwanted, but it was completely unnecessary.

"I'll have her call you when they get out of their activity," I said. I didn't even wait for her to respond. I pressed the "end" button and passed the phone back to Zaneda.

When I eased back onto the lawn chair, Zaneda frowned at me.

"You wanna tell me what that was all about?" she asked. The attitude had come back to her voice with a vengeance.

"Not really."

"Okay, well how about if you don't tell me and I'll call her back and ask her myself," she snarled. "The last time I let you handle shit as far as she was concerned, your daughter was born."

My eyes snapped open.

CHAPTER FORTY-ONE

Dani

The speed limit was the last thing on my mind as I flew down I-10 and quickly exited Highway 6. I wasn't about to be late to my very first gig. I was determined to make Savannah glad she took a chance on me. Even though I was still a little confused about the job, I figured if I showed up early, I could figure it all out.

As I drove, I waited for Lulu to get Niecy on three-way. A few seconds later, she clicked over and I heard Niecy's voice ring out.

"What is so urgent?" she asked. She sounded a little irritated, but I wasn't the least bit worried. What I was about to tell them was going to make up for any sidestep I'd ever taken before.

"Yeah. What's so urgent?" Lulu chimed in.

"Before I explain, did you guys do what I asked? Are you gonna be able to spare a couple of hours like I said?" I asked.

"Oooh, girl. If you don't get to it," Niecy said.

"Okay, next question. Can I borrow some money from both of you?"

"Whhhhhaaaaat? Is that what you got us on three-way for?" Lulu asked and sucked her teeth. "What kind of puckery is this!"

"I didn't call you guys for a loan, but if you want me to tell you why I'm calling, I need to know if y'all are gonna be able to lend me some money?"

"Um. Dani. I don't feel comfortable lending money to somebody who ain't working," Niecy had the nerve to say.

"Bitch, I got a job!" I said.

"Yes, she does," Lulu added.

"Okay then, why are you begging for money?" Niecy interrupted.

"I'm not begging for anything. I'm about to hook y'all both up and I want in on some of the action."

"Oooh, girl! Did a delivery truck lose its load again? Oh, God, please let it be electronics this time," Niecy said.

"Dani, you know the struggle is real out here; don't be playing with our emotions. Tell us what the hell is going on," Lulu said.

"So does that mean y'all got me?" I asked. My heart raced out of control as I pulled up in front of the mansion in the exclusive Memorial area neighborhood.

"Yeah, dammit. Now tell us!" Niecy yelled.

"Okay. I'm heading up to an estate sale at this bomb-ass house, and everything is ten damn dollars!" I announced in a grand way.

Silence.

I waited for a few seconds, then I said, "O-kay, obviously y'all didn't hear me."

"We heard you, but I just want you to know your punch line was an epic fail!" Niecy said.

"What the hell we gonna do at somebody's *estate* sale?" Lulu said.

Even though we were on the phone and I couldn't see their expressions, I could only imagine what they looked like.

"First of all, this estate sale is at some famous NFL player's house. His wife died and he wants to get rid of all of her designer shoes, clothes, and purses. But if that kind of estate sale seems like an *epic fail* for the two of you, maybe I can find some other chicks who would want to pay ten damn dollars for Gucci, Louis Vuitton, Prada, Michael Kors," I said. "But you know what, it's okay; let me get to work and y'all can keep slanging your knock-off designer labels with ya ghett-wah asses!" I added.

"Er…did you say Gucci?" Lulu asked.

"Damn that! What's the address?" Niecy asked. "I'm on my way."

"Come swoop me first," Lulu said.

Nearly an hour later, my jaw dropped as I walked around the massive, lavish home. I couldn't figure out which room I liked best until I walked into the master suite. It wasn't the custom-made bed that caught my eye, but the French doors, that led to one of the baddest walk-in closets I had ever seen. It looked like a small boutique.

"Now this is what the hell I'm talking about," I said to myself as I looked around. That chick had enough stuff to fill an entire department store.

When the doorbell chimed, I finally broke out of my trance and rushed out to the foyer to let the first few customers in.

"Um. I'm here for the estate sale," a woman said. She seemed nervous. "Is this the right place?"

"It sure is," I said, as I opened one of the double wooden doors that had stained-glass windows.

She walked in and looked around. "This house is beautiful."

"I know, right?" I closed the door. "So, here are the rules. It's only the women's items that are being sold. You can find them in the master bedroom's closet and the two smaller bedrooms upstairs to the left."

Her eyes were wide and bright. "And everything is ten dollars?"

I nodded. "Yup. Each item cost ten dollars each and we only accept cash."

"Oh, snap! Y'all not taking cards?" she asked. I looked at the flyer in her hand and pointed to the bottom where it said "cash only" bold as day.

"Damn! I knew that. Can I come back?" she asked.

"Yeah, but I'd hurry if I was you. This chick got lots of good designer stuff, and I don't know how long it's gonna last."

As she left, three other women strolled up. Before I closed the door, Niecy started to park, and I was finally relieved. I didn't want to miss out on the best stuff because they were gonna be late.

"What the hell is this all about?" Lulu asked.

"Shush," I shuffled them inside and whispered. "Start at the closet in the master bedroom to your left. She's got shoes in sizes nine, nine-and-a-half, and ten. I need the Jimmy Choos in a nine, and the Christian Louboutins in a nine-and-a-half."

"Oh you not about to be the only one stuntin' in red bottoms," Niecy said.

We cracked up at that.

The sale went smoothly. By the end of the shift, I had close to ten thousand dollars in cash, mostly ten-dollar bills.

Niecy and Lulu stayed with me until the end. They took our stuff out to the car and filled both my trunk and theirs and Niecy's backseat.

I didn't tell anybody about the jewelry. I got diamond earrings, bracelets, rings, and a few necklaces. I couldn't believe how I had lucked up.

Before I left, I made sure the whole house was clean, and nothing was out of place.

I called Savannah before leaving.

"Hey, Dani, how'd it go?" she asked.

"Oh, I think it went well. I did just like you said. We only sold the women's clothes, shoes, and purses."

"Okay, great job. Everything went well then?"

"Sure did."

"Wonderful. Dani, I want to thank you for your professionalism. We called you at the last minute and asked you to pass out flyers and I just want you to know that the client appreciates it. You will be paid extra for that," Savannah said.

"Oh, thank you."

"I'll look for some additional work for you and I'll be in touch," she said.

Savannah and I hung up, I pulled the door closed behind me and made my way to the car. That's when it dawned on me. Savannah never even asked about the cash!

CHAPTER FORTY-TWO

Arlene

The smell of the thick cigarette smoke, the constant sound of the bells that rang, and the machines that hummed non-stop made it hard to forget we were in a casino. In the middle of the week, there seemed to be more silver-haired ladies clutching small buckets than people who looked like Janet and me.

After we ran out of money, we posted up at the bar and decided to spend our last evening in Louisiana, getting drunk.

But things quickly livened up for me after I got the word that the gig had been a success. I couldn't help but feel elated. If I hadn't been sitting at a bar next to Janet, I would've jumped into a celebratory dance.

"Dani says everything went well. She said all of the women's clothes, shoes, and purses were sold. She also took the initiative to clean up and lock up the house," Savannah reported over the phone.

"That's great," I said.

It was hard to keep a steady tone. The phone call only made me wish I could be there when the happy family returned from their little vacay.

"Will you be picking up the keys?" Savannah asked.

"What keys?" I asked, then realized my mistake. "Oh, yes. Of course, I will. Can she drop the keys at your office? I'll come by and pick them up there."

"Yes. I'll have her report to the office tomorrow."

"Oh, not tomorrow; what about Thursday? That would work out better for me," I said.

"Not a problem. Thursday morning is fine."

I was glad when Janet's cell phone rang. She took the call and I wrapped mine up with Savannah. That gave me time to come up with a lie once Janet questioned me about who I'd been talking to on the phone.

By the time Janet finished her call, I had ordered another round of drinks for us and she didn't even ask about my call.

"What are these?" she asked, as she looked at the cocktail suspiciously.

"Just try it," I said.

She looked at the drink like she wasn't sure whether she should give it a try.

"What's in it?"

"Vodka, grapefruit juice and a splash of lemon juice with salt," I said.

She twisted her face into a frown, and dipped a finger into the drink. I rolled my eyes as Janet put the wet finger into her mouth. "Oh, that's not bad at all."

"I told you."

She picked up the glass, motioned for a toast with me, and we touched glasses.

"To our girlfriends' getaway, even if other girlfriends are having more fun than us," Janet said.

We sipped and savored our drinks.

"You seen your mama and her two gangster friends lately?" Janet asked.

"Girl, no! It's like they forgot all about us the minute we walked through those revolving doors. They were serious about their mission, huh?"

"I guess so." Janet looked around. "I hate casinos.,"

"Yeah, me too. I just thought we could get away for a couple of days, but not have to go too far."

"Oh, don't get me wrong, I've had fun with your mom and her friends. And you know anytime we get together, it's all good."

Instantly, guilt washed over me. A big part of me felt funny that I had left her out of the loop. But deep down, I felt that when I kept my business to myself, I didn't have to worry about whether anybody might slip up and share my dirt with anyone else.

When my phone rang again, I prayed it wasn't Savannah again. There was no way I'd be able to get away with a second call and no explanation.

Janet looked over. "Who keeps calling you?"

I glanced at the phone. "It's about damn time!"

It was Zaneda's number.

"Hello?"

"Mommy! This is the best vacation of my whole entire life! I saw Minnie, and Mickey and, Mom, you should see the water-slide. Our room is almost bigger than our house!" my daughter screamed in my ear.

"Oh, wow. I'm glad you're having such a great time, sweetheart," I said.

Janet smiled.

"Mommy, Daddy said we're gonna go…Daddy, what'd you call it again?" she asked. I heard Mark's answer in the background. Then my daughter returned to our phone call and tried to pronounce "snorkeling."

"That's nice, Sweetpea," I said.

"Mommy, where's Grams?" she asked.

"Oh, she's not here right now. We took a little vacation ourselves, your Grams, Janet and me. We're all in Louisiana," I said.

"You're in Louisiana?"

"Yes, we left the same day you left."

"You left when I left?" I was so glad Markeesa repeated everything I said. I knew Mark was nearby, and I wanted him to know that he wasn't the only person who could go on vacay.

I wondered what all they had done on the cruise. The excitement in my daughter's voice was very apparent. Mark had been right on point. She was having a blast and while I was happy for her, I hated that her good time was with Mark and his fake family.

"Okay, Mommy, we're going swimming," Markeesa said. "Have fun on your vacation!" she yelled. The next voice I heard was his.

"I'll get her to call back before we get dressed for dinner later," he said.

Was I supposed to say thank you for that? Did he expect me to pat him on his back for something he should've done from day one? I couldn't stand his ass.

"Arlene? You there?" he asked.

"Yeah. I'm here," I said coldly.

"Oh. Okay. Well, later then," he said.

I wondered why he had to call from Zaneda's phone instead of his own.

Again, thoughts of what would happen the moment Zaneda walked into their house ran through my mind. There was no way I could witness it, but because I knew she was an ungrateful label whore, I knew the loss of everything she valued would cut her deep.

CHAPTER FORTY-THREE

Keeling

Sounds of the NBA basketball championship game blared from the flat-screen TV. I watched the action on the screen closely, but my mind was on my real-life, soap opera-like situation. Time with the guys usually helped me focus on other things, but Dani and her antics stayed fresh on my brain. It had been the main topic of our discussion.

"What you gonna do, dawg?" Malcolm asked.

I shrugged.

We had been posted up at Roger's. After a few brews, we got on the subject of crazy-ass baby mamas. Nobody could touch Malcolm and his drama-filled tales, but I felt like I was close behind him. Dani was adamant that I better not turn her in, or force the DNA test on her and Keela. Of course, I didn't give two shits what she wanted, but getting the test done, wasn't completely up to me.

"So how you been, bruh?" Roger asked.

"Just ducky," I said sarcastically. "She makes me wanna…"

"I know, dawg; I know," Malcolm cut me off. "I'd be the same way. As a matter-of-fact, ever since you told me about that talk show, now, every time I see a show that involves ignorant people fighting, it just gives me the worst poverty porn vibe," Malcolm said.

We laughed. He was right. Because they replayed the stupid

episode so much, Dani had turned us into the equivalent of *those* people...the kind who made poverty porn.

"Man, she's on one, so she really thinks you're supposed to keep paying because she don't wanna live without your money?" Malcolm said.

In the short time I'd been on the job, Malcolm and I had become fast friends. We could relate to each other, and he hung out with Roger and me a few times, so we all hit it off pretty good.

"Man, she the type that make you catch a case," Malcolm said. "She do all that, then gets away with it." He shook his head before he took another swig from his bottle.

"Yeah, the only thing I can do is hope she agrees to the new DNA test," I said.

"Agrees? Hell, she can agree, but what if she never shows up?" Roger asked.

"Man, I dunno. You know I can't tell my moms that. If she knew Dani was tripping like this, I wouldn't be the only person on the verge of catching a case," I said.

"She wilding out. How she gonna tell you she ain't getting the test and nothing happens? It's bad enough she fingered you when she knew the kid wasn't yours," Roger said.

"When do y'all call the law on her?" Malcolm wanted to know.

"That's the crazy part. We could call the law all we want. Technically, she's right. I did sign the birth certificate as Keela's father," I said. "So, as far as the law is concerned, I'm her legal father."

"Yeah, but you signed because THOT lied and told you you were," Malcolm said.

"I know, but I'm only saying that to say, legally, she didn't break the law. She didn't tell me to sign the birth certificate; it's not like we were married. So it was like I volunteered to father her kid. Lying may be wrong, but it's not against the law," I said.

"These females make it hard for you to love 'em," Roger said. "She deserves her ass beat for what she's doing. I say you let your moms at her for thirty minutes," he added.

"Thirty minutes? Dani wouldn't last ten with my mom the way she's feeling right about now."

"Can you blame her? I'd wanna beat that trick too," Roger said. He stretched his legs and propped his feet up on the coffee table.

Malcolm rose from the sofa. "I need to run. You coming with me or what?" he asked me.

I jumped up. "Oh, yeah, I need to make that move."

"Dawg, why y'all rushing out?" Roger asked.

"I got a date," Malcolm said. I looked at him side-eyed. He shrugged. "What? One pony don't stop the show. Just because the others were bad, that don't mean I should let all the ladies suffer."

He and Roger fist-bumped, but we all laughed.

When Malcolm dropped me at the house, I noticed my moms' car wasn't there yet. That meant I'd have some peace and quiet before she came home pissed about Dani.

Ten minutes after Malcolm left, there was a knock at the door.

"What'd you forget, dude?" I said, as I pulled the door open. Dani pushed past me, and strutted into the house. I didn't feel like going there with her. She had on a short chocolate-colored trench coat, and really high heels. I wanted her gone.

"What do you want?" I asked, from my spot near the front door. I didn't trust her and was leery about being around her.

"Close the door and let me show you," she said.

Was she crazy? Did she think it was all good between us? And more importantly, did she know how she had risked her life by coming to my mother's house?

"What are you doing here, Dani?" I asked. I spoke with no emotion whatsoever.

She moved around the living room, then turned to face me. In one minute, she was covered up in that jacket; then in the next, she peeled it off and stood in front of me wearing nothing but a smile that looked fake.

"Dani, put your clothes back on! We're not about to do this again." I raised my hands and backed away from her.

"I think we should bury this thing between us and see if we can work it out," Dani said. I noticed how she tried to sound as sexy as possible. She must've been high if she thought it was about to go down.

"Naw. You should put your clothes back on," I warned her.

"Let's go back to your room," she purred, as she started to play with her nipples. I was glad the sight of her doing that had absolutely no effect on me.

"Dani, put your damn clothes back on, and get outta here. I ain't buying what you selling."

"I don't have any clothes," Dani said. "Let's go to the back. Besides, I'm offering it for free today," she joked.

I pulled my cell phone from my pocket.

"Hold up a sec. If you want pictures, that's gonna cost you," she said.

"What kind of nasty, disrespectful whore are you?" my mother's voice barked.

Startled, Dani and I jumped. We'd been caught completely off guard.

CHAPTER FORTY-FOUR

Mark

During our last day on Castaway Cay, Disney's private island in the Bahamas, we lounged around in a beachside cabana. Since our concierge team left the boat with us, we literally had people who were a phone call away when we needed them.

Inside, there were cushioned chairs, a chaise lounge, with a dining table, a refrigerator, and a lockable storage unit. On the shaded deck there was also a fresh water shower.

For as far as they eye could see, the pristine beach was lined with colorful umbrellas, and a few hammocks scattered here and there. There was a family beach, where we were, an adult beach close by, and even a teen beach.

Zaneda and I loved it because the crystal-clear water was warm and waist-deep, which made it safe for the kids.

Bright sunshine beamed up above. White sand beaches, turquoise water, colorful umbrellas and music in the air; we were in paradise.

Sadly, we were also at the end of our Disney cruise vacation and I hated to admit how the thought made me feel. The kids and Zaneda had the time of their lives. I enjoyed myself too.

Later, back on the ship, Arlene called again. Whenever I thought she couldn't get any nastier, she showed me that I should never underestimate her.

When we finally made it back to the terminal, the kids were still excited and talked nonstop about the great time we all had.

As I looked at my daughter, I wondered what it would be like once she was back at home. Arlene seemed determined to cause problems for my family.

"You're taking us home before you drop her off, right?" Zaneda asked as we buckled ourselves in the car.

I glanced in the rearview mirror and decided that would be best.

By the time we pulled up at the house, I thought about how cool it would've been if we had Markeesa for an extra night or two. But after all the hell Arlene had raised while we were gone, I knew that wasn't possible.

"Yeah, that's probably best," I said.

As I drove in reverse, I maneuvered the car into the driveway and pulled as close to the garage door as possible.

"Y'all go inside and I'll unpack the truck," I said.

I didn't have to say it twice. I'd barely parked, before the doors flew open and everyone hopped out. By the time I got out and popped the trunk, I heard a gut-wrenching scream from Zaneda that made me drop everything and rush into the house.

The kids and I made it to our bedroom at the same time.

"Mom! What's wrong?!" MJ screamed.

"Watch out," I said, and rushed into our bedroom.

"Everything is gone!" Zaneda cried. "My clothes, shoes, purses! We've been robbed!"

Her eyes were wild as she pushed past me and ran to the dresser. She flipped open her jewelry box, then passed out.

"Jesus!" I got to her just before she hit the floor. The kids crowded our door and watched in horror.

"What's wrong with Ms. Zaneda?" Markeesa asked.

By the time I got her to the bed, she came to, but she was still disoriented.

"Dial nine-one-one. Somebody robbed us," Zaneda said, as she raised her head.

"Are you okay?" I asked.

"Yeah. Yeah, I'm good, I'm just confused. All of our stuff, it's gone," she said.

I looked around the room. The sixty-inch plasma-screen TV was still on the wall; the surround-sound system and all of my electronics were exactly where we'd left them.

Zaneda pulled herself into an upright position and looked around the room too. I could see confusion as it settled into her features.

After I made sure she was okay, I went to the closet and realized what she meant. While all of my clothes, shoes, and stuff were neatly in place, everything of hers was gone. It was like only her side of the closet was targeted and completely wiped out.

Zaneda jumped up from the bed and screamed, "The other closets!"

"Dad, is Mommy okay?" Mason asked.

"Yes, son, she is," I said. I struggled to keep up with her, because I had to console the kids. "Why don't you guys go into the family room and watch a movie. Let me go check on Mom."

They turned to leave reluctantly, but could hardly move down the hall; they kept an eye on my every move.

"Jesus!" Zaneda screamed from one of the guest bedrooms.

I already knew what to expect. But on my way there, she nearly knocked me down as she rushed out and headed for the second guest bedroom.

"This bitch has got to be stopped," she snarled.

Her words made me stop cold.

"Zaneda, what are you saying?" I asked.

She was already gone. Her curse words floated from that room and out to the hall.

By the time she emerged from that second bedroom, her anger had turned to rage. She pointed a bony accusatory finger in my direction. "If you still wanna sit and act like she's not behind all this mess that's been happening to us lately," she barked in a hoarse voice, "I don't know what else to say."

"Babe, let's talk about this." I wanted to keep the peace. Cool heads could work together.

"Do you not understand what I'm saying to you? The only possessions I have are what's in the damn suitcases! Everything else of mine is gone! My jewelry; remember you didn't want me to wear my five-karat diamond on vacation? Well, maybe I should have, because it's gone too!"

"Let's check the security cameras to see what happened while we were gone. Was the door locked when you came in?"

"Yes. I had to use my key to get in. See, we've been slipping. I told you that a while back. How could we go on vacation and not even use the damn alarm?"

"Zaneda, let's not point fingers. Once the police come, we'll file a claim and you can go shopping to replace everything."

She froze, paused, then slowly turned and looked at me.

Her eyes pooled with tears and her lips trembled. "What do you mean?" Her voice cracked as she spoke.

"Babe, if all your things are gone, they have to be replaced," I stated simply.

Her eyebrows knitted together. "You mean I can…"

"Yeah, babe," I said before she could finish. I pulled her into my arms. "We're in this together. Your stuff is gone. You need new stuff."

I held my wife tightly as she cried. I didn't look forward to the conversation I needed to have with Arlene. She had finally gone too damn far.

CHAPTER FORTY-FIVE

Dani

C harlene fed the kids and that gave me the perfect opportunity to go over my plan. I meant to call Savannah right back, but a few things got in the way, and I looked up and several days had passed since the assignment ended.

I fully expected to hear from her about the money, but she never called. I locked my bedroom door and turned up the volume on the TV. Once I was convinced that everything would be okay, I dug under my mattress and pulled out the old plastic bag.

As I unwrapped it, I thought about everything I would be able to do with all of the money.

"There's like ten G's here," I muttered, as I ran my fingers through the stacks of cash. I organized it, stacked it up, and organized it again and again. The money looked so good and felt even better in my hands. I had prayed over it, and thought about what would happen if I decided to keep it all for myself.

I wouldn't have to wait. I'd be able to get my own place right off the bat. But then I thought about how I could go to jail if I kept that money. Savannah had all of my information and she knew how to find me.

Suddenly a thought hit me like a bulldozer attacking an abandoned building.

How would they know if I kept a few G's for myself? No one told me to keep any record of what sold, and everything did. If they sold all those designer shoes, clothes, and purses for ten damn dollars, it was obvious money was no object.

I picked up the phone and dialed Savannah's number. When she answered, I tried to play it cool.

"Hi Savannah," I said.

My heart felt like it had doubled in size. I needed to calm down and see if she'd say anything about the money.

"Dani. I'm still working to find another gig for you. You did great."

"Oh. Okay, that'll work. But it just dawned on me, I have a whole bunch of cash."

"Dani, I forgot all about the money from the sale. I'll bet my client did too. I need to call you back," she said.

Damn! I should've kept my mouth shut! At first, I was gonna keep two G's, but the way she rushed off the phone with me, really made me feel like there was no reason why I shouldn't keep at least three.

I took my cut off the top, and put the rest of the money back into the plastic bag. After I settled on three thousand and sixty dollars, I spread my cash out at the bottom of two dresser drawers.

After I put the money up and looked around the room to make sure nothing was out of place, I got up and walked out into the family room.

"It's about time you try to put in some quality time," my mother said.

I glanced in her direction, but decided not to say anything.

"Are those shoes new?" she asked when I crossed my legs. "And, are those the kind of shoes I think they are?" My mother's eyes were still on my shoes.

"Yeah, they're Jimmy Choos," I said nonchalantly.

My mother nearly spit up her drink.

"Are you freaking kidding me?" she asked. This time when she looked back at the shoes, her face was twisted into a frown.

I looked at her before I responded. Did she expect me to answer that or was she just reacting to the fact that my shoes were Jimmy Choos?

"You know what, Dani. I'm disappointed in you," Charlene said.

There was no way I was about to sit and listen to another woman going off on me. I'd had enough of that when Keeling's crazy-ass mother popped up at the house. The sound of my own mother's voice took me back to that moment.

What kind of nasty, disrespectful whore are you?

I whipped around and saw the hatred in her eyes as she looked at me.

"Keeling! How could you have this nasty bitch in my house after everything she's done to you, to us?"

"Ma. I ain't got her in here. She just showed up."

"You nasty bitch, you not even gonna try and cover yourself up?" Mama put the bags she was carrying down and put her purse on the counter.

"As far as I'm concerned, you trespassing, and I have a right to defend my home," she said.

Unsure of what the batty ol' witch was about to do, I snatched up my Michael Kors trench and scrambled to get out the door. I bumped into her as I made my escape, but she didn't catch her balance fast enough to react.

Outside and headed toward my car, I looked back at Keeling and his mama.

"And by the way, bitch, you two are the pathetic ones. Keeling is a grown-ass man, living at home with his nosey-ass mama," I said. "You need to mind your business and wean him off your titty."

As I closed my car door, something thumped the hood of my car. Had the bitch thrown something at me?

"You must think I'm stupid!" My own mother's voice screamed at me and snatched me back from the memory. "The minute you get a job, what's the first thing you do? You run out and buy a bunch of clothes and shoes! You are so damn irresponsible!"

I slammed the door on the rest of her insults. I'd had enough.

In my head, I wondered how far I could go with the money I had. Could the kids and I live somewhere else, like in Mexico? Shoot. I didn't speak Spanish and didn't know a single person in Mexico, so I quickly nixed that idea.

My mother made me so damn sick! I should've known she'd been snooping around in my belongings. I should've left all my new stuff with Lulu or Niecy, but I didn't want them all up in my new shit either.

We were all about the same size, give an inch or two here and there, and I didn't want any problems.

I was about to count the money again, but the sound of my mother screaming stopped me cold.

"Daaaani! Get your ass out here!"

"Who the hell she think she talking to like that? I'm grown just like her," I said as I pulled my bedroom door open and stormed out.

But my cell rang before I made it down the hall and it was Savannah. I stopped near the bathroom and took the call.

"Hello?"

"Dani, how much money do you have?" she asked.

"Um. I think around six thousand," I lied. My heart pounded so hard and fast, I just knew she was gonna question that amount.

But in an instant, she said, "Okay. Well, here's what we need to do. Come by the office tomorrow around three. And FYI, the client has agreed to give you another cash bonus outside of your pay and the other cash bonus for your Saturday work before the sale."

"Oh wow," I said.

CHAPTER FORTY-SIX

Arlene

It was about to drive me ape-shit crazy! Markeesa couldn't stop talking about that damn Disney cruise. And my mother didn't help the situation. She kept asking the child questions over and over again. I wanted them both to shut the hell up!

The new bright colorful clothes, shoes, and toys she had made me feel like if I didn't do something quick and drastic, those people were gonna try and buy my daughter away from me.

"Ma, I'm gonna go run an errand. I'll be back in a couple of hours," I said.

I couldn't be sure she even heard me. I left the two of them at the kitchen table as they looked through a photo album that had pictures from the cruise. I rolled my eyes at the thought. That was probably Zaneda's idea. She wanted so badly to believe that she was a devoted wife and mother, but I knew better.

A few blocks away from my house, I pulled into a strip mall parking lot and walked into the beauty supply store.

"Hello, can I help you find something?" the Hispanic woman asked. She and the Asian man, who probably owned the place, stood behind a counter that ran along the length of an entire wall.

"Yes. I need a wig, please," I said.

She pointed toward the back of the store. "Okay, I can meet you over there to help you find one."

It took about thirty minutes, but she helped me try on several wigs until we found the one that looked best on me.

"You gonna take this one?" she asked.

I looked at my reflection in the mirror and tried to think about what else I could do to go with my new look.

"Oh yes! I really like it," I said. "Does it look real?"

"Yeah, actually it does. That's why I thought the Beverly Johnson wigs would be better on you than the Iman ones."

The hair was a shoulder-length afro of spiral curls.

"You guys sell contacts here?" I asked.

She frowned and repeated, "Contacts? Like contact lenses?"

I nodded as I studied my reflection.

"We don't sell that here," she said. I walked around and picked up some leggings that had hips and booty padding. Then I went to Walmart.

After I bought a pair of hazel-green contacts and a new outfit from Tina Knowles fashion line in Walmart, I changed clothes in the bathroom. The padded clothes added something like thirty extra pounds on me.

People looked at me oddly as I scrutinized my reflection in the mirror. I looked like a completely different person and that was exactly what I wanted.

Finally satisfied that I had transformed into that chick, I pulled out the burner phone and dialed Savannah's number.

"Hey, Savannah, I'm running a few minutes late, but I'll be by there in about twenty minutes," I said.

"Okay, no problem. Dani and I will be here," she said.

The stares I got as I walked out of the store were nothing out of the ordinary. Once behind the wheel of my car, I put on the brown lace gloves and drove over to the temp office.

Savannah was the epitome of poise and professionalism. She

was a statuesque, brown-skinned woman with a blunt haircut. Her appearance said she meant business and she seemed very poised and confident.

"I'm Savannah Granger," she said, as she extended a hand for me to shake.

"Savannah, it's nice to finally meet you. I'm Penelope Jones. Thanks for all of your help with this assignment," I said.

"Oh. It's been my pleasure," she said. "Here, come with me; Dani is waiting in the conference room."

I followed behind Savannah as we walked down a narrow hallway. She pushed the door open and this young, ghetto-looking girl with a bad weave popped up from a chair. She seemed nervous.

Instantly, I recognized the Gucci shorts romper she had on, and couldn't help but howl with laughter on the inside. It was so hard to maintain a straight face.

"Hi," she said.

"You must be Dani," I said. I didn't have all day.

"Yes, ma'am. Um, thank you for the job, and I brought all of the money right here," she said.

She seemed far more anxious than me, but I didn't have time to hold her hands.

I took the plastic bag she extended toward me.

Savannah stood off and watched the exchange. I peered into the bag and saw the stack of cash. The entire time I planned the sale, it didn't dawn on me that we would make money. The money was an added bonus so, I turned to Savannah. "Is there any way you can give me the invoice now; I'd like to take care of it."

When Savannah left me alone with Dani, I talked with her for a little while. I used the cash to pay Savannah's bill, and gave Dani a thousand dollars and thanked her for her help.

My next stop was the bank where I deposited enough money to

buy the plane tickets. I left the bank and used a computer at a nearby Office Depot and booked the flights.

I wasn't stupid and I knew for sure that it was just a matter of time before Mark would use his money to put things together.

Once I completed all of my tasks, I was headed back to the house when my cell phone rang and Zaneda's number popped up. I rolled my eyes.

"Ah...hello."

"You think you're smarter than everyone else, don't you?" she asked.

My heart thumped so loudly I was scared she could hear it through the phone.

"Excuse me?"

"You can play that dumb role with Mark all you want, but I got your number, Arlene. You're not fooling me one bit and I just wanted you to know," she snarled. I pictured veins thumping at the sides of her head; the way she spat her stern words at me told me I had gotten under her skin.

"Zaneda, you must have the wrong number. I don't know what you're talking about," I said coolly.

She chuckled in my ear.

"Yeah, keep playing that role, but know this. Your time will come. It may seem like you're getting away with all of the shit you're doing to try and rip my family apart, but it's not working."

"Again, Zaneda, I don't know what you're talking about," I said. I was not about to let her get to me. She could've been recording the call. I had worked too hard to unravel after one nasty call.

"Of course you don't. But let me leave you with this. I hope you enjoy all of my shit you stole. The instant we realized we'd been robbed, my wonderful husband sent me shopping and I'm close to replacing everything! That's right. To the average chick, what you did may have been devastating, but unlike you, I'm a rich byoootch…so that means once again, you're stuck with my sloppy seconds and I'm having the time of my life replacing every single item you stole! You're such a non-factor, it's sad!" She snickered.

Her vicious rant did nothing except piss me off even more. It only added fuel and made me determined to show Mark once and for all that he really did make the wrong choice when he decided to stay with Zaneda.

But he'd find out real soon, and so would Zaneda and every damn body-else!

CHAPTER FORTY-SEVEN

Keeling

Nightmares stayed with me. All I could think about was what would've happened if I hadn't been there to snatch my mother away from Dani.

When I thought back to the tense and awkward moment, I was glad that everyone escaped with their lives intact. My moms was so riled up, we would've be on the news that night for sure. Even after Dani ran up outta there, my mother was still burning up mad.

I don't know who she was most mad at: me because I wouldn't let her get to Dani, or Dani for being in the house butt naked. My moms probably thought I was about to dumpster dive again and hit that, but I wouldn't touch Dani with someone else's junk.

"You should be glad I didn't touch her, Ma," I had said.

My mother sucked her teeth. "I would hope after all she's done, you wouldn't touch her if she was the last female on earth and your junk threatened to explode," she'd said.

My mother was a lost cause. I was mad about Dani and the type of foul things she had done too, but I knew better than to even think about laying hands on her. That would have been a whole new set of problems that neither of us needed.

"Ma! You ready yet?!" I yelled.

"Quit rushing me," she hollered back.

I threw my hands up and sat down. There was no point in trying to get her to move any faster than she wanted to. I thought about how Parker was gonna get Dani and Keela to take the DNA test.

A little while later, my moms strolled into the room and stopped a few feet from me.

The look in her eyes told me to sit and chill for a second. I was glad I didn't move; she had something on her mind.

"The next time I come home and find that nasty hoochie in my damn house, I'ma kill you both with my bare hands," she warned with a stern eye. "We're going through way too much to have you blow it by still associating with her. Do you realize how much she's trying to screw up your life? She knew from the beginning that baby wasn't yours, but still, she brought that child into our lives, looked us both in the eyes and lied every single day. She had you tossed in jail, for Christ's sake!"

I pulled in a deep breath and worked hard to hold my stoic expression in place. I listened and didn't say a word. When I thought she was done, and it was safe, I spoke.

"Okay, Ma," I said. I didn't need her being pissed off at me over Dani. I felt like my moms thought I wanted to get back with Dani, but I wish she knew, that couldn't be further from the truth. I hated that girl with everything in me.

When I stood, ready to go, the scrutiny still wasn't over.

My mother cocked her head to the side and she eyed me up and down. "I'm not playing with you, Keeling. I am putting in too much blood, sweat, and hard work to try and undo the mess she's created. If you're still screwing her, or even think you want to, you need to let me know now, because I got better shit to do with my time."

"Ma. Stop."

"No. You don't know how pissed I was when I walked in and found her in the middle of seducing you!"

"She didn't seduce me. She was naked, Ma, but you saw me. I had on all my clothes. I ain't nobody's fool. I'm not trying to fall for no trap with her."

My mother exhaled and looked at me for a few more seconds.

"I hate her with a passion," she said. She said the words with so much feeling, I knew she spoke the truth.

"I know, Ma. I know. But remember Parker is waiting for us, so can we please go?" I begged.

At first, she still didn't move. "You know when you hurt, I hurt, son. I hate what she did and I'm determined that somebody out there needs to make her pay."

"I know, Ma. I know."

The ride to Parker's office was quiet, except for the music that played. I was glad my mother didn't have anything else to say. She had gotten her point across and I understood.

All that stayed on my mind was what Parker would say since Dani let it be known she wasn't interested in taking a DNA test.

I was sick of worrying about what she would or wouldn't do. I pulled up at the front door to Parker's office and stopped. I threw the car into park and jumped out. I rushed to the passenger's side to open the door for my moms.

"Thanks, son," she said. I waited patiently as she eased out of the car.

"I'll be in after I park," I said. I drove around and found a space.

Once I pulled into the space, I paused for a moment and tried to get my mind together. Parker didn't need two emotional people to drive him crazy. I almost felt sorry for the man, because my moms was still wired. When she couldn't get what she wanted, she went on a rampage and I pitied whoever was in her path.

After too much time behind the wheel, I sucked in some courage and got out of the car.

I walked into Parker's business and heard my mother before I even made it into his office. Some of that courage bailed as I listened to her go off.

"She's in there," the receptionist said, and motioned over her shoulder. I was embarrassed, but I skulked toward the sound of her voice.

"So you're telling me there's nothing we can do to make her take the damn test?" my mother hissed, with lots of attitude.

I halfway knocked on Parker's door and eased it open. Silence fell on the room. Parker stood.

"Hey, Keeling, my man." We did the brother-man shake and back pat. "You doin' okay?" he asked.

"Yeah, it's all good," I said. I turned to my mother. "Ma, you not in here giving Parker a hard time, are you? I heard you all the way from the parking lot," I joked, and tried to lighten the mood in the office.

"Son, I don't understand what the hell is going on here," she said. "Y'all are sitting here handling this tramp with kid gloves, and I'll bet she ain't gave nary a sign of trying to do the right thing!" she exclaimed.

She turned to Parker. "It's like I told you. You're a professional. You talk all proper, and you probably go about business in a politically correct way. That ain't gonna work with a trick like Dani," she said.

Parker's face was instantly confused. He waited until my mother finished her rant, then he exhaled. "Trust me when I tell you. Whether it's from personal experience or some of almost anything that walks through those doors, I've seen, worked with and handled it all. I'm not new at this. Keeling and I have been talking about this and I've got it under control."

The creases between my mother's waxed brows deepened.

"And, no disrespect here, but let Keeling handle this. He's a man. He needs to work this thing, but you gotta let him do it," Parker said.

My eyebrows went up, and I fought the urge to duck; I expected my mother to start throwing things around the man's office.

Surprisingly, she huffed a little, adjusted her body in the chair, but didn't say another word.

CHAPTER FORTY-EIGHT

Mark

We were inside a Houston Police Department cubicle and I tried my best to focus on the discussion Zaneda had highjacked and had with the officer.

"Okay, tell me what happened again?" the detective who sat across from us asked.

"This woman is attacking our family and I believe she is using technology to do it," Zaneda said.

"What kind of evidence or proof do you have that she's the one behind the attacks?" he asked.

Zaneda looked like she wanted to jump over the desk and strangle him. When I noticed her jaw flinch, I reached over and gently rubbed her knee.

She looked at me and rewarded me with a strained smile, but her focus quickly went back to the officer. Timothy was a few feet away, but he was on the phone.

"First, we started getting hundreds of calls on my cell phone. People were calling about the Bentley ad we posted on Craigslist. It said we were selling the car for five-thousand dollars."

His eyebrows rose. He picked up a pen and started to write on a note pad.

"Five-thousand dollars? How exactly did you find out about the ad?" he asked.

"Callers started to get mad. Then one guy asked why I put the ad up in the first place, if I didn't want people to call," Zaneda said.

The officer whistled.

"After that, someone," Zaneda did air quotes with her fingers, "anonymously called and reported us to CPS." The statement was filled with judgment.

"Whoa!" The detective leaned forward. "You're shitting me."

Zaneda shook her head. "Oh, it gets even better. We come back from vacation, and every item I owned is gone from our house!"

His eyes got big, and his mouth fell open.

"So she cleaned out your entire house while you guys were gone?" His eyes darted in my direction, but before I spoke, my wife corrected him.

Zaneda shook her head. "No. She didn't clean out the house, oh no. She only took my things. She took it all, shoes, clothes, purses, jewelry, all of *my* things are gone."

"*Were* gone," I corrected.

She turned to me, smiled and said, "That's right, babe. You're right. All of my stuff was gone, but I've gone shopping a few times and bought some of the stuff back."

"That must've been costly," he said.

"Yes. The jewelry was insured, but it never dawned on me that I would need to insure my underwear," said Zaneda.

"Again, why do you think this Arlene woman is behind all of this?" the detective asked.

"She hates me, hates the fact that we're still married," Zaneda said.

They both turned to me, but it was only Zaneda's head that tilted to the side.

"Arlene and I hooked up for a short time. We had a daughter together and she felt like I should've been with her and our daughter, but I went back to my wife," I said.

"So this is a jilted lover," the detective said.

"I guess so."

"What do you mean you guess?"

"Yeah," I corrected my previous comment. "Yeah, she's a jilted lover."

"Umph," said Zaneda.

"We can get her on theft for the items she removed from the house, actually burglary, but we would have to prove that she is responsible," he said.

Zaneda leaned forward. "I know she did it. I feel it in my gut."

"We can't work on gut feelings around here. Did any of your neighbors see her by chance? Are there security cameras? You gotta give me something more to go on," he said.

"No cameras, and our neighbors aren't close enough to notice traffic on our property."

"How do you know? Did you try asking?"

Zaneda shifted in her chair and that meant she had become irritated.

"I tell you what. Maybe I can go and talk to her and see what she has to say," he offered.

"That's all we're asking. Maybe if she gets a visit from an officer, she'll know we mean business and she needs to stop!" Zaneda exclaimed.

"Listen, I have to warn you. I can go and ask her some questions, but with no evidence to directly tie her to the burglary, we would need her to confess," he said.

"Whatever you can do to help," I said. "If she's, er…I mean, we can't sit and wait for her to strike again."

I caught myself before I behaved like there was a possibility that Arlene couldn't be responsible for the havoc that had become our life.

We got up and the detective shook hands with Zaneda, then with me. Timothy walked back over to join us.

"Can I get your cell on the back of this card?" Timothy asked him.

"Sure." The detective took the card and scribbled his number.

We were escorted up to the lobby, and left. Outside, Timothy walked us a few feet away from the station's entrance.

"I was trying to set something up because I have a strong feeling I know where this is gonna go," he said.

Zaneda's eyes darted from me to him. "Are you trying to say he was just blowing smoke at us in there?" she asked.

"No. But remember what he said. He said if there wasn't any evidence, there isn't much he could do. The guy I was talking to finds evidence. He's a private investigator," Timothy said.

Zaneda looked at me with hopeful eyes. "Babe, please. I just feel it. I know she's behind all of this. We need to do this. We need to hire this guy," she begged.

"When can we meet him?" I asked Timothy.

"Let me see how soon we can get him started. He's wrapping up something right now, but I think by the time this cop gets back to us, we can have our guy up, and ready to go," Timothy said.

"Okay, keep me posted," I said.

"Well, after he calls, I'll tell the detective we've got some back up of our own," Timothy said.

"Let's go back in and tell him now," Zaneda said. "We need them to make this a priority."

"No, we need to give them time to do their job. In a couple of days, once he tells us what he's accomplished, which I'm sure won't be much, we'll let him know. Besides, his information could be helpful for us, and since our guy isn't ready to put boots on the ground just yet, we'll be ready when the officer finishes his work."

"That'll work," I said.

CHAPTER FORTY-NINE

Dani

"I hope you didn't cook nothing, Charlene!" I yelled to my mother from the front door, when I walked in after work. On my way home, I stopped off at her favorite restaurant and picked up dinner to go.

Savannah sent me on a three-day assignment, and today was the last day. It was boring as all get-out, and couldn't compare to the estate sale, but it still felt good to work.

There was nothing interesting about the assignment. I answered the phone in the lobby of a big fancy energy company in downtown Houston. I didn't want the job on a regular because I'd lose my mind. I also didn't make lots of money working for Savannah like I thought I would, but every little bit counted.

"What'd you get?!" Charlene screamed back. She sounded happy. But nothing beat the look on her face when she rounded the corner and saw me. "Oh Lord! You got Pappadeaux's? Whew! I just finished giving the kids their baths and was stressed out about what we would eat. You did good, girl," she said, as she rushed over and took one of the large bags from my hand.

"I got you some fried alligator, the catfish platter, shrimp étouffée, chicken strips, and fries for the kids," I said.

Charlene's eyes got wide, she was so excited. I never told her about the extra cash I had, but I took most of my designer clothes and shoes from the sale, and stashed them at Niecy's house.

If I knew the kind of peace that one move would've brought, I would've done it a long time ago. It finally dawned on me, Charlene was always gonna be Charlene. It seemed like when I was down and out, she was better. The moment she thought I had more than she did, she started to throw shade from every direction, and we fought worse than my kids.

"Ooooh, you go change, I'm gonna fix the kids plates," she said as she peeked into each bag. It was like Christmas had come early. I got the idea from work. I sat there being bored to tears when all of a sudden, a line of people walked in. Each had two Pappadeaux bags that they were taking up to the twenty-fifth floor.

Charlene fussed over the bags and what was inside them. The scent from the food made the entire kitchen smell good.

"Go on. Go, I got this," she said, as she shooed me away with her hands.

"Okay, cool," I said.

"Ooooh. You even got some fresh bread."

I still wanted to move out, but it would be hard because I didn't have patience with the kids like Charlene. She loved kids, period, so I could only imagine how she'd feel once we left.

As I changed clothes, I got another text message from Bernard. He had been texting for a few days, but I never responded. I knew my money wouldn't last forever, but while I had a few G's, using alum powder and vinegar to tighten up my coochie for Bernard was nowhere on my radar. He'd have to find some other broke, young chick to help him out.

Money made everything better, I was convinced. It wasn't like I had millions, or even a few hundred thousand. But still, the little I had, felt like the equivalent of a hundred grand because I had never held that much cash in my life before.

It was clear money meant nothing to people like Penelope and Savannah; neither one of them counted the cash. They just accepted what I gave them. Since I met Penelope and I felt like we'd be working together again in the future, I decided I'd hold all of the jewelry until my paper ran short or out. She never even asked about the jewelry. Besides, there was no way I could walk around with all that ice and not expect problems anyway.

I told myself that I'd have the money for a while anyway, because I didn't have to buy clothes, shoes, or purses. That's what females spent the bulk of their money on, and I was good in all those areas.

That lady had some bad stuff. She sure had good taste and it was obvious she didn't mind spending money either.

My phone had a mind of its own. I went to dial Lulu and heard a voice that said, "Hello, hello?"

"Yeah, who is this?" I asked, when I brought the phone up to my ear.

"Dani, this is Parker again," he said. "Listen, before you hang up, I'm trying to appeal to you. If you don't agree to the test, you'll leave me very little choice in this matter."

"Listen, dude! Your threats don't scare me! I've already warned Keeling. You'd better check the law! I'm on the right side of the law with this, so you can sit up and make all the threats you want. I know my rights and according to the law, Keeling is Keela's father, so he's gonna have to pay!"

"Are you that cold-hearted and greedy?" he asked.

That question stunned me.

Why did I have to be cold-hearted? Keeling was the one who wanted to end his relationship and support for his one and only child. How come everyone wanted to paint me as the bad person?

"Listen, ol' man, I'm not about to sit here and argue with you. I don't plan to put my baby through nobody's test. Keeling is the only father she knows and we plan to keep it that way."

He sighed in my ear, and I willed myself not to curse him out. He was foul for trying to get all up in somebody's business and he and Keeling had worked my last damn nerve.

"I hate that you've decided to make this difficult," he said.

I made a face I knew he couldn't see, but it expressed how I felt about the entire situation. Suddenly, my mind wondered how much of a cut he was getting out of this mess.

But then that didn't make sense, unless Keeling wanted to stop paying me so he could pay ol' dude. Either way, whatever scam they had going, they were gonna have to go at it alone., I wasn't about to take anybody's test and neither was my child.

CHAPTER FIFTY

Arlene

It was one of those perfect, mid-humidity weekends in Houston, perfect for being outside. I threw some meat on the grill. We had great music going, and a few drinks on ice. I was in a party-like mood and felt like having some company. When I ran the idea by my mom, she invited her girls Betty and Carol over. Janet brought her kids. We turned on the sprinkler so Markeesa and Janet's kids could run around and get wet.

"My daddy's house got a real big, pretty swimming pool," Markeesa said. "I don't have to play in sprinklers when I'm over there."

I bit down on my lip, but I didn't say anything.

My mother, her friends, and Janet had a fierce game of Spades going. But occasionally, I noticed Carol's eyebrow go up every now and then, mostly when Markeesa bragged about what all her daddy had.

She had already driven me to the edge about that damn cruise. And here lately, everything was compared to what her daddy had or what she had at her daddy's house. With every word, she disgusted me more and more.

For a change, it was good to hear laughter and screams of joy fill the air as Markeesa and the kids ran around. But a few minutes later, they quieted down.

"Mom, how come we can't get our own swimming pool?" Markeesa came over to the grill and asked. "Oh. I mean, Ms. Zaneda says you are poor, but I didn't think a pool would cost a whole lot of money. I don't like having to run around in the sprinkler."

Suddenly, Janet appeared out of thin air and jumped between us. I mean like quick. And I was glad she did. It took that kind of fast reaction for me to realize I was about to go *in* on my own daughter.

"Markeesa, honey, why don't you go towel off? Maybe you guys can watch a movie," Janet suggested. The tension in the air seemed to dissipate. My child tilted her little head, smiled, and then she took off toward the house. Only then, did Janet turn her focus back to me. But the damage had already been done. I was broken-hearted and mostly I was pissed.

I managed to swallow the bitter, foul taste in my mouth. The very thing I didn't want seemed to be happening right before my eyes. Mark's money had turned my only child into one of those snobbish, spoiled, slush fund babies.

"She's only repeating what she's being told and what she's heard," Janet whispered as she stood inches from my face.

My mouth dried. I blinked back tears, and forced myself to focus on what Janet had said, because it made sense.

"But this is the kind of shit I'm talking about. Anytime I say a cross word about Mark and what he's trying to do, you and Mama automatically jump in on his damn side."

Janet's voice was just above a whisper. She shook her head. "Honey, I had no idea it was that bad. I mean, who says something like that to a child?"

"That's why I don't want her over there. Mark can't be with her twenty-four-seven. There's no telling what other kind of poison Zaneda pumps into my child's head."

"I wouldn't have believed it if I hadn't heard it with my own ears," Janet admitted. She pulled me into an embrace and rubbed my back.

"Here." She took the tongs from my hand. "Why don't you let me take over here? Go see if you can snag some books, have a glass, or four of wine, and I'll finish up the food."

After a few hands with the ladies, I looked at my mom. "Ma, have you told your friends about my idea?"

"Gyal, dat da lone rass," my mother spat, and shook her head. She basically said I was talking nonsense.

Her nosiest and most outspoken friend said, "I think it's a good idea. Why stay here and live foot to mouth when you don't have to?" Ms. Carol said.

My mother looked at me. "Da how you di go aan so?"

"You make it seem like I always bring it up, but I don't. I just think you should consider it. Look at what's happening to Markeesa. I don't want to stay here, struggle, and lose my daughter, that's all."

"If y'all went to Belize for a little while, that would give me an excuse to run off whenever I felt like it," Janet said, from the grill.

No one knew I had already bought our tickets. I wasn't about to sit around and wait for anyone's approval. If I couldn't be with Mark and we couldn't be a family, I didn't want to be here.

If he didn't have to play by the rules, I saw no reason why I should.

Later, after everyone had gone home, my mother and I sat and watched one of those unbelievable, but based on a true story movies on Lifetime.

"Was that the door? Who's coming over at this late hour?" I asked as I got up to answer.

When I opened the door and saw the man in a cheap suit, I swallowed the massive lump in my throat. When he flashed his badge, my legs went weak.

CHAPTER FIFTY-ONE

Keeling

I rushed out to the car because I wanted to get to work early. Since it was going to be my last day with Malcolm before I started my own route, I wanted to make sure I was ready.

After I locked the front door, the moment I turned around, I could see something wasn't right with my car. When I got to the curb, all four of my tires were flat. They had been slashed.

"Shit!" I didn't have to guess who was responsible. I was pissed. I wasn't about to call my moms because I'd have to listen to her rant.

Malcolm answered his phone after the fourth ring.

"What's up, dawg?" he asked.

"Dude, you at work yet?" I asked.

"Naw, I haven't even left the house. Shoot, dawg, it's early as hell."

"Yeah, sorry about that, but I need a ride, bro. Can you help me out?"

"Yeah, I'll come scoop you," Malcolm said.

I went back into the house and grabbed a bowl from the cabinet. I turned on the small TV my moms kept in the kitchen and put the volume on low.

Thank God, my moms had overslept. That meant there wasn't enough time for her to grill me about anything. She rushed into the kitchen, looked over at me like she was baffled, then said, "I thought you had to be at work early today."

At that moment, a horn sounded outside and I was glad. I jumped up, and leaned over to kiss my mom's cheek.

"Yeah, car trouble, so I'm riding with Malcolm," I said.

"What happened to your car?"

I didn't get a chance to answer because Malcolm honked again.

"Have a great day, Mom. Chat later."

"Daaayum, dawg, what happened to your ride?" Malcolm asked the moment I closed the passenger door of his car.

I shook my head, and used my hands to dry-rub my face.

"I don't know what to do about her. It's like she's determined to fuck up my life. She'd better be glad I was raised to respect women," I said.

"You damn right, she's lucky. She's stupid, too, because she already knows sooner or later, that money train is gonna stop. You'd think she'd try to be nice."

"Naw, Dani is a predator, man. She's the type that sees your weakness and continues to add pressure to it every minute of the day."

"Yeah, she's a real ball buster, dawg. I hate that she's got you caught up like that."

We rode the rest of the way in silence. I had to do something. I was sick and tired of Dani doing whatever she wanted to me and I turned the other cheek. Everyone always expected me to do the right thing, but she did what she wanted and didn't have to answer to anyone.

During lunch, I called Parker and ran my idea by him to see what he thought. It had been on my mind the entire morning and I felt like I might snap if I didn't do something, soon.

"I don't think I like that idea," Parker said, and sank my hope in an instant.

"I'm about to lose it here," I said. "Man, she gets to literally take money from my pocket, and we both know the test would change that, but there's nothing we can do to make her take it. I can't think of anything else," I said.

"I understand your frustration. But I think if you pursue it the way you just told me, we'd be opening ourselves up for even more problems."

"But, Parker, hear me out. Seriously, she's already tried to come on to me. That tells me if I made her think there was a chance we could get back together, it just might work," I said. I did more than said. I all but begged him to see my suggestion as a real option.

For a while, he held the phone, but he didn't say anything.

"I think it would do more damage than good," he warned, when he finally spoke again.

"Not if I did it the right way. Look, after all I've been through with her, I'm not thinking about being with another woman right now. I can act like there's a possibility of us trying again and I really think I could be convincing."

"I've got a few friends at HPD. Let me talk to them and see if maybe they can help us add some pressure to her," he suggested.

"Parker, my moms already tried that, dude, and nothing. As a matter of fact, I think she had an officer who said he'd go talk to her, you know, to try and scare her a little, but Dani simply ignored his calls and never talked to him."

"With all due respect, Keeling, your mother can come off more than a bit pushy," he said. "And I could see someone telling her exactly what they think she might want to hear. Let me talk to my guys. Believe me, we've seen it all and I can assure you some of them are used to dealing with Dani and lots worse," he said.

I sighed hard. Nothing about the conversation made me feel hopeful. I felt defeated and weak. But most importantly, I felt trapped and like nobody understood what I was going through.

Once I hung up with Parker, I felt worse than before I called.

My work day felt longer and harder because I couldn't stop thinking about how Dani had gotten over on me.

"What he say?" Malcolm asked. We were in his car on our way home, after work.

"He said it's not a good idea, sort of like playing with fire and thinks it could screw things up even more," I said, dejected.

"So, whatchu gonna do, dawg?"

My head whipped in his direction. Malcolm kept his eyes on the road and drove, cool as ever.

"What do you mean what am I gonna do?"

He shrugged. "Just like I asked, whatchu gonna do? I mean, Parker's cool and all, but Dani ain't like any of those prim and proper females he's used to dealing with. She's basically a thug in a skirt," Malcolm said. "Think about it, how is what she's doing any different from extortion? Seems to me like that should be against the law. I don't know why nobody else sees that."

Everything he said made sense. Dani was basically strong-arming me and taking my money. She knew the kid wasn't mine. She had already admitted so in front of a national TV audience, so why the hell did I still have to pay?

CHAPTER FIFTY-TWO

Mark

I should've known bad news was right around the corner. First, when we arrived at the police station, we had to wait an obscene amount of time before we were seen.

Zaneda was already anxious, but I tried to keep it cool and not give her any reason to blow a gasket. Her expectations were sky-high, and I didn't have the heart to say what I suspected—that she was about to be disappointed.

After we waited for more than an hour, the detective strolled over and flopped down into his chair. He looked nervous to me, and I knew good news never made people uneasy.

We exchanged pleasantries, and his eyes darted between mine and Zaneda's. That told me where this was headed, but I sat there and hoped for the best. When I heard the words fall from his lips, I wanted to get up and walk out. My life as I had known it for the last couple of weeks was about to take a turn and not in a direction I wanted.

Zaneda's neck began to swivel and I almost felt sorry for the officer.

Suddenly, her back became erect and she squared her shoulders. "So lemme get this straight: you questioned her, she denied it and you turned around and left?" Zaneda asked. "Just like that?" she spat.

It wasn't what she asked, but how she asked it. She was pissed, spoke through gritted teeth and her words sounded as if each and every single one had been dipped deep in sarcasm.

"Ma'am, I told you guys that this was a long shot. I tried, and like I said before, without any evidence whatsoever to tie her to any of these things, it's hard to do much more than I did," he said.

Zaneda blew out an angry breath and frowned. I didn't want things to get any nastier. So I leaned forward and asked, "Did it seem like she was trying to hide anything when you talked to her?"

He looked at Zaneda when he answered. "I know you believe this woman is behind all of this, but I gotta tell you, after I talked with her and her mother, I'm not so sure."

That was all it took. My wife popped up from that chair, tossed him one final nasty glare, and all but dragged me up out of there.

Outside, she collapsed into my arms.

"It's gonna be okay, babe," I said.

"It's so fuc-king unfair! She screws with our life and she gets away with it!" Zaneda pulled back and I wiped the tears from her cheeks.

"I know I haven't been the very best wife. I probably took you for granted for far too long. But honey, once I rededicated myself to you to us, to our family, I didn't expect it to be this hard," she sobbed.

"I know, babe. I know."

"And you know what else? If it was a situation where we were doing things to sabotage our own marriage, then I could halfway understand it, but you can't tell me she's smarter than every single body in the damn room!"

People walked by and looked at us oddly.

"Zaneda. Please. Let's get in the car and go home. We can talk about this there."

She wiped her face with the back of her hand and we held hands as we walked to the car. I opened the door and let her get into the car.

Once I got in and buckled my seatbelt, she looked over at me. "I'm sorry about the meltdown. I didn't mean to lose it like that back there. But I just knew this was going to be the answer to our problems."

"Babe. I know you're disappointed, but I'm working on something else. We will get to the bottom of this. I promise you we will."

Zaneda looked at me with hopeful eyes. For the first time since we'd left the police station, it seemed like her spirits had lifted a bit. "What are we gonna do?"

"Well, remember Timothy said he had that guy?" I reminded her.

"Oh, yeah!" Her eyes actually lit up and that gave me some hope.

"I'm gonna ask Timothy to meet us at the house after the boys are asleep, so we can talk and set up a meeting with his guy."

Zaneda snatched my hand and squeezed it. When she pulled it up to her lips and kissed it, that made me smile.

I was glad to see the hope in her eyes again.

"I love you," she said.

"I love you too, babe."

Hours later, after Zaneda put the kids to bed, my cell phone rang. I expected it to be Timothy, but it was Arlene instead.

"You got a whole lotta nerve!" she screamed.

That was how she greeted me after I said, "Hello."

I was in my office, so I got up and closed the door.

"Arlene, how's Markeesa doing?" I asked. I struggled to keep my tone even. The key to dealing with her was to remain calm and cool.

"You son-of-a-bitch! Do you really think you will ever lay eyes on her again?!" she screamed in my ear.

"Arlene, why wouldn't I see her again? She's my daughter, our daughter. I don't understand."

"You send the fucking police to my house to accuse me of all kinds of bull and now you wanna sit here and act like you don't know what's going on? Oh puh-lease! But that's okay, because I've got something for you and that rusty-ass wife of yours!" she screamed.

I took a deep breath and tried not to let her get to me.

"Oh. Is that what this is really all about?" I asked calmly.

For a second, she didn't respond.

"W-what are you talking about?" she asked.

"Arlene, it all makes sense now. I don't get why it took me so long to figure this whole thing out."

"You're on drugs. What are you talking about?"

"You were supposed to be my wife, right, Arlene?"

I could sense her pause through the phone.

"If I had left Zaneda and married you, none of this would be happening right now; isn't that right?" I asked.

CHAPTER FIFTY-THREE

Dani

"**W**hat do you mean the cops are here?" I asked. Buckets of sweat poured down my back like I had robbed a bank. At that moment, it felt like I could have shit bullets. I was pressed about what my life had become.

When I saw strobe lights in my rearview mirror, or saw the police for any reason, I immediately became paranoid. Maybe they were looking for me. Did someone sic them on me? Would I be able to get away?

This time was no different. All of those familiar thoughts ran through my mind, as I got ready to face the music. I was pissed at Keeling. I couldn't believe he'd let that man talk him into sending the cops after me. And then, they pulled this crap right when it looked like things had gotten better for me.

Lately, Charlene and I had been on good terms and I hated that the mess with Parker and Keeling was about to ruin all of that. The kids were asleep and I needed to get ready for a night out with my girls. It had been a long time since the three of us went out and wreaked havoc on the single men in H-town. I was looking for something to throw on until I got to Niecy's house.

"Charlene, did you call them again?" I asked. It was a legit question to ask. Her track record meant I needed to be clear about which side she was on. I talked to my mother through the crack of my bedroom door.

"Dani, will you throw on some clothes and come on out here," she said.

"So you didn't call them this time?" I asked, again.

She sucked her teeth. "Why would I, silly?"

"Okay, I'll be there in a sec," I said.

Quickly, I sent a text message to Lulu and Niecy that let them know I'd be later than expected. I put the phone down, pulled on a floor-length, maxi dress, and walked out of my room to see what the hell was going on. Each step I took was heavier than the next, because regardless of how much *ish* I talked to Keeling, I really was scared.

It wasn't until I walked up front and saw Savannah standing there that I became really, really confused. My movement stopped and I looked around in utter bewilderment. What was really going on? Was it about the jewelry?

"Yes. That's Dani Patnett," I heard Savannah say.

My eyebrows probably jumped up to touch my hairline.

"Dani Patnett," the man with Savannah said. "I'm a private investigator and I understand that you helped to facilitate a recent estate sale—"

The rest of what he said came in a blur because I was so relieved that this had nothing to do with Keeling or Keesa.

"Um. Yes. I handled the sale," I said.

But my heart felt like it was about to bust out of my ribcage. I wasn't sure how much to say or whether I should keep my mouth shut. If they found out about the jewelry I had, could I go to jail? Something told me to get it and give it to them so they would leave me alone. But before I played my hand, Savannah suddenly rushed to my side and whispered, "You've done nothing wrong.

He's investigating the sale and I told him that you were doing what you were supposed to do."

The guy wrote something down on a notepad. But when he pulled a picture out of the breast pocket of his jacket, I was even more confused.

"Do you recognize this woman?" he asked and shoved the picture in my face.

At first glance, I thought I recognized the woman, but something in me clicked.

"No. I don't," I said.

"Look real hard. This is an older photo, so maybe she's changed her hair," he suggested.

I knew exactly who it was, but I wasn't about to tell him, or Savannah. I didn't believe in being a snitch.

"I don't know her. Never seen her before," I said.

I could've been mistaken, but I thought I saw signs of a smile on Savannah's face.

Just as quickly as they'd arrived, Savannah and the cop, or private investigator, were gone. I turned and looked at Charlene.

"What was that all about?" Charlene asked.

I shrugged. "I don't know, but that was my boss, so I hope she's got it all together."

"That's your boss?" Charlene asked. "She looks good. I like that dress and those shoes she had on."

"Yeah. She's sharp. But now I'm like, what the heck is going on with her business? That's wild, for her to come here with the police."

"Well, technically, he's not the police. He said he's a private investigator. That means he's hired by someone with money," she said. Charlene looked at me like we were best friends with secrets.

I shrugged. I didn't know anyone with money so it meant nothing to me.

"Hope he finds what's he's being paid to look for," I said. I returned to my room and finished getting dressed to meet up with my girls.

But in the back of my mind, I wondered whether there was a way I could hook up with Penelope and tell her what was going on. I felt like if she knew how I had held it down for her, I could get more assignments like the estate sale versus the oil company lobby gig.

CHAPTER FIFTY-FOUR

Arlene

"Okay, since my vehicle is going to be shipped, does that mean I can put all of my belongings in it?" I asked.

"Yes, you can, but you want to use the same type of rules you would if you were sending something through the U.S. Postal Service."

"Okay, so, clothes, shoes, and things like that," I said into the phone.

"Yes, and I don't recommend you pack any valuables. We can't be responsible for damages or loss," he said.

Once I finished my call with him, I looked down at my checklist. So far, it looked like everything would be fine. A part of me wanted to see the look on Mark's and Zaneda's faces when they realized that I had gotten the last laugh after all.

I thought about his smart comment the last time we were on the phone, I'd admit. Back in the day, he would've hit it on spot. I did want him. I wanted us to be the epitome of what I thought would be a perfect family. But when he crawled back to Zaneda and allowed her to basically run him, that confirmed that he could never be the man for me.

It was gonna be a challenge, but once my mother was back in her Belize, she'd be okay.

I had two weeks to pull everything together and knowing they had hired a private investigator made me work that much harder.

By the time they pieced everything together, I planned to be thousands of miles away.

I closed my notepad and got up to go talk to my daughter. She was in her room playing with some of the expensive toys her father had given her.

"Markeesa, I need to talk to you about something."

She looked up.

"We are going on a little vacation, but it's a secret and I need to make sure you understand that this is family business."

"Okay, Mommy," she said.

I expected her to ask questions about where we were going and what we'd be doing, but the child turned her attention back to the life-sized doll house that Mark had assembled inside her room.

"Don't you want to know where we're going? Or aren't you curious about when we're leaving?" I asked. "I'm surprised you don't have any questions at all."

"Oh yeah, Mommy. I have questions."

I felt like maybe things wouldn't be as difficult with her after all. She was a kid and once she knew she was about to start a new adventure, I was sure she'd be able to enjoy herself.

"So what kind of questions do you have?" I asked.

"Oh. Can Mason and MJ come too? I know they would have a really good time, and, Mommy, when we were on the cruise, Miss Zaneda said we were the best kids ever!" she exclaimed.

This had to be handled in a delicate way. I couldn't say exactly what I felt, but I also wanted to make sure that I kept the upper hand.

"I think bringing Mason and MJ would be a great idea. That way your brothers would be there for you to play with. You know what, honey, the next time I talk to your daddy, I'll ask him if he'll let them go."

Her little eyes got so wide it looked like they might pop from their sockets. She rushed into my arms so fast and hard, she nearly knocked me down. "Thank you, Mommy! I can't wait for this trip."

"Good. Now remember this is a family trip, so you can't talk about it with anyone, especially people who are not part of this family," I explained.

"Okay, Mommy. But can I tell Mason and MJ?"

"No, not yet. You have to let me talk to your daddy first, okay? If you say something about it too soon, he might not let the guys come with us."

Her little face looked like it might crumble. I needed to put some fear in her because I couldn't have her blow the plan out of the water before I had a chance to execute it.

After I was confident that Markeesa understood she couldn't tell anyone about the trip, I left her to go and talk to my mother. She was still reluctant about going, but I had convinced her that it was best for us all. When I finished painting Mark as the monster that he was, she had started to dislike him too. He thought he was being slick by sending the police to question me, but that had completely backfired. It also let me know that I needed to kick things into high gear and get the hell out of Dodge quickly.

Officer Smith was a potbellied, chocolate-faced, short man who wasn't ready for me. I allowed him to come in and talk with my mother and me and that proved to be a great move.

"The Clyburns have had a series of bad events happen here recently," he said.

My eyebrows went up because that was a shock to me.

"Oh, that's too bad," I said.

My mother simply nodded.

"Well, they recently returned from vacation, only to find their house had been burglarized," he said.

"Oh, wow! That's a shame," I said.

He cut his eyes at me. Then he looked over at Mama. She shook her head and gave him a sorrowful expression.

"So where were you on Sunday, July sixteenth?" he asked.

"Oh, my best friend and I took my mom and her friends on a little vacation. We drove to Louisiana. They love the casinos," I said.

Again, my mother nodded for good measure.

His face cracked. I could see the color drain from his features as he stumbled over his next question.

"So, um, how long were you guys out of town and did anyone see you?"

"We came back, let's see," I said. "Oh, we were supposed to come back Tuesday, but we took our time, stayed an extra day and came back late Wednesday. And of course people saw us!" I exclaimed. Then I leaned over. "She may seem quiet and harmless now, but you put her with Betty and Carol, and they're quite the hell-raisers! I'm glad we got out of there when we did," I joked.

He cracked a smile, but if I could read minds, I would've guessed he knew his little case had fallen apart.

"What else happened to the Clyburns?" I asked.

"Oh. Um, someone called CPS on them, and Mrs. Clyburn's—"

"Hold up! What did you just say? They have a CPS complaint against them? Oh, Mark never told me that," I said.

His expression told me he realized his mistake and suddenly he brought the little interview to an abrupt end. That's when I decided to call Mark.

Now that I knew he had been or was being investigated by CPS, I finally had grounds to keep him away from my daughter for good.

Sure, I definitely wanted to see the look on their faces when they came to pick up Markeesa and found nothing but the copy of a detailed letter notifying them that I had taken her into hiding after I was made aware that they'd been under investigation for possible child abuse.

Here they had sent someone for me, but had no way of knowing that move played right into my plans.

CHAPTER FIFTY-FIVE

Keeling

I walked in from work exhausted. It was Friday, payday, and my moms was cooking in the kitchen so that made me feel better.

"Damn, what you got brewing in here?" I asked as I tried to remove a lid from one of the pots. She popped my fingers with the wooden spoon.

"Get outta my pots! You didn't even wash your nasty hands," she said.

"Oh, my bad, Moms. You right, you right," I said. I moved closer to the sink and was about to wash my hands. Suddenly she pinched my ear and squeezed tightly.

"Ooouch! Ma!"

"Go to the guest bathroom. Act like you got some home training, boy!"

I scooted out of the kitchen and headed to my room. The aromas from whatever she was cooking danced in my nostrils and I couldn't wait to get cleaned up and change.

"Ma. I'ma 'bout to take a quick airplane bath. I'll be down in a few!" I yelled.

"You are nasty!" my mother joked.

I only said that to get at her. When I was little, she used to get after me because she said I wouldn't wash my behind properly and she didn't want no stinking man under her roof. She would ask whether I took a bath or an airplane bath. At first I didn't know what she meant until she explained that it was a half-ass way of cleaning, when you took a wet wash rag and hit only the tail, and under each wing, meaning your crotch region and the armpits.

Later, we sat and ate catfish, with red beans and rice. It was slamming too.

"So, did Parker make any progress yet?"

"Naw. He says he's gonna run it by a few of the guys he knows down at HPD," I said.

"Did you tell him, I've been there and done that? They don't wanna get involved. But I'll bet if you went upside the skeezer's head, they'd be quick to throw a pair of cuffs on your wrist and drag you back to jail."

"Yeah, Mom, I told him. But he also reminded me that he's got a good relationship with some of those guys. So I hope we have a different outcome. Remember, Ma. This is what this man does for a living. He probably knows way more people than us, so I say let him work his jelly."

My mother's expression told me she wasn't totally convinced.

"Look, Ma. It's way better than the plan me and Malcolm came up with," I said.

"What plan was that?"

"I don't wanna tell you. All you're gonna do is tell me how dumb it was. Just forget I even said anything."

"No, son. Tell me, what did you come up with? I'm open to anything that might work."

"Well, I told Parker that I was thinking about dating her, not for real, but just so I could get next to her and convince her to take the test. Look, I'm desperate," I said.

Surprisingly, my mother didn't upchuck at the sound of that

idea. She chewed her food and kept her eyes on me. Suddenly, a sly grin appeared on her face. "What did Parker say about that idea?"

"He didn't like it. Told me it was the equivalent of playing with fire. Then he told me to let him try his contacts at HPD before I took such a dangerous and drastic move. But Malcolm pointed something out. He reminded me that Parker was probably used to dealing with those prim and proper women. He probably don't know what to do with someone like Dani."

"Well, son. You guys are all right. Malcolm is right. Dani is sewer trash, but Parker is right too. I think your idea would've led to more problems. But it does give me an idea," she said. "C'mon, let's finish up dinner. We're about to go for a ride."

"Ma. I don't feel like hoo-bangin' with my mama," I joked.

"Come on here, boy!" she fussed.

Not even twenty minutes later, we were in my mom's car and flying down the street. When she turned on to Dani's mother's street, I wanted to jump out of the window.

"Ma! This is not a good idea," I said.

"Look here. I'm sick and tired of this foolishness with this girl. I know Charlene don't know what the hell this chile's been doing. It's about time we have a real woman-to-woman talk."

"We can't just show up at someone's house unannounced like that, Ma." But there was no point in trying to reason with her. Her mind was already made up.

She pulled up in front of their house and turned to me. "Now who's scared of hoo-bangin'?"

Honestly, I was stunned to see Dani's car there on a Friday night. Reluctantly, I climbed out and followed my mother up the walkway that led to the front door.

"Dang, Ma," I said after she banged on the front door like she worked for the law.

"When you're unannounced, you gotta enter with confidence, son."

I didn't get to respond, because the door flew open. It was Dani's mother, Charlene.

"Kelsa, Keeling, what brings you two by this evening?" she asked.

"Charlene, we should've come a long time ago. Can we come in?" my mother asked.

"Oh sure. You just caught Dani. She's on her way out," Charlene said and stepped aside to allow us in.

The house was clean, quiet, and dark. My mother walked in and looked around.

"The kids are asleep, so we can talk in the kitchen if you want," she said.

"Where's that, uh, your daughter?" my mother said. I was so glad she checked herself. The woman never had anything nice to say about Dani.

Even in the kitchen, signs of the kids were all over. Artwork and wallet-sized pictures were stuck to the refrigerator door.

We sat, and a few seconds later, Dani rushed by only to stop and do a quick double-take as she headed for the front door.

"What the hel—"

Charlene turned to her. "I knew you were on your way out so I didn't get a chance to call you, but Keeling and his mother need to talk to us," she said. "Come on in here."

Dani made a face. Her eyes darted between my mother and me. "I ain't got shit to say to neither one of 'em."

Charlene's face was instantly embarrassed.

She moved closer, snatched Dani by her shoulder and all but shoved her into a seat at the kitchen table.

"I wasn't asking you whether you wanted to talk. I told you these nice people are here to talk. The least you can do is listen."

CHAPTER FIFTY-SIX

Mark

I felt like a special kind of fool as I glanced over the evidence the private investigator laid out for Zaneda and me.

He had pictures, copies of receipts, copies of contracts, travel itineraries, and much, much more. He had earned every single penny of the six-thousand-dollar check I signed for him.

"As you can see here, she's been very busy," he said.

Zaneda sat upright, with a look of sheer satisfaction across her face.

"I see these tickets are for next week," I said.

"Yes. It looks like she plans to take your daughter to Belize. The minute I found out, I took a quick trip there and did some digging. This folder contains information about where they planned to live and all the details surrounding that plan."

"Wow!" I shook my head in sheer disbelief as my eyes gazed over all of the information. It was all too much to take in.

"I told you that bitch was behind it all! And she's about to try and kidnap Markeesa! Oh, wait 'til I get my hands on her!" Zaneda was fired up. I felt lost. What the hell could Arlene have been thinking? Did she think she'd be able to get away with all of this?

Timothy walked over and patted me on the shoulder. He gripped me tightly and I knew he understood the sheer shock I felt.

"Edward, as always, you did a great job," he said.

"Did you ever talk to her?" I asked.

"Yes, Sir. Briefly. But I didn't tell her who I was or what I was doing. She thought she was solidifying plans for her move. I wanted to be sure she was actually planning to relocate and take the minor child with her." Edward pointed at the CD that was included inside the folder that contained his detailed report. "That's a recording of the phone call where she's trying to find out exactly what items she can pack inside the vehicle that's being shipped to Belize."

There was no denying what his pile of evidence proved. He had it all covered.

"So she didn't break in, but she was responsible," I said.

"Yes, sir." Edward pulled large glossy photos of three women. "This is Savannah. She runs the temp agency Arlene hired under the alias Penelope Jones. This young lady who is in the middle of her own paternity issue is the one who actually executed the sale. Her name is Dani Patnett."

"Has she been around my daughter?" I asked.

"No. From what I can tell, she's trying to establish something with Arlene." He flipped through another stack of pictures and pulled out one of Dani and Arlene having lunch.

"I wasn't sure what they were up to, but I think Ms. Patnett is trying to get Arlene's help with her own paternity battle. There have been several calls from the offices of Don't Force Fatherhood, a fathers' advocacy group. When I talked with Parker Redman, he told me Dani is extorting money from a man she fingered as the father of her child, but that's where their connection ends."

"She's got her nerve. So, now she's trying to help this little trick get over on someone? Did you find my jewelry?" Zaneda asked.

"No traces of the jewelry, but," he fished out additional pictures, "you can see these are Dani's friends. The designer clothes and shoes they're wearing may have come from the items that were stolen."

Zaneda snatched the pictures and released an eardrum-bursting scream. "These hood rats are walking around wearing all of my stuff!"

"Who else was in on this?" I asked. I needed all of the details and information he had.

"Honestly, outside of the help she hired, Arlene seemed to be the mastermind behind it all. There are receipts for the burner cell phone she bought, the gift cards she used, and of course, a search of her IP address found the sites she used to find the temp agency as well as the company to ship her furniture, vehicle, and appliances to Belize. That's how I was able to call and confirm the move with her."

I shook my head because I couldn't find the words. She gave this plan serious thought and consideration.

"So all of it was part of her strategic plan all along?"

"It looks like it, sir. She was going to use the CPS complaint, the Craigslist ad, the burglary, and paint you and your wife as an unstable couple. It would provide the foundation for her fear of allowing her daughter to spend time with you. In her mind, she wanted to justify leaving the country because of your family's instability, and fears of what that instability might do to her daughter."

He looked at me and said, "Everything is detailed in the summary. That pretty much concludes my report."

"Wow," I said.

"Great job; thorough as always, Edward," Timothy said.

Zaneda sat quietly, and flipped through the stack of pictures. I didn't know what else to say.

"If you need anything else, simply let me know," Edward said.

"Timothy, thanks for the business." Before they shook hands, the private investigator turned to us.

"Thank you so much for your hard work. You have completely validated everything I suspected all along. Here, let me show you out," Zaneda said.

I was glad Zaneda decided to walk him out.

The minute they left, I turned to Timothy.

"What should I do with all of this?" I swept my arm across the desk. My entire desk was covered with evidence of Arlene's devious, well-crafted plan. And it made me sick to my stomach.

"It's up to you. Remember, the police have nothing. You can take this and have her thrown in jail, or you can use it to confront her. It's completely up to you," he said.

"So if I don't want to turn this all over to the police, I don't have to?" I asked.

"It's completely up to you. That was a private investigation that you paid for. You need to understand, if you turn this over to the authorities, she can face charges and could go to jail."

"I know. And that's what's the toughest with all of this. I hate that she went to such lengths, but there's no way in hell I can have her sent to jail," I said.

"And why the hell not?" Zaneda burst back into the office. "Better yet, if you don't press charges, I will," she said adamantly.

Timothy and I looked at each other, but I was speechless.

CHAPTER FIFTY-SEVEN

Dani

Charlene always picked the worst times possible to try and play the mother role. She got on my last damn nerve with that mess. I sat there and drummed my fingers on the table top. I wanted to be anyplace else but there.

"She knows he's not the father. She needs to do the right thing," Kelsa, the bitch, said.

I rolled my eyes at her. I hated her more than she could ever hate me. All she did was try to live her life through her son. We probably could've made a real go at it, if she had kept her nose out of our relationship. But he wasn't man enough to tell his mama to mind her own.

"Dani, this ain't right and you know it. It's not gonna end well for you. I'm trying to avoid you going to jail," Keeling said.

"You not scaring me with that jail bull. I didn't do nothing wrong."

"You lied!" his mother screamed and sprayed us all with spittle. As dramatically as I could, I wiped her droplets from my arms and shoulders and shot her a death-like stare. I hated her with a serious passion.

I kept my frown in place as I listened to Charlene take sides with them, against me. I'd tell her about herself later for sure.

"We talked about this, Dani. I asked you how come Keeling

wasn't after you to go down there and tell those people he wasn't the daddy. And what did you tell me?"

I couldn't believe her.

"Charlene, don't you have something you could be doing right now?" I asked.

"Baby, I'm trying to keep you out of jail. If these people go and tell the police you lied, we don't know what could happen. Do the right thing. I don't care who Keela's father is. She's always gonna be my granddaughter, just like you'll always be my daughter. Right or wrong, I'm gonna love you regardless. But I can't sit back and let you ruin things for this young man," she said.

Did Charlene just say she loved me? I couldn't believe she had allowed Keeling and his mama to get to her like that. I couldn't remember the last time she said she loved me.

I looked at Keeling. "You are so pathetic, such a poor excuse for a man. When are you gonna stop hiding behind your mama's skirt and be a real man? It's time for you to stop being such a mama's boy," I said.

"I am a man," he said. "That's why you still sitting here with your face fully intact, and all your limbs," he continued, "You see, a real man handles his anger with words and not his might. But you've pushed me close to the edge more than a few times."

A tingle shot down my spine. His words literally made me shiver with excitement. I had never heard Keeling talk with that kind of raw intensity. But of course, I had to play it off. I kept my cool and held my poker face.

"I know you ain't threatening me," I said to him.

"You are such a simple little girl. What the boy is trying to tell you is other guys would've got in that ass long ago. You sitting here playing games and you don't even get the ramifications of what you're doing," his mother said.

"Who the hell was talking to you?" I asked.

She pursed her lips like it was a struggle for her to keep it together. I couldn't care less what she thought. And since I had the money and my secret stash of jewelry, I knew I wouldn't go to the poor house anytime soon if I lost Keeling's money. But they didn't need to know that.

"Dani, I'm tired of the games. If you don't go take that test, I'll take Keela down there myself," Charlene said.

She made me so sick sometimes.

"Charlene!" I screamed, and crossed my arms over my chest.

"Charlene, nothing! You think I wanna go down to the morgue and identify your body one day?" she asked.

I frowned. What the hell was she talking about? That's why I never liked having her in my business. My mother couldn't keep up for nothing.

"What does a morgue have to do with this conversation? You are always going way left." I snickered.

My cell rang.

It was Lulu.

"Girl, y'all may as well go on without me," I said into the phone. All eyes were on me, and I wanted to tell them all to find some damn business.

"After we waited all this damn time, what's up?"

"Keeling and his mama," I said. "They popped up over here."

"Whhhaaaat? At your house? Oooh. What Charlene say?"

"Oh trust. She's got a whole lot to say, all of a sudden," I said.

"Umph. Bye, girl!"

I ended the call and put the phone down.

"Where's Keela's real daddy?" Charlene asked.

For a change, I was glad when Keeling's mama stuck her nose in where it didn't belong.

"You two can have that conversation after we're gone. For now, all we want to discuss is this DNA test that needs to happen. We know who's not the child's father, so we need to make that happen ASAP."

They all looked at me. But it was a completely different voice that pulled our attention away from the conversation at hand.

"Daddy? You're here!" Keela rubbed her eyes as she stood in the doorway. Before we could do or say another word, she rushed and jumped into Keeling's lap and threw her little arms around his neck.

"Oh, Jesus," Kelsa said.

"Dammit, Charlene, I thought they were asleep," I barked at my mother.

Whap!

My face stung, but I wasn't sure whether it was the pain or the utter shock that left me speechless.

"Have some respect for your mother," Kelsa said. "I'm sick of you talking to her like she's the child!"

Oh, but no! That bitch actually slapped me?

CHAPTER FIFTY-EIGHT

Arlene

At first, my mother was a little upset that we had to leave right away. She said it was too sudden, like we needed to run from someone or something. I ignored it all. She wanted to know if this was really a surprise why I sprang it on her the way I did, but in the end, she came along. I pulled out my notarized letter that proved Mark had given me permission to take our child out of the country and we were on our way.

As we shuffled through the international gate at Bush Intercontinental Airport, my mind raced with all sorts of thoughts. But there was one that was more prevalent than the others.

We could make one helluva team.

Her words haunted me.

It don't even matter why you're doing what you're doing, but I wanna help!

Who was this girl?

Days after my meeting with Dani Patnett, her words stayed on my mind. Initially when she called me, I didn't know if I was being set up, or what was going on, but I figured I should at least meet with her to see what the hell she thought she knew.

We met at Blue in Sugarland. I opted for a seat out on their sidewalk patio. We had lunch over colorful cocktails and expensive half-dishes.

"How did you find me?" I asked.

"Well, I gotta admit, it wasn't that hard. Remember, I did the estate sale for you. Well, I Googled your baby daddy, Mark Clyburn, read up on y'all on Mediatakeout, and WorldStar Hiphop," she said.

I had forgotten all about those trashy websites. Back in the day, they kept up with the drama between Mark, Zaneda and me like somebody was paying them to do it.

"Wow. So what did you learn?" I asked. As I sat there, I prayed this little girl wasn't about to try and blackmail me. I had too much on my plate already with the move.

"I learned that, as with me, there's a man who did you wrong. When I figured out who you were and realized you had done what many women like me and you would like to do, you became my shero," she said.

That put my mind at ease a bit.

"So, you wanted to meet with me for—"

"Because, I just wanna let you know, I'd be down to help you. Whatever you're planning to do, I want in. That's all," she cut me off and said.

Everything she said had me skeptical. What if somehow Mark had found her? Well, not Mark, but Zaneda and she worked for them. I couldn't trust her, but she didn't need to know that.

"Oh, I should also let you know. There's some guy who's been asking questions about you," she said.

That's when she got and held my attention.

"Who, Detective Smith?" I asked.

"No. This guy is a private investigator. He's not with the police. He had a picture of you and he came to my house with Savannah," she said.

Dani's phone call and the meeting couldn't have come at a better time. So Mark had hired someone to dig up dirt on me. I knew what that meant and if I could've, I would've kissed Dani Patnett.

After that meeting with her, it was more obvious than ever, I had to move fast. I thanked her and told her I'd be in touch. But the truth was, I had no intentions of ever seeing her again. Instead of leaving in a week-and-a-half, we'd have to leave the very next day.

Since I suspected Mark knew my plan, I didn't have much time to wait for him to make a move.

"Mommy, where's Mason and MJ?" Markeesa asked, as we boarded the plane. She kept looking around as we sat at the gate and waited to get on the plane.

I didn't have an answer at that very moment, but once we took our seats, I kept my eye on the plane's door. Any moment, I expected air marshals, or even Mark himself, to board the plane and pull us off.

My daughter tugged on my sleeve. "Mommy, where are Mason and MJ?" she asked again.

Once the flight attendant announced the door to the aircraft was closing and we were headed to Belize, I released a huge sigh of relief. I had done it!

I turned to Markeesa. "Oh, honey, your daddy said he's gonna bring them once we settle into our new house."

My mother sat there and cut her eyes at me, but she didn't say anything. I was glad, because I didn't have the energy.

"So, they're not coming with us now?" Markeesa started to cry.

"Markeesa. I need you to get it together. I told you, they will come once we get settled."

She pulled her arms up to her chest, crossed them, then pouted her lips. "Then I don't wanna go! I wanna go live with my daddy!"

Thank God. After the pilot greeted us and told us we'd make it there in a little under two hours, I knew that meant we'd been cleared for takeoff.

It wasn't until we were airborne that I finally felt relieved. After about ten minutes of crying, Markeesa fell off to sleep and I had some peace. I thought about how Dani helped salvage my plans.

What if I had no idea Mark had hired a private investigator? I would've been sitting there waiting to go and he would've ruined everything I'd worked so hard to pull off. And he would've done it at the very last moment.

But thanks to Dani, I was able to move three steps ahead of him. The letters I had written would be delivered tomorrow instead of a week and two days from now. In it, I told Mark everything and said that I hoped once he read it, he'd forever regret the way he treated me.

Then there was Zaneda. I knew that deep down, she'd probably be more than happy that we were gone. There was a part of me that hated to give her the satisfaction of seeing us leave, but the ability to really hurt Mark appealed to me more.

I adjusted the headrest on my seat and leaned back to enjoy the flight. In two hours, I was prepared to embark on a new life, or at least that was what I thought.

If I had known what awaited us in Belize, I may have done things differently.

CHAPTER FIFTY-NINE

Keeling

The day of our DNA testing came faster than I'd expected. But it still took forever. Once Dani agreed to do it, I wanted it done the very next day, but of course that couldn't happen. I had every reason to doubt that she would show up.

First thing Monday morning, I called and gave Parker the great news. He told me to give him a couple of hours and he'd call back with information about where we needed to go to be tested.

Parker was cool. He even got my supervisor to give me the day off. I told them, I'd be able to come in after the testing, so I only needed a half a day.

It was agreed that my moms and Charlene would come along. When we exited Kirby off 610, I was a little nervous. My moms was so happy, it was crazy.

"Son. This is like the first day of the rest of your life. I'm so excited for you."

"Ma. I'm glad, but did you have to smack the girl like that?"

She started to laugh.

"You know good and well that little tramp deserved it. You heard how she was talking to her mama! She'd better be glad all I did was slap her behind!"

We both laughed at that. I laughed because my mama wasn't

exaggerating. She turned into the parking lot for the large tan-colored building that had the numbers *2646* embossed in large white numbers.

Once she parked, I jumped out of the car and rushed around to open my mom's door. She got out and we walked into the building together.

"Parker! Hey, man, I didn't know you were gonna be here," I said. I was so happy to see him. His presence instantly put me at ease.

"Ms. Lake," he greeted my mother dryly.

"Hi, Parker. Which floor is Houston Medical Testing on?" she asked.

"We're going up to suite 550," he said.

I looked around the lobby.

"Don't worry. They're already up there. They got here about five minutes ago," Parker said.

"Wow, she showed up," I said. I was excited and happy at the same time. I couldn't believe that she'd kept her word.

"Yup. Let's go up so we can get this over with," Parker said.

Nearly an hour later Dani, Keela, my mother and I were escorted into a back room. I signed a form, and watched as they told Dani to sit and have Keela on her lap.

The little girl screamed so loudly when that needle pierced her skin, I felt her pain. Once they drew her blood, it was Dani's turn. We signed more papers and soon, it was my turn.

Keela stood between my legs as the technician strapped my arm and searched for a vein. I hated what this meant for her because she was very attached to me.

"Daddy, it's gonna be okay," she said.

That took me back to the last time I was at the house. She refused to go to sleep until I read her a bedtime story. I felt like such a fraud when I walked into the room Dani shared with her children. But it was obvious that if I didn't read the story, she wasn't about to let up until she got what she wanted.

"Okay, results will be back in about two weeks," the technician said.

After that, we were all on our way. Parker asked my moms and me to fall back so that Dani and Charlene could leave with Keela.

"No need to create a scene. I don't want the little girl to get upset all over again. The way she clung to you tells me this is going to be devastating for her," he said.

I understood, but there was still a part of me that felt connected to her too. I just didn't want to pay. And honestly, if Dani wasn't so ignorant, she could even call me if she needed something. I wouldn't say no. It was just the idea of being forced to pay for a kid who wasn't mine.

"Here's how this is gonna go. We'll get the results back. I'll send it off to the judge and she will order you be freed from all financial responsibility. Once we get that court order, I'll send it to the AG's office and payments will stop."

"How long will all of that take?" my mother asked.

"Oh, about four weeks total. You know the wheels of justice rarely move at the speed we want," he said.

"So, they're gonna keep taking money out of his check until when?" my mother asked.

"Ma. He just went through it once. I'm good. They'll take money out for another couple of pay periods," I said.

She gave me that look and I knew that meant she'd soon be swinging if I didn't watch my tone.

"C'mon, boy. Let's go," she said.

When I got to work, I stayed in the warehouse since I didn't get there early enough to go out on a route. The trucks came in slowly and I saw some of my coworkers I rarely saw because we were in and out so quickly in the mornings.

By the time Malcolm's truck pulled in, I knew he'd have something to say.

He jumped off the truck and rushed up to me. We did the brother-man handshake with the pat on the back and he came in for another hug.

"Man, how does it feel?" he asked.

"Damn good now, but believe me, in about a month, it's gonna feel a whole lot better," I said.

"That's what's up, dawg! That's what's up. Let's go throw back a few. My treat."

"You ain't said nothing but a word, playboy," Just knowing the test was done made me feel better.

"Aye, I already called Roger. He's meeting us at Sugar Hill, so get it ready, get it ready," Malcolm sang, as he darted toward the locker room.

CHAPTER SIXTY

Mark

Our house was big, but it felt ten times bigger when Zaneda decided not to talk to me. She was mad because she overheard me say I didn't want Arlene to go to jail.

She didn't get it.

"Do you still have feelings for that bitch?" she asked.

Timothy's wide-eyed stare made him look more like a trapped deer.

"We can talk about this tomorrow," he said, and scrambled toward the door. "You guys let me know how you want to handle this and I'll take it from there," he said before he turned to leave. "Oh, I can find my way out."

"I'm sick of this shit with you. You think the fucking grass is greener? What, you sit up and wonder what life would've been like if you'd stayed with her? You spent damn near three years on the fence. I waited for you to figure out that this was where you wanted to be. I'm done," she said.

"Zaneda. You finished yet?" I asked.

She exhaled heavily.

"I know I made the right choice. And I'm sorry Arlene did all of this stuff to us, to you, but putting her in jail ain't gonna solve anything. If anything, all it's gonna do is create more problems for us. Is that what you want?" I asked.

"What I want is for her to pay for what she's done," Zaneda said.

"Zaneda, how much should she pay?"

"What?" She twisted her face when she looked at me.

"How much should Arlene have to pay for all she's done?" I asked. I got up from my chair and moved toward her. "You tell me, what exactly do you want her to do? How do you suggest we make her pay?"

"She needs to go to jail! That's how much she should pay. Send her simple ass to jail, and until you do what you're supposed to do, don't say another damn word to me!"

She pivoted on her heel, and stormed out of the office.

That was three days ago. She hadn't said a word to me since.

It still amazed me when I looked at the stacks of information Edward had collected. I didn't want to be at war with Zaneda, but I also knew jail wasn't the answer in this situation.

The following day, I met with Timothy at his office, and we went over my options. Timothy agreed jail wasn't the solution so the other option was what brought me to the most unlikely place.

Zaneda's silence kinda worked out for the best, because I didn't have to explain anything to her. I made the decision and that was all there was to it.

From the passenger's seat, I grabbed the large envelope that contained copies of Edward's report, pictures, and receipts. There was no way to deny all the tangible evidence he had collected.

Armed with everything I thought I needed, I climbed out of my car and looked around. Something didn't feel right. I knew I was headed for a battle, but the thing was, Arlene didn't know she wasn't going to jail. Timothy and I discussed that I would confront her with all of the information and let her know that there was more than enough for the police to bring her up on charges. But the real joke was on me. Not only did I not panic when her car wasn't there, but it never crossed my mind that she'd be gone.

I walked up to the door and knocked a few times, and there was no answer. That's when I walked to the edge of the porch and peered into the window. The entire house was empty! My legs felt weak. She wasn't leaving for another week! What the hell? My hands trembled as I dialed Timothy's number.

"Mark, what's up? You met with her already? How'd it go?"

"Tim, man, she's gone."

"What do you mean she's gone?" he asked.

"She gone. The house is empty, my daughter, her furniture, her car, everything. She's gone."

"I'll be damned. How did she find out?"

"I have no idea, but Tim, man, we need to find her. We need to find my daughter. Call Edward," I said.

Alone and behind the wheel of my car, I felt empty but completely filled with rage. In that moment, Arlene would've been sentenced to hard time if I were the judge.

She took Markeesa and moved to another country.

When Timothy called back nearly an hour later, I was still at their house, or what used to be their house.

"Edward is ready to meet. He's also prepared to go back to Belize if you need him to. But, Mark, you have to know that this now changes the game. I don't think you can handle this without bringing the police into it," he said.

"I just want to see my daughter," I muttered.

"Well, we already know where she is and we know we can be there on the next thing smoking, but what if we get over there and she refuses to let your daughter come back?"

"I, uh...I don't know the answer to any of that yet," I stammered.

"These are the things we need to think about before we make

our first move. It wouldn't be smart to go there without a plan," he said.

Everything he said made sense, but it didn't help me feel any better.

"Edward is free tonight at eight. That's the earliest he can meet us. Can that work for you?" he asked.

"I'll make it work. I'll be at your office by seven thirty. I'd rather meet there. I don't want Zaneda to know about this until it's absolutely necessary."

I pulled a couple of papers from the folder. I'd do some investigating of my own. I pulled up in front of the modest house and got out of the car.

A few minutes after I knocked, a woman pulled the door open.

"I know you." She smiled. "You're that football player."

Her expression quickly changed.

"Wait, why are you here?" she asked.

"I'm looking for Dani Patnett," I said.

The woman rubbed her temples and sighed loudly. She leaned against the doorframe and asked, "What has she done this time?"

"She's been working with my daughter's mother and I think she may have some information about a kidnapping."

"Oh, sweet Jesus! She's not here. She's at work. But I can call her if you want," she offered.

Moments later, I listened as Dani's voice rang out on the speaker phone.

"What, Charlene?" she said.

It was kind of odd to hear her call her mother by her first name, but that wasn't my issue.

"Dani, this nice gentleman, that football player who's from Houston but plays in Los Angeles is here. He says you know something about a kidnapping," she said.

That wasn't the way I would've done it, but what could I say?

"Charlene, will you stop talking to strangers, please. I don't know nothing about no damn kidnapping. Don't tell him nothing," Dani said.

"I can hear you," I said.

"Oh God, Charlene! What's wrong with you?!" she screamed at her mother.

"Listen. Arlene took my daughter to Belize. I know you know her. I know you met with her the other day, and I know you helped her clean out my house. That's accessory, if not worse," I said.

"Whoa! Hold up. I ain't an accessory to a damn thing. I met with her because I wanted her to hire me for another temp job. I don't know her and honestly, when I met with her, she didn't seem interested in anything I had to say," Dani said.

"What did you tell her?"

"Nothing. I told her I needed more gigs like the estate sale," Dani said.

"That's it?"

"Oh, wait. I did tell her about the private investigator that you guys sent to my house," she admitted.

"Okay. Thanks," I said.

"Hey, wait!" Dani yelled.

"Yeah?"

"That doesn't make me an accessory to anything. I didn't know she was gonna run, so I'm good, right?"

After a few seconds, I let her off the hook and left. She had given me more than she knew. Once Dani told Arlene about the investigator, she got spooked and ran earlier than planned.

I arrived at Timothy's office and he poured us both a shot of cognac. By the time Edward arrived, I felt a little relaxed.

"How can we handle this without bringing in the police?" I asked.

"We would have to go over there and talk to her to see where her mind is," Edward said.

"The only way we have to bring the authorities in is if she refuses," he said.

"And you'd be able to go with me?"

"Sure, Mr. Clyburn."

"Let me get a refill," I said to Timothy.

"How long will it take?" I asked.

"I could be cleared to leave within twenty-four hours. It's only a two-hour flight from here, so we could be on the ground by Wednesday. I'll make some calls ahead of time and find us a driver who knows the area."

"Thank you, Edward. I appreciate you," I said.

I felt better knowing that when I got to Belize, I'd be able to confront Arlene with an ultimatum: either she gives up Markeesa or she goes to jail. I wouldn't settle for anything else.

EPILOGUE

Thirty Days Later

Dani

"I don't know who he is," I said. The words felt heavy on my tongue, like they didn't wanna come out. I was still pissed about the whole thing, but I didn't care what people thought. It wasn't none of their damn business anyway. I noticed how Kelsa's eyebrows went up when I said it, but so what. If her son knew like I knew, he'd try to keep his mama under control.

Why did that trick mouth the word "bitch" when I looked at her. I hated her even more. If she woulda had some business of her own, we wouldn't be here today.

"Ms. Patnett, speak up," said the judge. She was nasty too.

I sucked my teeth, rolled my eyes, and pulled my death stare away from Keeling's side of the room. That judge knew good and well she heard me the first doggone time.

"I said, I don't know who my baby's father is," I repeated.

"Okay, but you do acknowledge that this affidavit is true and correct. It states that Keeling Lake is not the biological father to the minor child in question."

"Yeah. It's true," I said.

The rest of what she said may as well have been in Portuguese, because I didn't hear nothing but the words I never wanted to hear.

"Okay, Mr. Lake, your request is hereby granted. You are no longer legally required to provide financial support for the minor child."

Kelsa squealed so loud, the stupid judge banged her gavel like that would do something. The last thing I remembered was Kelsa doing some kind of stupid-looking dance around her son and that man who bugged me to pieces over this mess.

"C'mon, Charlene!" I called over my shoulder as I stormed out of the courtroom. I didn't know what the hell she was standing around for. We lost. I lost. I wasn't gonna be getting Keeling's money and I was pissed. I didn't need to watch them celebrate like they just won the doggone lottery.

I wanted to get as far away from there as I could, and I didn't feel like being bombarded with the ton of questions I knew Charlene would be asking.

Arlene

Getting settled in Belize was harder than I expected. It was so hot there and the place my mother's family owned was nothing like our condo back at home. Then, Markeesa had a hard time adjusting.

She didn't understand the Creole the rest of our family spoke, and she kept asking when her brothers would come. The first few weeks were miserable.

"Mom, I'm going to the store," I yelled toward the back of the house. We lived in the back portion of a four-bedroom house we shared with my mother's sister and her daughter. They lived up front. The house was on the upper level of a two-story structure with a long set of cement stairs.

"All right," my mother yelled back. Her adjustment wasn't smooth, either, but I could tell she was going to be fine.

I closed the door behind me and walked down the stairs only to nearly lose my balance at the sight of Mark and a man I didn't recognize. I grabbed the banister and steadied myself as I made my descent.

With wide eyes and my heart racing, I looked around even though I wasn't sure what I was looking for. I knew guilt permeated from my body and my nervous actions didn't help.

"You can run, but I promise, I'll be right here when you get back. Where is she?" he asked.

I couldn't find my voice.

Mark's eyes locked with mine.

"Kidnapping, forgery, theft." Mark used his fingers to count down as he approached me. I took unsteady steps backward until I bumped into the railing, and couldn't move.

I didn't want him to go upstairs. I didn't want him near Markeesa. Fear gripped my heart and threatened to squeeze harder. But I knew my gig was up. He had won.

"Where is she?" His eyes darted all around. I could tell he couldn't be stopped.

"You need to go!" I said.

"I'm not leaving 'til I see my daughter. I don't know what you thought you were doing. But I'm warning you. You got five minutes to bring my child or your ass is going to jail today, for sure."

"You'll never see her again," I stammered. Even my threat sounded shaky. I wasn't ready for this. My plan didn't include him following us to Belize.

"Like hell I won't." Mark pushed his way past me and stormed up the stairs.

"Okay. Okay, wait," I yelled.

The desperation in my voice must've moved him because he suddenly stopped. He didn't turn to face me right away, but at least I had his attention. "Can we, um. I wanna work something out," I said. I rushed up the few steps to meet him where he stood. "I know what I did was wrong, but I felt like I didn't have a choice."

Skeptical eyes stared back at me. I saw the determination in his twisted features. I knew without him saying it that he wouldn't give up until I gave him what he wanted.

"Why should I trust you after you lied, and stole my child?" he asked.

It was hard to hear those words. I did what I had to do. He turned his back on us when he went back to his wife. If he would've kept his promise, we'd be together as a family here on vacation in Belize. Instead, we were at war.

"You know where I am. You said it yourself, I can't run. I just want to talk to you. I'll let you see her, but she's gonna be confused. Let's go somewhere and talk for a little while, then we can come back together and I'll let you see her," I said. "I swear I will, Mark. You've gotta believe me."

Mark turned to the man who stood near the gate. The guy shrugged. He was a big mass of a man, with a bald head and a pair of reflective shades that hid his eyes.

"I can stay here while you go," he said to Mark.

"I promise I won't try anything. I just think we should talk before you see her."

"No one will leave this gate until you come back," the man said. "It's up to you."

"There's a restaurant not far from here. Let's go sit, so we can talk. I'm willing to try and work this out," I said.

"Arlene, if you try anything," he said. "I mean I will have your ass thrown under the jail."

"Mark. Please, enough with the threats. I just told you, I want to talk. You will see her. I just want us to get our story straight and get on the same page."

For a second he looked at me like he couldn't be sure whether I was lying. I put my hands up. "Please, Mark. Don't do it for me, do it for Markeesa. If you burst in there now without the boys, think about what it will do to her."

His eyes softened and I knew he'd agree before he nodded slightly.

Nearly an hour later, we sat across from each other at a small table. The conversation was friendly and surprisingly, calm. I was encouraged because it looked like we were headed toward an agreement.

"Why didn't you come with the police?" I finally asked him.

"Arlene, I don't want you in jail. You're the mother of my daughter. We both need you. But if you can't get over Zaneda and me, we won't really solve anything."

"That's why I've gotta stay here, Mark. I can't be over there and sit on the sidelines while you live your life with her; I'll never be at peace. I'm just being honest."

Keeling

"Speech!"

"Speech!"

"Speech!"

They wouldn't let up. My moms insisted on a birthday party and when I told her not to, she did what she usually does. Exactly what she wanted to do.

When I walked into the house and people jumped up and screamed, "surprise," I nearly passed out.

"Ma!"

"Oh, boy, cut it out. We've got a lot to celebrate and you better be glad all your prayers are being answered."

I walked in and said hello to the friendly faces that smiled back at me. When they started clapping, cheering and whistling, for a second, my mind went back to the last time a crowd had made such a fuss over me.

That was months ago, when I was on a stage in front of a studio audience. But today, there was nothing to fear, I was hyped, and looking forward to keeping more money in my pocket.

"Congrats, Bruh," Roger said as we did the brother-man greeting. Malcolm was there too.

At first, I wanted to stay in Keela's life. But the more I thought about it, dealing with her meant I'd have to deal with Dani and that was not an option.

Besides, my moms said Keela was young enough that soon, she'd forget all about me.

Malcolm placed a beer bottle in my hand and the real celebration got underway.

Mark

I'd have hell to pay when I got back to Houston, but for now, I felt good about my decision. Zaneda would probably threaten to leave me once she found out, but I decided not to press charges against Arlene and we agreed we'd work together to raise Markeesa.

"So you forgive me?" Arlene asked as I pulled the iron gate open.

"For now. If you do what we've agreed to, we'll be good," I said.

We returned from our talk at the restaurant and I had the chance to do something I never considered before.

After Arlene opened up and told me about the resentment she still held over how our relationship had ended, I took her hands into mine and apologized.

"I'm so sorry for everything I put you through. I wasn't a good person back then; I took advantage of you because I felt like I had lost control of my marriage. It was wrong, I was wrong and I'm truly sorry."

When the tears streamed down her cheeks, I wasn't sure if a scene was about to follow. But instead of going ape-shit crazy on me, Arlene seemed relieved. That helped me to understand why she needed to put so much distance between us.

It took another hour or so for us to work out the agreement that would have Markeesa and me shuffling between Belize and Houston.

I didn't think it was fair that she should be the only one traveling, so I told Arlene my family would spend some of the off-season there and we would work it out.

"What's Zaneda gonna say about this?" Arlene asked with a grimace.

I shrugged, then said, "She won't like it, but sometimes in life, we've all gotta do things we don't want to, and just like everything else, we'll all get through it."

Edward and I waited at the bottom of the stairs while Arlene went up to get Markeesa.

We agreed, she'd go in and prepare my daughter for what we were sure would be the surprise of her young life. I finally felt good about the future with the women in my life.

ABOUT THE AUTHOR

By day, Pat Tucker works as a radio news director in Houston, Texas. By night, she is a talented writer with a knack for telling page-turning stories. A former TV news reporter, she draws on her background to craft stories readers will love. She is the author of seven novels and has participated in three anthologies, including *New York Times* bestselling author Zane's *Caramel Flava*. A graduate of San Jose State University, Pat is a member of the National and Houston Association of Black Journalists and Sigma Gamma Rho Sorority, Inc. She is married with two children.